the Other Side *of* Life

The Eleven Gem Odyssey of Death

Susan D. Kalior
M. A. in Education in Counseling
Human Relations and Behavior
B.S. in Sociology

Blue Wing Publications, Workshops, and Lectures
Tualatin, Oregon

The Other Side of Life: The Eleven Gem Odyssey of Death (Profound Metaphysical, Philosophical, New Age, and Spiritual Insights into death, afterlife, spirits, ghosts, and angels, for Personal Growth and Transformation)
Visionary Fiction
Copyright©2009 by Susan D Kalior
First Printing: June 6, 2009
ISBN 978-0-979566356

All rights reserved, including the right to reproduce this work in any form without permission in writing from the publisher, except for brief passages in connection with a review.

Published by Blue Wing Publications, Workshops, and Lectures
Cover Design by Laura C. Keyser
Logo by Sara C. Roethle
Author Photo by Stephen Roethle

Blue Wing Publications, Workshops, and Lectures
P.O. Box 947, Tualatin, OR 97062
sdk@bluewingworkshops.com
www. bluewingworkshops.com
Readers' comments are welcomed.

Other Books by Susan D. Kalior

The Other Side of God: The Eleven Gem Odyssey of Being
Growing Wings Self Discovery Workbook:
17 Workshops to a Better Life-Vol One
Growing Wings Self Discovery Workbook:
18 Workshops to a Better Life-Vol Two
Johnny, the Mark of Chaos: An Urban Dark Fantasy
Jenséa, an Angel's Touch: Into the World of Johnny
Warriors in the Mist: A Medieval Dark Fantasy
The Dark Side of Light: A Medieval Time Travel Fantasy

Manufactured in the United States of America

Dedication

This book is dedicated to my touchstone,
my father,
Robert V. Kalior,
a great old warrior who will never fade away.

ACKNOWLEDGEMENTS

Thanks to my beautiful sister, Cindy, whose pure heart embraces me so warmly, and for her eager interest in all my manuscripts. Thanks to my lovely daughter, Sara, who shares my creative adventure and proofreads my books with inspiring support. I appreciate my son, Stephen, for keeping my computer in top shape for writing and for cheering me on like a ball of sunshine. And I ever appreciate my wisdom buddies: my father, Robert, and my brother, Mark, who spark my mind to new heights. I salute my mother, whose mother's heart cloaks me still, even though she, what people call—died, a few years ago. Thanks to Laura Keyser for her brilliant cover design and loving support. Special thanks to the Myers family for inviting me on a beach trip whereupon I had a meditation that became the ending for this book. I am grateful for my dear friend, Karlyn Myers who enthusiastically reads my works, and bestows me with the greatest compliment by being inspired by them. Thank you also to my dear friend, Dr. Cyndi Myers whose reaction to my work further inspires me, for being a scientific reference, and for curing my tendonitis and back pain. Both Myers women gave valuable feedback and suggestions which I implemented into the book. Their eager reception of my work, along with Helen Levison, (a lovely lady I had known as a child), moves me deeply. Thanks to Aaron Myers who so colorfully educated me about the workings of rip currents. Thanks to Linda Post for the wonderful trip we took last year that inspired the beginning of this book, and my dear old friend, Paula Warren who I used as an example in the workings of synchronicity. And thanks to those who have believed in me, Jennifer Kalior, Matt Keyser, Gail Barton, Mary Thompson, Linda Post, Anita Savi, Karol Roethle, Sarah Nevin, and my recently departed friend, Anita Mitchell, who also shifted her focus from one world to another.

Prologue

Some people have psychics. Some people have gurus. And some people have life coaches. I had a Fool on the Hill.

I found Him one day when my life overwhelmed me. I was laden with the responsibilities of motherhood and wifehood and just making life work—hood.

I had put myself on the backburner, living for everyone else, but not for me . . . not—for *me*. So, one warm winter day in the Arizona desert, I journeyed up a shallow incline of a mountain. My brown hiking boots crunched pebbles and bramble, and my navy blue, long-sleeved tee shirt and jeans protected me from the sun.

When I reached a plateau, I hunched down under a mesquite tree and I began to cry. My long, light brown hair fell over my face, as I took my tears into meditation. And in this meditation, I stumbled into a state of mind, an inner world, as real as the outer world. I had arrived in a place that would help me find my real self, buried alive under piles of personal expectation and social criteria.

I had left behind the focus of my ordinary self in my ordinary day, in my ordinary life. For this short while, I wasn't a mother, a wife, a psychotherapist, a writer, or an all around do-gooder. I journeyed beyond those things into my quintessential self, whatever that was. I had crossed into another level of being.

I heard a voice that said, "Welcome to the real world, Susan."

When I looked to the voice, I viewed a semi-incorporeal man in a violet sweatshirt, white pants, and jogging shoes with the toe part cut out, showing bright orange socks. His short gray-white hair, beard, mustache, and twinkling brown eyes gave Him a wizardly appearance. Headphones cupped His ears, and an outdated Sony Walkman was clipped to His pant's waist.

"Why are you less solid than others?" I asked.

His eyes sparkled brightly. "I am half in this world, and half somewhere else. My focus is on a new adventure on the Other Side of Life. But I must finish the old adventure first."

"What is your name?" I asked.

He replied, "I am The Fool, and in the course of my life, before I began to become incorporeal, I had often been referred to as the Fool on the Hill, which was seldom a compliment."

After that, He guided me on an odyssey into the inner realms of human life. I learned about perceptions of reality, alternate worlds, and how everything is Creative Energy, and therefore, one energy. I was shown how most people serve image. I learned how to find inner balance, and how to turn loneliness into independence. I learned the merit of strife, the meaning of love, and how to confront the shadow self. I learned about life and death transitions, how to self-actualize, and how to behold the synchronicity of existence. These psycho-spiritual adventures led to me into a new life within the life of Susan. I was no longer ordinary, my days were not ordinary, and my life would never be ordinary again.

Five years hence brings me to this day, and this is where my story begins. Come, adventure with me beyond the boundaries of everyday life, into the realms of ghosts, spirits, and hobgoblins—multiple realities and multiple selves. We will jump off the precipice of fear into life's mysteries, and we will dance across the meridians of time and space, traversing diverse dream worlds, and parallel other worlds. Let us explore the world of *A Thousand Me's, Counterbalance,* and *Compression.* Let us move into the world where memory comes before the event and where music lives before it becomes music. Come, let us grow together on the Other Side of Life.

The Wall of Remembrance

"What we remember seems alive,
what we forget seems like death."

Gem #1 TRANSITIONS

It was my birthday. The sand was soft under my bare feet as the seawater swirled around my ankles. There was a fresh water stream near me, flowing into the sea, the lovely sea. This created wave currents from several directions that pushed against my calves at varying convergences, creating several shades of blue colored water that sparkled in the warm morning sun.

I was divorced, my kids were off to college, and I had begun a new life in Oregon writing books and lecturing. I was a content single woman, happily married to myself.

I was wearing my one-piece aqua bathing suit. The sequins on my matching sheer, sleeveless, cover-up, glittered in the sun. My long, light brown hair hung loose over my shoulder blades. A strong breeze blew a tress over my shoulder, tickling my arm as it went by. My heart lifted as always it does when I visit the ocean. And a meditative song rose to my lips as it ever does when seawater touches my skin. I call it "The Song of the Sea."

I began singing, "I am you, and you are me, the cradle of life resides in the sea." I stepped further into the water, up to my knees, chill liquid cooling me on this unusually hot May morning. *The day is hot for me*, I thought like a child, *hot to warm up the sea, just for my birthday.*

Oh how I loved the water! Even though my mother had died in a rip current two and a half years ago, the water still impassioned me. I imagined that my mother's spirit was the heart of the sea, still loving me, still embracing me as her baby.

I continued my song. "The currents of life can toss and turn our lives and identity. And that is when, and it is then, I sing the song of the sea."

And I felt it then, as I always do when I begin a meditation, that familiar tingling at the crown of my head, that queer chill that stimulates a sensation of opening. I sang on, reaching my hands out to the sea. "I call for you, the ocean blue, because I know you're me. And when I'm lost, you bring me home, home to the womb of the sea."

In merging with ocean energy, my ideas of how I perceived myself, loosened. *I am more than the flesh and blood of Susan. There is more to me than I know or can understand.* The best meditations that embrace the quest for inner balance often require the softening of our intellect that we may transcend the beliefs that *cement* us into a certain reality. *All that I have ever been in any time or place . . . and all that I will ever be in future time or space, melts into a great ball of the moment, encompassing me.* In opening to what was beyond myself, I felt heightened, expanded, and free. I had never died and I was never born. Everything was now.

My arms drifted back to my sides. Breezes brushed my face, and cold water moved about my ankles. With eyes closed, my mentor, my sage, My Fool came to mind. His whimsical smile and twinkling eyes warmed my heart. He had shared much insight about how Creative Energy makes the world what it is, and how we, as that energy, have made ourselves as we are. I thought about the eleven gem rainbow wand He'd bequeathed me before He died. It represented the odyssey of being. I still carried it; it burned in my soul, the wisdom of which spilled out into my books and lectures.

Oh, it wasn't that I parroted Him, per se. What He touched beyond everyday life was also what I could touch, and in that we sang a song together. The song of 'the fool.' The song of those who dissolve boundaries to expand their realities, even though the social world might deem them misfits.

I moved into the water, deeper, until it reached my knees. The frosty sea clamped my lower calves. It was quite cold, but the coldness enlivened me. It woke me up, I mean from the inside. It woke up that sleepy human part that goes through the motions of everyday life, missing the many miraculous occurrences popping up before us all the time. Everything is in constant change no matter how stale one's life may seem—and when we 'awaken,' the monotony seems to disappear.

But I needed to get all the way into the water to wake up completely. I needed to feel the liquid on my face, drenching my hair through and through, to let the energy of it soak into the numbed corners of my existence into the complete identity of Susan. I didn't want to walk out any deeper to get wetter. I feared undertows and rip currents. I thought of my mother drowning. My face welled with pain. No. I mustn't think of that. I loved the sea, but even as a child, before my mother died, I had frequent dreams of the ocean taking my life. So I just sat where I'd been standing. Clear water bobbed around my ribcage beneath my chest.

I deepened my meditation while also retaining an awareness of my identity as Susan. It is strange, but when I loosen the idea of who I am, who I am—strengthens. By lightening the boundaries of who I *think I am*, I become more translucent. In a way, it's like, 'letting in the light,' and who I *really* am—sharpens.

A clear unbroken wave welled up over my chest and moved past my throat. Even though joy was my primary emotion, I had a pang of fear. I pushed past my fear of the water by focusing on the greater picture of Creative Energy everywhere, in everything, all the time—that I was all things, and all things were me. I inhaled a deep breath of salty sea air, sighed heavily, and relaxed. My fear subsided.

I almost scolded myself for having been afraid, but then I softened, recalling something My Fool had taught me. He said, "The human experience, fear inclusive, is a gift that we, as Creative Energy, give ourselves."

What My Fool meant was that the purpose of life was to have experiences rather than to strive for some state of ascension. I loved that. If, as many wise ones have experienced in meditation, we are all One, then nobody is more or less ascended than anyone else.

However, I could see the appeal in the concept that we *must* spiritually evolve, given we, in general, experience ourselves as separate identities, somewhat lost and alone, trying to survive, and hoping for something better.

I smiled lightly. My Fool had shared many luminous insights that brought me into a new plateau of being. So no, I would not be mad at myself for feeling fear. In the words of My Fool, "Live the mystery."

A wave rolled back exposing my wet legs to the sun. I moved my fingertip in a tiny swirling pattern over my shiny wet thigh, feeling my commitment to live the mystery. To that end, I tried not to close-mindedly interpret matters, especially spiritual matters. My Fool had said, "Subjective interpretation cements personal beliefs—diminishes insight, and masks the deeper gifts available."

Case in point: Many religions have sprouted from what one might term, a spiritual experience. People flock around the one who has the experience. Interpretations follow. These interpretations serve the needs of the social group, eager to believe in a supreme power that can ease their suffering. Therefore, a pure 'spiritual' experience is often clouded by subjective interpretation.

The water covered my legs again, moving over my chest. And as the sun beat hot on my head, I cried out inside myself, *I open to Creative Energy, unfiltered by my beliefs!* And like a camera flash, I experienced a moment where Creator and the Created were One, rather than supreme and inferior.

I heard some kids laughing. I looked over my shoulder off to my right, just behind me. Two little boys, maybe two and three years old were running away from a wave that tried to catch their ankles. When the wave receded, they chased after it, giggling as they played their game with the sea. The younger boy in red swim trunks would slap his thighs with delight every time a wave came toward his ankles. Then a woman standing next to them, their mother I presumed, said, "Come on kids. It's time to leave."

The older boy in blue and yellow striped swim trunks hollered, "I don't want to go!" and proceeded to throw a tantrum.

I had to laugh. I had to, because this was what life was all about: winning and losing, acceptance and rejection, safety and fear, love and hate, happy and sad, and all the other pairs of opposites that are the makings of any great story. These challenges enrich our life experience, which in *every* case, is a decent undertaking. Thus, the so-called 'evolved' person is no worthier than the bum drinking whisky on a city sidewalk.

The mother grabbed the little boy's hand and dragged him away, grabbing her other son's hand as she passed him. They were living their story. And when we are ready to finish a story, as in ending a phase, a life, or a pattern that has been carried on for multiple lives, it is then that the light of wisdom, (unfiltered Creative Energy), flows into us. The beliefs that have cemented us into a particular story begin to dissolve. We change our views. Our old way of being changes, and a new way is in place—for we are *enlightened*, that is, before we take another trip into the dark for a new adventure!'

The little boys and mother were finally gone. The beach was quieter now. Time to get my head wet!

I leaned back flat as the gentle waves washed over me from three directions. I held my breath so they could slide over my face. The cool liquid soothed and refreshed. I let my face surface, staring at the sky so blue. A seagull flew overhead. Its underbelly made me think of the eggs it might have lain, and the babies that may have hatched. I thought about the womb of life, the belly of creation, Creative Energy always creating, even if our perception held us captive in stale realities.

I floated there in the shallows on my back. I closed my eyes, bobbing gently with a faint smile and teary eyes of joy. I gave myself to the sea. I was . . . the sea. With my ears beneath the water, a quiet hush absorbed the chatter of humans all over the world who felt they had all the answers. It absorbed war cries, cries for help, and the cries of the silent, screaming lonely who feared an empty night.

Only in the quiet of where all things are created can I find clarity. My Fool used to call it 'being in The Zone.' He had taught me how to get there, and stay there if I chose, while living my daily life.

I lifted my head into the dry air, preparing to sit up, but I had to stand to keep my head above water. I had floated a bit deeper into the sea than I had wished. I was waist deep, my sheer cover-up clinging to my body. I know it's more comfortable to swim in a swimsuit with no cover-up, but I hadn't quite steeled myself against the strong social manner in which the female body is so often objectified. My pet peeve was being viewed as a 'thing,' or seeing anyone viewed as a thing instead of a viable human being rich with unique wonder. I was working on not being affected by all that, because I was tired of being affected by all that, but I *was* affected by all that. And I was more at ease covered, so why pretend I wasn't? My Fool would have said, *That is part of your story, Susan. It is okay.*

I decided that waist deep water was okay too. Waist deep, so what? The fresh air braced my wet body, and the hot sun warmed my cold skin. I dipped my hands into the water, and flung them upward, throwing a shower of plump water droplets into the air, watching them sparkle in the sun.

Then I closed my eyes in a meditative trance and reached my hands out to the distant ocean. My heart cried, *Live the mystery. Open. Behold. Become.*

Two wave currents converged and crashed hard against me knocking me down. I lifted my chin so I wouldn't swallow water. I shook my head, a bit dazed by this incident. I started to rise, when a strong current knocked my feet out from beneath me and sucked me toward the sea so super slide fast and hard, I could not fight it.

My meditative state faded fast. My Fool used to call that 'falling out of The Zone.' I feared I was in a rip current, and the identity of Susan became my focus with a thud. The song of the sea had left my lips. My mind flashed upon my mother's death, along with scenes of tidal waves sweeping me out to sea. Oh that I could love and fear the sea with equal measure!

I flashed then upon a gathering I was at just last week, when a friend was telling me how to survive a rip current. Rip currents were not foreign to him and he'd in fact saved others who'd been caught in that perilous situation. He'd said, "Swim parallel to the shore if possible. Stay calm, and conserve energy. Don't worry if you can't get out of the current; eventually the current will run out of steam once it gains passage to the deeper sea. From there you can swim diagonally to get back to shore."

Okay. I tried to calm myself. *Okay. If my friend can do it, so can I.* It was odd that as I faced possible death, or as My Fool would say, a shift of focus from the reality of Susan to another world, all I could think was, *I am not done writing my books*! *I am not done*! With that thought, I returned to a meditative state, to the quintessential vibration of Susan, to my identity and the story that I had not yet finished. I usually had to soften the edges of my identity to get to the quintessential depths of wisdom. This was a rare time in which I felt I must *strengthen* my identity if I was to keep it.

It was difficult not to panic when viewing the beach getting farther away. I tried to swim parallel to the shore, but even with all my strength, I couldn't escape the current. And my friend had warned to conserve energy, so I wasn't sure what I should do. I was already so tired. I just needed to stay afloat. I might have to let the current take me out to sea and then try to swim back once it faded. However, that was a very scary thought given all those fish out there. My mind kept drifting to the old nightmares of drowning in the sea, and my emotions kept gravitating to feeling doomed. Was I to die? Would I write no more books?

I realized then that the real struggle was less about surviving the rip current than it was about being committed to the story of Susan.

We are such complex beings. We think when we say 'I', we mean our singular self—yet no self is truly singular, for there is always a parent and child in us, a saboteur and a hero, an idiot and a sage—and so much more. And there is more to these selves within us than is generally comprehended by the psychological profession. These selves, or facades, as My Fool called them, are aspects within us that can temporarily hijack our persona. For instance, a shy, repressed person might uncharacteristically hurl insults at someone with the energy of something like *the best defense is a good offense*, and could be labeled something like, 'The Flamethrower.' Often these facades pop in when we least want them to make an appearance. And so it was with me in my rip current trauma when the facade I referred to as 'My Nun,' surfaced.

She said sternly, "It is well to sacrifice yourself to the sea and *not* finish the story of Susan. It is better to have a life where one is *not* noticed, because being noticed is a sin."

A stream of water moved into my mouth, and I choked. After a minute of wide-eyed coughing, I could breathe clearly, but I was panting hard. Listening to My Nun had made me choke; that is how easily I could be absorbed into her reality.

She spoke again. "Do not fight death, Susan. Let yourself die. It is the spiritual thing to do."

I almost started arguing with her, but I had learned long ago to avoid dialoguing with aspects of myself that seemed to work against me. Such engagement kept the unsavory dialogue going. So I ignored My Nun, and gave all my energy to the pure intent of what Susan was to become.

I strove to keep my head above the rushing water. I couldn't feel my body and I feared hypothermia. I tried now and then, to no avail, to move sideways out of the rip current. I peered only through the slits of my eyes, for if I opened them fully, I'd see the expansive ocean and how distant I was from shore. I mustn't deepen my fear; I was afraid enough. It seemed like a long time had passed, though it was probably only minutes, and it took everything I had not to give up.

I know in times like these many would pray to some idea of God to save them. My salvation however came from chanting, "My books, my books, my books. I have to write my books."

I was exhausted, my arms hurt, and it was getting difficult to catch my breath, and harder still not to panic. I might sink—I might. I just couldn't hold out much longer. But . . . my books. I visualized myself at my computer writing, but the vision faded. I was so tired. I needed help. I opened to receive aid, even if it was from a sea turtle. I squeezed my eyes shut and cried because this was it. The moment was now. If help was to come, it *must* come now.

The idea of surrender was overpowering me. It would be so easy to give myself to it, to just give up and die. I thought about it, because fighting the panic monster was just too hard. I hated battle. And I disliked all it entailed: confrontation, repelling, attacking, or harming anything, even a fly. Though this was a natural part of life, it was so unnatural for me. Given this, I was entranced by those who *could* repel easily and fight without compunction. I admired a strong survival instinct, attracted to what was pale within me.

It was then I heard a voice near my face, a man's voice. "Look at me, Susan."

I cracked my eyes open. It was a man, a spirit man, treading water next to me. Even with an ethereal body, his sharp-lined facial features exuded determination, and he seemed to have long black ethereal hair. "Look into my eyes."

Deeply fatigued, water lapped into my mouth and throat. I coughed it up.

"My Warrior," I whimpered, "are you My Warrior?"

He replied, "You know who I am."

Five years ago, My Fool had helped me reclaim a part of me that I had shunned. This part of me was the energy essence of my collective yang. I call him My Warrior. After reclaiming him, I was able to guard my boundary and repel those who wanted something from me that was not in my own best interest to give. However, it was still a great challenge for me to choose The Warrior instead of My Nun. I always found it interesting that the sword and the cross looked similar—just different ways of using the same energy.

I stared into My Warrior's penetrating eyes. I moved into the pure vibration of all that he was. I saw a medieval knight on the battlefield, his weapon maiming flesh, drawing blood. I saw a tribesman chase away offenders who were trying to steal women. I saw a grossly wounded man dragging himself through a forest with what seemed to transcend human endurance.

My Warrior was strong in the way of survival, in the human existence thing– while I felt like a puff of smoke.

"Draw from me," he said.

I did; I inhaled the strength he was lending, *he* that was *me*. I felt cradled in his yang, the yang of my own beginnings. I felt like I was being rescued, rescued . . . by myself, by the me that I'd been trying so hard to integrate these last five years. Feeling this energy, this warrior energy as now I did, made me realize that though I'd come far, I had far to go.

And then quite suddenly, I broke free of the rip current. With a second wind, I swam on my side, diagonally toward the shore. I was still staring at the spirit warrior who was swimming on his side, facing me.

I smiled at him, and he smiled at me. "There, there," he said, "See now . . . you have survived."

And then he disappeared, or at least I could not see him. Oh, some people might say that an angel helped me. But what is an angel anyway?

It seemed only a blink of time passed, though I'm sure it was more, and I was trudging out of the surf onto a stretch of dry vacant beach. I pulled my clinging wet cover-up over my head and dropped it at my feet. My body buckled with exhaustion, bringing me face down upon the dry sand. As I lay there, flat on my stomach, arms bunched beneath me, head turned to the side, bedraggled and panting with wildly beating heart and numb limbs, I wondered if I was going to lose any toes over this. I hoped the sun was still hot, and that soon I'd have that assurance.

I was staring at my shoulder in brilliant Technicolor. Sand crystals and water beads dotted my skin on either side of a water-plumped tress of hair. I closed my eyes, still panting. My head throbbed, and my mind was spinning with images of rushing sea currents, and wet hands treading water. I was still unable to feel myself, except for my heavy breathing and chattering teeth.

After a while, my breathing calmed and my teeth chattering lessened, only to be replaced by the burn of thawing skin. But I guess that was a good sign. I seemed to be coming back to life, and I still couldn't believe I almost died. I was proud, however, that I'd used My Warrior to rescue me. Every time I used that energy, I became a more balanced person against the stark contrast of my extreme passive propensity.

Thank you My Fool, for teaching me that. I missed Him. In some ways He had never left me. I knew Him well, so I could ever hear Him talking in my head. But He always told me what He had already taught me. And when I dreamed of Him, He told me what I already knew He knew, as if reminding me. And sometimes I felt His presence, and sometimes I saw His spirit, but all in the form and way that I had known Him, and all in the words He'd once spoken.

He had told me once that this was how people experienced the dead, beholding them as they *were*, as if they had stopped the continuance of their own adventure. He called this place of interaction The Wall of Remembrance, a non-physical location found by honing in on the deceased. Whether we found them at The Wall in our dreams, in meditation, or in other states of mind, the experience would be colored with how we perceived them when they were alive, along with our personal beliefs about an afterlife.

For example, I recall my mother with a bright face, eager to nurture her children no matter how old they were. And I tend to believe that her afterlife would be nicer than the life she left. In this, her spirit would appear bright, nurturing, and happy to me. If one perceived the deceased as bad and believed in hell, then the spirit might appear mean and anguished, suffering for his sins. Therefore, experiencing the dead, though viable in its way, will be somewhat skewed. My Fool had shared this and so much more, yet there was still so much more He didn't share. So much more I wanted to understand.

Given my near demise, I wanted to know more about life beyond death. Even though I only knew how to reach My Fool at the Wall of Remembrance, maybe He could help me go *beyond* The Wall and teach me something new.

As I rested there on the beach, waiting for the sun to further warm me, I went into a meditative state, and arrived at The Wall, infinitely long and tall. Psychics might call it a veil.

Scenes of My Fool as I knew Him played on The Wall. Then His spirit appeared before me, short in stature, gray-white beard and mustache, violet sweatshirt, white pants, and jogging shoes with the toe part cut out, orange socks peaking through.

I was delighted to see Him, as always.

Before I could speak, His hand swirled in a Ferris-wheel circle, landing palm up. He said, "In addition," as if my previous thoughts had been part of a conversation we'd been having, "communication with the so-called dead requires the impression that we are separate from each other."

"Hmm," I said, "I never thought of that before. When we communicate with the deceased, we are not in our deepest state of expanded awareness, for if we were, we'd be one with them."

"Yes, but the experience of talking to the dead has value and serves its purpose. We see what we want and need to see in the deceased, just as we experience our own death the way *we*, on a deeper level, choose."

"Does that apply to *near* death experiences?"

"Yes," He said, "you nearly drowning in the ocean served the purpose you needed it to serve. When you were in the rip current, you considered shifting focus from Susan's reality to another. If you had decided to do that, consciously or unconsciously, you would have, what people call—died. But as it is, you used the experience to affirm and strengthen your current life."

"And if I would have chosen to die, what then?"

"Death," His voice sounded funny, like in slow speed, "and," then high speed, "birth are . . ."

I became aware of my body on the beach, stomach to the sand. My Fool's voice sounded to my right, "—the same."

My eyes flew open. My Fool was laying flat on His stomach, hands folded under His chest, head turned toward me.

I jolted, startled. Since He died, I'd never experienced Him this vividly. "Can other people see you?"

He said with a lilt of cheer, "Probably not."

"Are you really . . . here?" I stretched my sandy hand to His cheek. It went through Him. I shook my head, even though it was resting in the sand. "Am I crazy? I mean, this is not typically how I communicate with you. You look 'flesh and blood' real. How are you doing this? How can you be here like this? I mean . . . you're dead."

"What is 'dead?' Nothing is 'dead.' "

"I know we always exist somewhere, but . . . no death, no period of time between here and there?"

"Death is but the blinking of an eye. We have a focus. We blink. We have another focus. We focus on being here or there, in this identity or that, in this world or another, in this reality or a different one. I have blinked, and I am here with you. When you perceive that something has died, it is as if watching a Christmas tree with blinking lights. When a light goes off, it is still there, but we look at the ones that are lit. The one's that are lit seem alive, and the one's that are out seem dead. When something cannot be seen any more, society in general, claims it dead. But it has simply slipped out of focus, and is only seemingly nonexistent. But just like a Christmas tree light, whether it is lit and in focus, or not lit and out of focus—it is still there."

I said, "So, when a light goes out, doesn't it die, kind of at least, before it lights up somewhere else?"

"Though death is perceived as an exit or a disappearance, and birth is perceived as an entrance or an appearance, death and birth are the very same, there is no in-between."

"Not even for a second?"

He said, "Think of it like this: Beyond the concept of linear time is an infinite net of identities. Each little opening in the net is an identity. When we live, we are completely focused into our own space, our little opening in the net, our own identity. When we die, we simply move from one opening in the net to another. We move from one identity to another."

"So we just change location."

"Yes. Everything is always somewhere in constant change, dying and birthing simultaneously—Christmas tree lights, blinking. Nothing has really gone anywhere because everything is always everywhere. No thing has truly and solely ever been *just* here, regardless if it is a person, an ocean, a mountain, a planet, or a universe. We are always One Creative Energy, always in existence, just flitting about from focus to focus."

"But when you so-called died, I watched you leave your body and exit earth, for you were finished with the earth experience. If that is so, how can you be in focus with me now?"

He narrowed an eye. "You will uncover that mystery before the next chapter in your life is complete."

I furrowed my brows impatiently. "But, you're actually here, right?"

"I *am* here as you remember me."

"But, you are real?"

"What is real?"

"You have told me that everything is real. I guess that means imagination too. So even if I am imagining you, you are real?"

"What we imagine is what we have witnessed in some realm of life. Envision the infinite net of identities once more. This net is one of countless layers of nets. Each layer is a different realm of existence with its own vibration. These varying vibrations yield different experiences of reality. So, having an otherworldly experience is about jumping from one net to another."

I gasped. "Wow!"

"Furthermore," He said, "using another net analogy, envision layers of nets that line up one under the other, the net holes in perfect alignment. One identity, if falling through that one hole, aligned with all the nets below it, would experience itself as the same identity living out different versions of the same life."

"You spoke of that once in the cave of alternate realities. I remember I saw multiple 'you's' fly out of your body in a silver streak."

"Yes, however, each self is generally only focused on its own reality."

"So, there are many worlds, and we have many selves, we just are not aware of them because we only experience the world that holds our focus?"

"Indeed," He said, "the world we feel alive in is our Focus World. And the identity we are focused upon is the Focus Identity. And the life that we currently live is the Focus Life."

"So, my Focus World is earth in this day and age. And my Focus Identity is Susan. And my Focus Life is as a mother of two, a writer and lecturer, living in Oregon."

He nodded. "We usually believe that our Focus World, Focus Identity, and Focus Life *are* reality. If a bat stays in a cave, it might not know that stars exist, but it doesn't mean the stars aren't there. If the bat were to shift its focus to the stars, and experience them, at that moment the cave is less real. When we dream, we feel that the dream world is real. When we become conscious and live our daily lives, we feel like daily life is real. When we have a powerful spiritual experience, we feel like that is real. So what is not reality? *Reality to us is where we are located at any given time.* Just because we are all in different places, does not make anyone's world less real than another—even the so-called dead."

"I want to journey *beyond* the Wall of Remembrance and gain new insights about the other side of life."

"Ah, you speak of the death odyssey."

"The death odyssey?"

"On the other side of what humans call—life, what many call death, is all that creates and sustains reality as humans know it."

"Can I take that journey?"

He cocked His head. "Perhaps."

"Would I still be Susan?"

"Yes, however, you must attune your sense of self to resonate to a vibration conducive to time travel."

My eyes widened with excitement. I rambled, "Time travel? Can I time travel to my mother? Can I find her where she is now in her current reality? Can that be our first adventure beyond The Wall?"

He chortled, "Given you can traverse The Wall, of course, my dear, of course. We will attempt it when you can be in a quiet place without distraction, perhaps tonight. Meet me at the Wall then. Sit up, my dear." He sat up in a half-lotus.

I sat up to face him, hugging my upward bent knees, wondering what might happen next."

"Open your hand.

I opened my palm to him.

He placed in my hand an ethereal silver key. It looked like an old skeleton key from ancient times. Even though it looked singular and inert, I had a sensation that it was an energy moving through multidimensional halls and doors and worlds.

He said, "This is the Gem of Transitions. It unlocks every door in existence so that we can explore."

"Transitions?"

"Transition from one body to another, from one identity to another, between the conscious and the subconscious, between parallel worlds, and between separation and wholeness. Transition, often viewed as dying, is the key that connects everything."

The key absorbed into my palm, and My Fool faded slowly before me. And just before He disappeared, He left me with these words. "Life and death are a state of mind."

He was gone, or seemingly so. And it was time for me to go too. I rose, feeling warmer, teeth no longer chattering. I didn't bother to brush the sand off my dried skin. I was yet traumatized by the sea beating me up, and the sand felt like my friend. I reached down and grabbed my cover-up, no longer feeling the need to wear it. I felt vibrant and empowered. If I was objectified in my bathing suit, I just didn't care.

I walked back toward where my towel was before the rip current took me away. It, along with my sunscreen, and straw hat were just as I had left them. They seemed like children unaware of my ordeal, and unaffected by my return.

I had a childhood flashback of me as a little girl, on a flowered towel, basking in the sunshine on a beach in Florida, with my brother and sister. Our mother was cooling off in the waves when an undertow caught her, and she disappeared from the surface. A man happened to grab her, and he helped her to the shore and brought her to us. I remember her little scarf was all lopsided on her drenched short, blonde hair. And then I thought of how the sea got her at last, two and half years ago, lost to the sea, lost to the sea forever.

Or what was I saying? She never went anywhere. She just changed her focus. A light gone out here, but lit somewhere else. Even so, even with this awareness, my throat became a lump and tears wet my eyes. I so wanted to find my mother *beyond* the Wall of Remembrance. Could I do it? I *so* wanted to be able to do it. Today was my birthday. And it was almost my death day. But is there such a big difference?

Perhaps tonight My Fool would show me.

And who has not experienced transitions? When something leaves us and is replaced with something else, the transition is complete. An old house to a new house, an old job to a new job, an old mate to a new mate. Sometimes transitions involve coping with the death of a relationship, or way of life, a dream, an ideal, or even hope. The transition might involve coping with the loss of money, or a home, or a treasured object. Or perhaps the transition involves healing from the assault of some aspect within us, such as the innocent child. The greatest transition, however, often involves coping with the death of a loved one.

Sometimes we feel the loss, but have difficulty recovering. Instead of completing the transition, we get stuck in heart wrenching grief, bereft in an emotional wasteland. When stuck in the wasteland, no matter what the loss, focus is blurred.

Focus on a loss in your life from which you have not recovered, no matter how small or big. Shift your focus from that loss to what was born from your loss. *Loss always brings a gift equal to the loss—always.* Peer into the shadow, the unknown. Behold your gift. You might behold it in a vision, or in words, or as an insight beyond vision and words. You might realize the gift in your dreams tonight, or in your future days. But the gift *is* there. Keep your mental radio dial tuned to the gift and not the loss. This gift is yours and yours alone. A lost opportunity may have yielded the gift of sparing you from an early demise. A lost home might have yielded the gift of a new adventure. A broken relationship might have yielded the gift of self-reliance. The death of a loved one might have yielded the gift of self-reflection. Perhaps the gift in your loss is that you will have to face your fears or strengthen your sense of self. Or the gift might be that something new and better is around the corner, courtesy of the loss. As things slip away from us, we are forced into new ways, ideas, and the stirrings of dormant treasures within us.

Focus on the gifts. Keep your eyes there, hold on tight, and don't look back. You will feel yourself on a new plateau. Then the transition will be complete—a new perspective, a new reality, REBIRTH.

Dancing on the Timeline

"We are never anywhere, because we are always everywhere."

GEM #2 TIME TRAVEL

After returning home from the 'fighting for my life in the sea' ordeal, I showered, slipped into my soft, midnight blue pajamas and fuzzy blue socks, and fell into bed to get some sleep. I wanted to be refreshed for my evening adventure with My Fool. Waking up hours later in my bed, I stretched, sore from my oceanic escapade. I was staring at a surrealistic Wizard of Oz poster on my ceiling. It seemed to mirror the journey I'd begun this morning at the sea and would continue tonight in search of my dead mother.

The room was almost dark, hence the sun was almost down. I rolled out of bed and crossed the bedroom floor. My twenty-year-old caramel-colored cat, Jensen, followed with an arthritic limp and hearty meows. When I got to the kitchen, I flipped on the light, opened a small can of cat food and emptied it in a white china bowl on the floor. Only the best for my beloved cat. As he sat to eat, I ran my hand over his bristly hair from head to rump, knowing he was soon to die.

Death was such an odd thing, a seeming good-bye that most often elicited in the survivors dire pain, a healthy dose of fear, and perhaps a shot of religion. We commonly call out for the deceased to return—even if only in the heart, or in spirit, and even if only for a moment. We might even enlist a clairvoyant to make contact with our deceased loved one. But I was soon to employ a less popular method to find my mother. I would *go to her* in whatever world or world's *she* resides. I was ready, My Fool's protégé, through and through.

Excited to move into the 'I'm going to find my mom' adventure, I rose. Angel, my fluffy white cat, and Baxter, my long-haired black cat with white fur masked face, approached and nudged me. All right, okay, they were important too, so I took a moment to open two more small cans of cat food. I dumped the food in the other two white china bowls next to Jensen's, and left them there to eat.

I grabbed my Walkman on the kitchen table, and attached it to the waistband of my pajamas. I placed the headphones over my ears and clicked on Gustav Holst's orchestral suite, *The Planets*. The first track played, "Mars, the Bringer of War." The outdated Walkman was old-fashioned, I know. Even so, the little machine was precious to me, for it was a gift from My Fool.

He had once told me, "Music is always playing everywhere."

I had asked, "Then why do I need the Walkman?"

He answered, "Because it reminds you to listen."

I headed out into my yard and walked into the balmy May night. It had been an unseasonably hot day, and the heat wave yet warmed the air. My socks padded through the grass as I traveled toward my spacious, forest green netted hammock, strung between two mighty cedar trees.

I was deeply anxious to find my mother. I missed her badly, and the anticipation of seeing her in another world was almost more than I could stand. Then, an unexpected cold, and I mean very cold, wall of fear hit me. I froze in my tracks. What if I find her in a wretched situation, screaming in agony? What if I find her as a war victim of incessant rape, or see her murdered cruelly by a serial killer, or de-armed by a farm machine? What if a wild bear is eating her, or she is sobbing because her mommy just died? Would I be able to return to my life and live without feeling horrible forever? "Mars, the Bringer of War" still played in my ears.

Oh, how I wished I could behave the way the music made me feel—like a full-blown warrior with the ability to detach when necessary. However, my extreme sensitivity deemed the path of the mighty warrior inaccessible to me. Detaching from others was difficult, and using the metaphorical sword even harder. Feeling intimately connected to all, I reacted empathically to small things in a big way, and to big things in a humongous way. My throat twitched, and for a moment I couldn't breathe.

My eyes closed and my palm flew over my chest. My heartbeat raced beneath my fingers. Was I brave enough to find my mother no matter what her current experience? Was I willing to endure my acute reaction if I discovered something unsavory? I needed to think about this. Hothouse orchid traveling into death realms . . . hmm.

I sighed with a quivering breath frustrated by my fear, fear of my self really, fear of my sensitivity. My sensitivity had often felt like a curse, rendering me constantly empathic to all the sadness and madness of the world: the rape of a woman a world away, the secret pain hiding in a friend, a child's bumped head, a cat's anxious cry, the fly drowning in a puddle, a spider sucked up in the vacuum cleaner, the flea collar poisoning a flea. Oh! "Calm down, Susan," I murmured, "calm down."

I opened my eyes. The next track of *The Planets* played in my ears, "Venus, the Bringer of Beauty." Beauty was easy for me to behold. By the soft light cast from my kitchen window, I looked about my lovely dark yard, soaking up the splendor: majestic cedar trees, quiet and tall, looming in the mystical night; clusters of yellow wildflowers flirting with the earth; and rich green grass blades curling around the edges of my fuzzy blue socks. A soft breeze cupped my face, as if to say, *It will be all right, Susan.*

I inhaled a slow jagged breath, and exhaled more smoothly. I focused on the sound of my deep breathing, aware of the rise and fall of my chest beneath my hand. My sensitivity had also enriched my life, bequeathing me with gifts of beauty great and small: a tiny country gaining freedom on the other side of the world, a child's authentic smile, an orange butterfly fluttering past my kitchen window, the bright rich yellow of a lemon rind.

I sighed. If I had to risk touching ugliness to behold beauty, it was worth it. I wanted to find my mother. Fear be damned. What was life if not to live it? What good could come from cowering when an adventure beckoned? I murmured, "Live the Mystery."

With shoulders back and chest out, I walked to the hammock feeling secure, sure, and prepared to journey to the other side of The Wall. Oh, what lurked beyond known world? Just call me Columbus. Or Dorothy. Or Susan, the Fool.

I crawled into the green twined cradle, lying on my back gazing up at the stars in an opening void of tree branches. The darkness was beautiful. So beautiful it was, I could barely breathe. It was one of those nights when you are happily alone because you feel connected to everything.

The next track on *The Planets* began playing, "Mercury, the Winged Messenger." I positioned my legs into a comfortable half lotus, and rested one hand over the other upon my solar plexus. I closed my eyes with a deep sigh, and focused on the essence of My Fool at the Wall of Remembrance. I would soon find out if I could get beyond it—or not.

The imprint of stars was fresh in my mind. My Fool's face emerged against the imprint—wizened features, short gray-white beard and mustache, eyes bursting with all that is. But the image was just an imagined reflection. I still needed to get to The Wall, so I deepened my trance. I could 'see the ethereal dead' while in my physical body, but my experiences usually proved more pure if I allowed my ethereal body to execute the task.

So, my physical body remained in the hammock, while my ethereal body moved into an ethereal realm (of which there are many). I appeared at The Wall of Remembrance. Multiple scenes involving My Fool played upon The Wall. If I were to be contacting a different deceased person, it would be their life scenes that I would see. I had done it with my mother too, but I was tired of talking to a wall, and I sure hoped My Fool and I could do something about that.

With that thought, My Fool appeared, standing before me in violet sweatshirt, white pants, and jogging shoes with the toe part cut out, orange socks peeking through. "Hello Susan." His eyes twinkled. "Are you ready to find your mother beyond The Wall?"

I nodded eagerly. "If I can find her, will she recognize me?"

He replied, "When identities die, or rather change location, life memories can be retained for a long while, a short while, released at the moment of death, or released *before* death. But sooner or later the so-called deceased continue their adventure in another consciousness, and the old one becomes but a dream. So, in answer to your question, will your mother recognize you if you find her *beyond* The Wall—well, you might seem familiar, but no, at this point, she would not recognize you as her daughter."

His answer disappointed me.

"Remember," He said, "you cannot transcend The Wall with the strong Focus Identity of Susan pursuing the Focus Identity of your mother as you knew her. That experience is for this world in which you already reside. If that is what you desire, you need nothing more than the Wall of Remembrance. You have already met your mother as you have known her in dreams, and in trance states. You have already talked to her as one would talk to the dead. If you want more—you must first release the heavy sorrow that goes with missing her. If your child went to a foreign country to have the experience of a lifetime, would you be sad? Think of your mother the same way."

My heart *was* heavy. "Yes, I do need to work on that."

"Secondly, you must lighten the boundaries of your identity and focus on who you are *beyond* the persona of Susan."

"You mean, like I do when I go into deep meditation?"

"Not quite. I know you generally preface your meditations with *whoever I am, whatever I am, whatever I need, I open to this.* In this, you have no focus destination. This time, you are shifting from your location, (your idea of yourself), to your mother's vast essence wherever she may be."

"You mean vast, because our essence really isn't singular?"

"That is exactly what I mean."

I nodded lightly. "Okay, I will try."

I focused on my mother's essence in its purity beyond her identity as my mother. But the minute I did that, tears dripped from my ethereal eyes, and my physical eyes too.

"Perhaps," He said warmly, "you are not ready."

"No, wait," I exclaimed, "I fell out of it for a moment, missing her, and I know that keeps me on this side of The Wall. But I very much want to journey beyond The Wall of Remembrance to see what is there."

He said, "Then you must transcend the notion that you have lost her. That notion thickens your identity as Susan, grounding you to your current location in time and space."

I nodded and said forlornly, "I know, I know."

He said, "Besides, *your* mother began dissolving her identity long *before* she died. Even if she had remained in the identity that you knew her, in time, she would not have recognized you anyway."

"Do you mean, like—age related memory loss? Isn't that a function that happens in the brain?"

"Everything is connected, my dear. Chicken nor egg comes first—whether understood or not, the business of spirit and body are simultaneous."

"So is memory loss always involved when one dissolves their identity before they die?"

"No. Sometimes people just change the way they think and behave because they are, on some level, releasing their life as they have known it. They are readying to end an old adventure and embark upon new one."

I said, "I think that is what happened with my mother. Unbeknownst to all of us, including her, it was as if she were saying her goodbyes before her unexpected death. She had told each one of her children how proud she was of them, and all the old issues that had once bothered her seemed to fade into thin air. She had taken heirloom diamond earrings and made them into two necklaces, one for me, and one for my sister. Her old friend, who hadn't called her in decades, called to wish her a happy birthday on her *last* birthday. And for some reason, people out of the blue were paying special tribute to her, and she to them. Then she unexpectedly and to everyone's shock—died."

I started crying. I didn't mean to cry. It just came out.

My Fool said, "You are experiencing what looks like your mother's departure, and responding emotionally as humans do. This emotion, as it should, colors the experience of a loved one dying. Death is viewed as tragic. People, in general, are sad."

Tears dribbled down my cheeks. I sniffled as I wiped them away.

He continued, "That is how it is supposed to be. As you well know, the impression that we are separate from each other allows interchange that produces emotions such as love, joy, hope, fear, anger, and sorrow. Without the impression that we are separate from each other, there would be no relationships or experiences generated from relationships. Hence, the impression of separation affords us great opportunity. You can take that opportunity, Susan. It is unnecessary to go beyond The Wall."

"I know it is not necessary, but I am *compelled* to make this journey."

He brought His hands together in a silent clap. "Very well. Then let us begin with where you are at. When you first heard the news that your mother had died, you were in shock. Shock turned to grief. Your world shattered. Your mother had been ripped away from you, and you felt a part of yourself die too. This partial death catalyzed you to birth into a new level of being. Your existence became more defined."

"Yes," I said, "my whole world had changed. It was like I was in a different world without her. And I just wanted her spirit to visit me so that I could see she was all right. But even when she came to me, I still pined for her physical presence. But because I could not have it, I had to compensate for her absence. I drew closer to the rest of my family, and I further developed my own life, moving into levels of creativity I didn't know I had."

He said, "That is the way of it. Losing a loved one feels devastating, yet it is really not so tragic, not even for the deceased. Common perceptions of those who have 'passed away' are that their spirits visit us, watch us from heaven, or upon our death greet us and accompany us into the afterlife. While these perceptions might carry a measure of truth, is our essence really that finite? Is the whole purpose after death to comfort those yet living. Is the fate of the so-called dead simply to hang around in a heavenly realm waiting for their loved ones to die? Is everyday life really so big, and existence outside everyday life—so small?"

I shook my head. "No, I'd think that existence outside everyday life would be quite vast."

He continued, "Then consider this: What greater love could we have for our deceased loved ones than to emotionally release them to the infinite scope of existence *beyond* our personal beliefs? What is love? *What* is love? In the name of love for your mother, would you not wish for her many great adventures in many exciting worlds?"

"Yes, yes I would."

"Then know too that while your mother's multitudinous Being (that is Being with a capital B) is experiencing many realities, in your reality, she also remains here as your mother, even though her body isn't visible. She simply stopped *expanding* the story she was living as your mother in your current reality. Knowing that she is here with you, and also in other realities in multiple existences having many adventures, can diminish your grief. And then, with emotions in balance, you will be able to traverse the Wall of Remembrance."

I nodded, trying to align myself with His words.

He said, "Your mother, in the inner sanctum of her essence, now and always, will be able to find the joy of the story she lived with you. She can see, and has seen her story in an overview from her greater essence, rather than through the eyes of the identity she was (ever is). She is now and will always know who she was, and what she did to help make the story of the earth what it is."

His beauteous words touched me so. Tears dripped like rain in sunshine. Sensitive, sensitive me.

He said, "And you will always know that you were to experience your mother and she you. You brought each other, and are always bringing each other what you need."

I sniffled, tears still dripping. "I guess there *is* beauty in death. Accepting death is kind of like accepting change, and by accepting change we actually open our world a bit and invite new experience. Besides, eventually *everything* goes through the door of so-called death, so how can death be bad? If death is bad, then birth would have to be bad. If things kept birthing and never died, eventually the world would be destroyed by gross overpopulation of everything. We need death."

He said, "Death *is* needed. When we finish our life story and we, what people call—die, we are released into something new."

"When we die, do we know it?"

"We experience so-called death the very way we expect to experience it. Some continue to perceive themselves still alive in their everyday routine, unaware that they have died. Some perceive nothingness. Some perceive a heavenly state. For others, it is more like a dream. Some shift focus fast and move into a new reality. Others first examine their old reality, and take care of unfinished business. However, eventually the identity's consciousness changes, and the essence of that identity moves on to a new adventure."

"I wonder," I said, "when my mother so-called died, what *she* experienced."

"After your mother 'died,' she examined the story she lived as that identity. She then went through a process of dotting the I's and crossing the T's—unfinished business so to speak. These are times when people might sense the newly deceased in their room at night or have vivid dreams about them."

I gasped. "Just after my mother died, I had a dream that she was at her high school trying to release an age old resentment of a person she knew growing up. She was pulling clothes from her teenage years out of a closet, the clothes that she had worn when she knew that person. She piled the old clothes into my arms, as if giving them away. When she was done, the clothes in my arms vanished. Then she vanished. Cleaning out the old clothes must have represented getting rid of the old resentment she had worn. The clothes vanishing, and her disappearance after, must have meant she had completed the intended task."

"Yes," My Fool said, "she was concluding business before she shifted her focus to a new reality. She continued that process for about a month. Then she journeyed on into new adventures."

"I have to keep remembering that my mother is alive, even though to the world, she is labeled dead."

"Your mother is as alive as the air we breathe in multiple existences. And she is here, in every moment she ever lived in her identity as your mother, and in every moment she has ever lived or will live in any world—anytime."

I furrowed my brow, trying to grasp the abstraction. "This is immensely hard to assimilate!"

My Fool said, "It is as simple as this: We are everywhere, always. What can leave that never really came? What can die that was never really born. Beyond the perception of time and space, we all exist in one homogenized state, eternally and infinitely. Time and space are the shifting of focus from here to there, moment to moment, from this identity to that identity, but everything remains. Whenever we shift focus, it is as a death of one thing and the birth of another. Even if we shift focus from working on the computer to going into the kitchen to eat dinner. What we leave behind no longer seems as important or real as what our new focus has become. Who we are this moment feels more real than who we were five minutes ago. As birth and death occur simultaneously, our perception of what is being born or what is dying depends on which side of the door we are focused upon. A bird dying (shifting focus) is to someone else a bird being born (coming into focus). In perceived separation, we are all on the move, continuously dying and birthing with no real ending or beginning."

"You mean, like the blinking Christmas tree lights you explained to me on the beach today?"

"Yes," He said. "Since we are always everywhere, we continue to exist in every moment in our lives, and all our lives, past present, future. When a light goes on, that is where we are focused, and hence it feels like that is where we are. That is what time travel is . . . a shift of focus."

I said, "Can we time travel to ourselves in other so-called lifetimes, in ways other than hypnosis?"

"Yes. It occurs quite often in dreams and in the strange little experiences we have."

I flashed on an experience I once had. I was writing, trying to think of a way to express something, and I had a vision of a Russian man imprisoned for a book he wrote. Completely immersed in his experience, my physical hand inadvertently stretched out in the air, but in my mind it was stretching to him. We touched. I received his words, the expression of what I sought to put in my writing.

"Yes," My Fool said, having read my mind. "The Russian was you."

"But I thought I had to loosen my identity to time travel?"

"Where were your thoughts when you struggled to express yourself on the computer?"

"Hmm, my thoughts were on the character in the book, and I needed to express something that would uplift the human spirit from oppression."

"Yes, and so, who was your vision of?"

"A repressed Russian. Oh, I see. When I was writing, I wasn't in the identity of Susan. I was in my character searching for expression."

"You see," He said, "time travel happens with ourselves even when we don't view it that way. All our identities interrelate, though seldom do we realize it."

I said, "But tracking someone who is not one of *my* identities, like my mother, seems like it would be harder. I mean, how would I find her current focus?"

"That is the beauty of time travel," He said. "Of her multiple selves, each self will feel like its life is the only life. So, when you go to her, no matter where you go, she is in her current focus."

I held my head, frustrated. "I'm puzzled, if she only feels alive in the focus she is in, how can she feel alive in all focuses at once?"

"She, like everyone, is one of multiple identities housed in a Being. While each identity feels that they are the one and only, the Being experiences everything that its identities experience."

"Oh," I said, "I kind of get it."

"You can see then why time travel to locate the deceased in their current reality requires traversing The Wall of Remembrance. Your mother can't be found in a new identity and location if you continue to behold her in the old identity, which grounds you to this location."

"Yes, I think I understand. This is very exciting!"

"If you succeed in passing through The Wall, you will be able to view her in more than one existence, even though her consciousness experiences one existence after another. You will be dancing on her time line. Hence, you will be able to peek in on her . . . in time, from no time."

"So then, to contact my mother beyond The Wall, I must be open myself to travel into any of the many locations where she might be?"

"Yes, release all your current imaginings so that they do not interfere with what is."

"Given I've waited two and a half years, will locating her be more difficult?"

"No. As all her existences coexist, they are always where they are."

I said, "Viewing it that way, it makes sense that she is also with me now even though I can't see her."

He replied, "She is. You have merely slipped out of her focus, and she, yours."

"So, because any identity that has ever been, is, or will be—coexists, we can locate the so-called deceased in any identity, at any 'time?'

"Yes. A Being is like a book with an identity on every page. For an identity to exist, it must vibrate *in* time and space at a specific location. By leaving your location, you can flip through the book of her various identities existences. The pages can be turned, going from one identity's reality to another, but the pages never go away. They are always there to revisit and experience again."

I was growing deeply anxious to explore the book of my mother's Being. "Can we transcend The Wall now?"

"Not yet. There is more. The degree to which you loosen your sense of identity (which cements you in your Focus World) is the degree you will experience yourself in a different location of space and time. If you loosen your identity in a minor way, then you might only glimpse your loved one in the past or future. If you loosen your identity substantially, you might appear as a ghost or maybe an angel to the one being visited."

"Can we ever be fully seen by whom we are visiting?"

"Only in dreams. In this state, not only can we appear fully visible to those we visit, but we can appear fully visible to those visiting us."

"Dreams excluded, why can't I appear solid when I visit my mother in her current locations?"

"Because each identity is cemented by the location they are in. So, when we visit them or they us, the visitor would not appear dense with flesh and blood. If they became solid, it would mean that they completely left the location that their identity is focused in. And if they did that, they would no longer be that identity. In a sense, that Christmas tree light would have gone out."

"Do you mean they would die?"

"There is no death—only a change of focus."

"But would their bodies dissolve?"

"In perceived time—yes."

"Is it possible to loosen too much?"

"Our identity's life intent pulls us strongly into focus, like gravity. And until the intent is fulfilled, the focus on that identity cannot be broken. Likewise, when that life intent is fulfilled, the identity will move on, no matter what. This is what happens when people survive impossible situations, or when they die in freak accidents, or die suddenly for reasons unknown. So . . . no, we cannot *fully* shift focus away from our current identity, no matter what the circumstance, until our story is done."

'Well, how can we know to what degree we must loosen our identity for balanced time travel?"

"Go into neutral, and trust that the vibration of your identity will adjust to take you where you need to go in a manner that is right for you."

"So, I just need to set the premise that whatever is right for me will be, and *know* that it will be."

He affirmed, "Yes, then you will be in a state of mind for time travel. Remember, time travel experiences are more about touching upon insight, rather than trying to understand the complete workings of time and no time. To get a hint of what lies 'beyond the box' is enough to add fuel to a story, and meaning to a life. It is enough to enable one to embrace their worth, forgive what seems unforgivable, and to find a sense of centeredness."

I said, "It's ironic in a way, that to understand ourselves better, we have to let ourselves go."

"That is true. Loosening the sense of self as a solid identity, not only makes time travel possible, but once we have journeyed and insight is gained, the Focus Identity is more reverently beheld."

"So, when we visit my mother, I will know that I am Susan, but softening the boundaries of who I think I am, will keep me in a time travel mode?"

"Yes, but you cannot visit her until you finish releasing her. Do this now."

I closed my eyes and concentrated. I saw clearly that if I truly loved my mother, then my focus would *not* be on what she could do for me, but on what I could do for her. And the greatest gift I could give her was to release her and wish her well on her journey. And in so doing, I gulped back a forthcoming sob. "I wish you well, mother, on your journey. I wish you—well." I felt a strong building sensation in my heart. Something shot out of it, and I felt a great release, as if a weight had been lifted. I had a vision. My mother drove past me in a red convertible with the top down on the highway, zooming joyfully along, without noticing me.

And I knew My Fool saw her too when He said, "Now you are ready to transcend The Wall. Open your hand."

I stretched my palm to Him.

He placed in it miniature high-powered binoculars. "This is the Gem of Time Travel. Given we are all always everywhere, the gift of time travel enables vast experiences by creating the ability to shift focus from here to there, from one moment to another, and from one world to another. In this, we experience time and place, hence the setting for stories to materialize."

The binoculars absorbed into my palm, and I felt the power of time travel within me. I was about to say, *I am ready to time travel,* when He said, "Experience the joy your mother feels in the red convertible without needing her to recognize you. Loosen your mind, Susan. Do it now. Focus on your essence, rather than yourself as Susan. Focus on your mother's essence, rather than your mother as you knew her. This is vital if you want to transcend the Wall of Remembrance and see your mother in her other worlds. If you go after her as the mother of Susan, this will not work."

I focused on what lay ahead on the Other Side of Life. I went deeper and deeper into meditation, feeling the edges of my identity fading. I knew who I was, but it was as if I were casting myself out into the ocean while anchored to the shore.

Everything around me blurred. Boundaries faded. Then My Fool's wise and timeless hand reached through the vagueness. I thrust my hand toward His. He took my hand and pulled me through the other side of The Wall. A rushing sensation overcame me, so intense that I almost jerked back into my physical body. But just then, My Fool whispered in a rather god-like way, "Keep focus. We are jumping the linear thread."

I felt queasy when scenes of life drama flashed in front of me. Not my life drama per se—just frames from the play of life like a woman in labor, two people hugging, one man shooting another, a person hand gliding. But I was feeling increasingly nauseas, and I wasn't sure I could go on—such movement, or such rapid shifts of focus seemed too much for my system, like a ballerina spinning around and around without spotting.

Then a man's face came before me; my eyes locked with his ethereal orbs: deep-set blue, impenetrable to invasion, burning ice-fire to survive. Was this the spirit who helped free me from the rip current? No, it felt like another. Then he vanished and the rushing stopped.

There was only quiet stillness. My heart pounded.

"Be calm," My Fool said, "stay centered."

I calmed my heartbeat and practiced an open state of mind. And then a scene came into focus. I was standing with My Fool in a bright clear meadow of green grass. Beyond the meadow was a clean and manicured neighborhood.

My Fool was beside me in a form that flashed many forms. The flashing sickened me, so I held my focus on the form of Him in which I was most comfortable, My Fool.

We walked across the field. I felt less solid then I normally do, and I assumed, in this world, I was incorporeal.

I asked My Fool, "Can psychics in this world see me? And if so, would I be perceived as a dead person?"

He replied, "It depends upon the psychic. You could be perceived as a dead person, a spirit helper, or maybe even an evil entity."

I gasped. "Really?"

"The beliefs of the psychic will at least, in a minor way, influence how they experience you. The psychic is called upon to interpret psychic events, and therein lies the possible skewing of what is at hand."

My Fool and I neared the neighborhood. I asked, "Are we going to see my mother?"

He said, "We are going to witness one reality of your mother, but remember, her Being is the whole book, pages and pages of identities and realities."

"Yes," I said, "I understand."

As we approached the houses, cars were coming and going in the noonday sun. Children played in yards, dogs barked, and birds sang. This world did not seem much different from the one that the identity Susan lived in.

We moved toward a white brick house, a typical upper middle class home in the suburbs. We went through the wall of the home into a living room. On a beige sofa sat a woman with shoulder length black hair, in tan slacks and a dark green dress shirt.

I asked My Fool, "Is that my mother?"

He replied, "Yes, it is one of her."

"I guess time really does work differently than we imagine," I said, "given she died two and half years ago, and here she is a grown woman."

"Remember," He said, "time is not really linear."

"Yes, but it is hard to keep hold of that insight. I keep wanting to think of my mom as I knew her." I wanted to cry out to the lady on the sofa—*Mom, it is me, Susan.*

He said, "She can't recognize you in this consciousness."

I felt sad.

She suddenly hunched over, and seemed upset.

A man walked in the room. He looked like a professor. He sat next to her. "What is wrong, Lee? You seem distraught."

She replied, "I feel sad suddenly, for no reason. Or, maybe I feel sad for someone."

Then two teenage boys strolled into the room, one tall and blond, the other shorter with dark hair.

"They can't see us at all, even as spirits?" I asked.

He replied, "Not in their current mind state, however, they might sense us."

One of the boys said, "I feel weird."

The other teenage boy said, "You are weird."

I looked to My Fool and said, "Maybe we should leave. Can we go to another reality of my mother's essence?"

He nodded. "However, you are on the verge of returning to the world of Susan because you are focusing on your mother as you knew her—too hard. If you want to see more, you must once again loosen the edges of your identity as you know it, and you mother's identity as you knew her."

I immediately deepened my meditative state, and focused on my quintessential being, rather than my human life as Susan, seeking to visit the essence of my mother rather than the mother I knew. I had the odd sensation of moving against stillness, or perhaps things were moving past me. I could not tell.

Then the sensation ceased, and everything felt still.

My Fool said, "Look."

We were in a backyard with seven playing children accompanied by their mothers and fathers. A round birthday cake was brought out to a female toddler whose bright smile made dimples on her cheeks. She was told to blow out the candles from the pink iced cake. She blew them out, and then suddenly looked our way with interest.

"Can she see us?" I asked My Fool.

"Yes. Many children see beyond the physical realm."

"Hi," I said to the girl.

She mouthed with audible breath, "Hi."

Her mother said, "Who is she talking to?" And then the incident was ignored and the cake was cut.

I said to My Fool, "I'm glad to witness this. I know in the life she had with me, her childhood was fraught with neglect."

My Fool said, "We all experience everything, eventually. We each have our turn. And the dark times are just as precious, for they set the scene for amazing discovery and deep self-embrace."

Even so, I liked this life for my mom. I wanted to hold the little girl, even if she seemed more like my child than my mother. I loved her still.

"Shall we move on?" My Fool inquired.

I nodded. I loosened my knowing, released anticipation, and had a mind-set to experience of my mother what was right for me. I felt that zooming sensation again, then stillness.

Before me and My Fool was a mystical setting resembling an expansive cloud. An energy form approached us, female, I think. This form seemed spirit-like, and apparently it could see us. The form waved her hand toward herself, inviting us to follow her.

We were guided up to an energy fountain of predominantly oranges and pinks. A cool yet warm energy entered our feet, surged through us, and flowed out at the top of our heads. I felt like I was being cleansed. I glanced up at My Fool in His many changing forms within a form. He just smiled.

I was wondering if the spirit-like form was an aspect of my mother. In my head, My Fool answered, *Indeed.*

Again I missed my mother and as I knew her. I wanted to tell the form who I was, that I was her daughter.

My Fool replied in my head, "Again, she will not recognize you in her current consciousness."

I felt frustrated, much like the two-year-old crying out with all my heart, *I want my mommy.*

I suddenly snapped back into my body, into Susan lying on my hammock outside in the dark, no mommy and seemingly no Fool. Holst's "The Planets" had ended, and the stars were covered with clouds.

Well, He did keep telling me that if I focused on the identity of Susan, I couldn't travel to these other worlds. I would try to do better next time. I decided to go back inside and sleep in my bed. I'd had enough adventure for the night, and for that matter, the day. Right now I just needed to ground myself in the familiar.

I journeyed inside, removed my Walkman, placed it on the bed stand, and fell into bed. Lying there in the dark, I felt my old cat, Jensen, crawl onto my stomach. I stroked his bristly fur as I lay there drifting to sleep thinking of my mother. She was living in me, around me, and away from me, all at the same time. She was here, there, and everywhere. This concept was more beautiful to me than the concept that she *just* died and is under the ground in dirt, or *just* hanging around waiting for me to die, or *just* in some paradise somewhere with all adventure ended, or *just* reincarnated into another body. Why cannot *all* these be true? Only in the concept of linear time would this perception present glitches. But, if a crystal with numerous facets can radiate light in all directions, why can't the many faceted us, do the same?

As I nuzzled my head deeper into the pillow, I felt like I was sinking into an etheric crystal. From there, looking about the facets, I saw the many faces of myself, all reflections of my other existences elsewhere, some inside me, some across the world, some in the seeming past, some in the seeming future. A thousand me's, I thought. Layers of dimension seemed to converge, and I sank into unremembered sleep.

We all lose loved ones, and we are all lost by loved ones, in one way or another—and yet, in the greater scheme of things, no one leaves anyone ever. We dance together in a myriad of ways in a myriad of realities. We breathe in; we breathe out. We are the caterpillar, chrysalis, and butterfly, moving on, ever changing form, but ever present in whatever form we focus upon. But all identities exist at once. There is no death. There is no time.

Close your eyes a moment and behold yourself as a vast energy that is everywhere. If you like, you can open to this vast self to enable you to have a time travel experience that would lend insight into your current reality. This experience might entail beholding a deceased loved one in another reality. Or it might be to visit another identity in your own Being.

The easiest way to have such a journey is during sleep. Before you sleep tonight you might say to your vast self, something like this: *I open to a time travel experience in sleep that will bring me peace regarding the death of my loved one, or an experience that would lend insight to my own life journey.*

Do not hope it will happen. Know that whatever is right for you *will* happen. *Bon Voyage*!

A Thousand Me's

"In vastness I separate; in separation I am vast."

GEM #3 MULTIPLICITY

My eyes opened to my bedroom ceiling viewing my surrealistic Wizard of Oz poster in the early morning light. Dorothy in her crazy world . . . . Was she really so different than each one of us? Oh, how we toil through the maze of life to reach a happy ending!

It was the day after my birthday. A brand new year. A year of what? It was always kind of exciting not to know. I sat up in bed. I scanned the three square cat beds in a row at my side. Usually every morning they were filled with one cat each, little ears peaking up over the cat bed rim. My eyes caught a bed with a different sort of cat. A dead cat.

My twenty-year-old caramel colored cat had died.

Jensen, oh my Jensen! He was on his side stretched out. His small shell was empty of life. I stroked him as if he were alive. I wailed, "Jensen, I love you with all my heart!" And then I thought of what My Fool had been teaching me about death.

So, I shifted my focus from viewing Jensen as the cat I once had, and instead viewed him as energy, always alive . . . somewhere. I wondered if I could locate Jensen's essence as I had my mother's last night.

I reached to my bed stand to my Walkman and changed the disc. I slipped on my headphones, and clicked on the music. Lying down, I took a deep breath and let Gustav Mahler's *Symphony No.10* wash over me. I whispered, "Susan is a cloak I wear, but I am pure energy beneath. This pure energy has wings to find you, Jensen. Wherever you are, whoever you are, whatever death is, whatever life is, beyond all belief systems, I seek you now."

A sensation grabbed me. I felt like I'd blasted through a giant swinging door, and that fast, my etheric body was inside a giant crystal with numerous facets, similar to the one last night where I glimpsed my many identities. As I looked around from inside the crystal, I saw countless kaleidoscopic pictures. Keeping my focus on Jensen, his essence came into view.

The facets now were as tiny windows. Through one tiny window, I saw myself as Susan petting Jensen with his little rump pointing in the air as I scratched down his back. Jensen and I were still together, even though he was so-called dead, just as, according to My Fool, my mom was still with me though she was dead. Through another window, I saw Jensen as a gray and white long-haired cat, chasing a mouse. In another facet, I saw an anxious leopard in a zoo pacing its cell. Through another window, I saw a monkey scampering up a palm tree. It occurred to me then that a cat, in its multilevel existences, is not always a cat.

My Fool had told me that if we should tap into our other realities, they will usually seem akin to our current reality because our other worldly experiences are *still* filtered through our current identity's conscious perception. Thus, our experience is influenced by who we know ourselves to be. I, as one who identifies with female oppression, most readily glimpse times and places of myself as an oppressed female. People who identify with domination, quite often witness their other lives in times of experiencing supreme control. And if we should glimpse into the lives of another, it too will be flavored with how we have known them. I knew Jensen as a cat, therefore my view of him in other realities does not stray far from that image.

I know what My Fool would say about that. He'd say, *that it is the way it is supposed to be. We must retain our Focus Identity and its perceptions if we are to finish its story.*

As the music of Mahler's tenth symphony sounded sweeping tones, I sank deeper into my meditation, dead cat at my feet. Still inside the crystal of Jensen's essence, I moved inside a facet, like going through a window. I was in darkness. I heard muffled liquid sloshing. Next to me was a cat fetus. Jensen was incubating in another cat!

Unexpectedly, I zoomed inside the fetus, into cells, into atoms. I began to feel uncomfortably disassociated with my Focus Identity. *Stop!* I commanded myself. Though still in a trance, I felt the bed beneath me once more. This is one reason I opted for drug free metaphysical exploration. I could stop and start experiences as I liked, and control the direction of my experience if I chose.

I wanted to speak to My Fool, so I deepened my trance once again. I came upon the Wall of Remembrance, only I was already on the other side of it! Apparently, I was getting good at time travel. Ironically, My Fool was on the mundane side of The Wall in violet sweatshirt and white pants.

"Hey," I said playfully, "what are you doing over . . . there?"

He stroked His beard in a scholarly fashion. "Before we proceed to the next adventure, a review is in order. Even when we review what we think we know, we can see the old view in new and more profound ways *if* we are open."

"I *am* open to gain fresh insight," I said.

He arced His arm toward Himself. "Then come on over."

"Okay," I replied. I focused on strengthening my sense of identity. I was Susan, the writer and mother of grown children. Just like that, I appeared next to My Fool on the mundane side of The Wall.

In His hand, there appeared a crystalline pointer. And before us there appeared a map of the Universe. He arced His pointer across the map. "Everything vibrates to numbers."

The map changed into a map of earth. "Earth vibrates to the number eleven; when Beings enter earth, they vibrate to this number." He arced the crystalline pointer across the earth image. "In the vibration of eleven, a Being assembles numerous identities to experience earth in many lifetimes."

As I stared at the earth image, an orb of light touched upon it. He pointed to the orb. "For instance, a Being might want to experience a zealous Roman warrior." The orb expanded as something began to happen within it. A vast array of tiny energy particles mixed and matched, and came together like a mosaic with specifically cut chips arranged into a beautiful, one of a kind, multi-colored pattern. My Fool said, "*Voila*, an identity is created!"

I cocked my head, awed by the demonstration.

He continued, "And that same Being might want to also experience an overbearing business man, an African activist, and so on."

Energy particles conglomerated inside the expanding orb as identities assembled into one of kind mosaics.

I said, "So, the Being houses all of the identities that it wishes to experience in earth life."

"Indeed," He said. The mosaic identities began to glow. "Each identity has a spirit, a driving force that makes them who they are. The spirit is the essence of the identity. All these essences, or spirits, are the soul of Being."

"So the spirit in each identity makes up the soul of our Being, or is the Being an over soul of the spirits?"

"Both. Even so, these depictions do not fully reflect a Being's complexity, but it will do."

He pointed to a chip in the Roman warrior mosaic. Each chip in the mosaic of an identity represents a reference, personalized for the spirit. References are varied and many. Examples are: measures of intellect (smart, slow, scientific, clever, deep thinker, problem solver, mastermind, etc.). Measures of emotion (sensitive, detached, feisty, shy, aggressive, temperamental, paranoid, pessimistic, optimistic, nurturing, passionate, etc.). And physical traits (height, eye color, skin tone, features, health, etc.). These references also include unconscious emotional motivators, such as fear of water or love of rain, or a leaning toward science or art."

His crystalline pointer tapped an identity inside the now very expanded orb. "Each identity has a mandate, which is comprised of the life circumstances needed to set the scene for that life. Examples of mandates are: being born into an unstable family, or into a third world country, as an only child, or to be the child of a politician."

I was absorbing these insights more deeply than I had five years ago, mostly because 'I' had changed since then.

His crystalline pointer touched another identity. "Each identity has an intent, which is its purpose for living. An example of an intent might be to go through a lifetime seeing what it is like to develop personal power. Again, I am radically simplifying."

Then the Being and the identities within it changed into a massive tree. My Fool's crystalline pointer started at the trunk and moved upward. "Every master intent, like a tree trunk, has multiple sub-intents like branches. The sub-intents have sub sub-intents like leaves on the branches."

Just seeing the massive tree made me realize the complexity of intent.

He pointed to the trunk again. "The master intent of a Being will be fulfilled through its identities, for example, Susan, Laurie, and Joe." His pointer outlined several branches. "Each identity will explore a different branch of the same theme. For instance: if the master intent is to experience sensitivity, then the identities, Susan, Laurie, and Joe, will have sub-intents that serve that master intent. Susan's sub-intent of the master intent might be to experience life as an ultra sensitive person who exposes herself to the world. Laurie's sub-intent of the master intent might be to, as a sensitive person, be a great healer. Joe's sub-intent of the master intent might be to, as an ultra sensitive man, learn how to shield his energies in order to make it in a man's world. Yet each identity is experiencing sensitivity."

I said, "So a master intent of a Being, such as developing personal power, would be explored by all identities in the Being. Each identity would have a sub-intent. One identity might have the sub-intent to build a business from scratch, another . . . to be one's own person rather than following the dictates of others, and so on."

"Yes," He affirmed. "Then an identity's master intent, such as exploring personal power, might have a mandate to be born in a slum, (escaping the slum would require the identity to develop personal power), and personalized references such as a weight problem, or a race that invites prejudice, or a passionate drive for something that exceeds convention (thereby facilitating the fulfillment of the life intent to develop personal power)."

"Wow," I said, "we really are exactly the way we are supposed to be, and so are our parents, siblings, children, friends, and even our enemies."

His pointer disappeared and His hands came together as if in prayer. "Yes, every identity is lovingly designed by *us* as Creative Energy, to have experiences that we may further explore what we are."

I said, "It is as you once told me, Creative Energy wants to know itself by exploring individuality."

His face seemed cosmic for a moment, as if it were a backdrop of stars, and His voice took on a resonance potent with inspiration. "If one takes multiple colors and mixes them together, there is a new color. A similar thing happens when we construct our identities. We stir in multiple intents, mandates, and references. Then, when we are finished, we are like no other identity that has ever been, or will ever be. We are . . . an original."

My heart warmed. "What a pretty way to think of it!"

"Then if we like or hate rain or sunshine more than most, it is because that special mixture has created a reference of joy or punishment due to the rain or the sun. With massive references in countless combinations, creating innumerable interactions, no two identities will feel *exactly* the same about any thing, even if it is close."

"So when someone says, *I feel that way too,* they might feel similar but never exactly the same."

"We cannot be like someone else. When we try, we are unwittingly ignoring the true gift of life, of our life, the point of our life. Everyone is a true one of a kind."

"And because we can't fully understand all our references, which is the same as us trying to fully understand ourselves, we can't really ever *fully* understand any one else either."

He said, "And *not* understanding allows surprises that make life exciting."

"Or scary," I added.

"It is often the not so pleasant surprises that spark the greatest explorations. Your cat died, and you were exploring his other identities. Would you have done that if he had lived?"

"No, I wouldn't have. And I am glad I did. It further drives home the realization that death is not an end, experience always continues, and that we are all multiple, including my dead cat."

"Yes," He said, "our constructed references guide us into the living experiences we seek. An identity who hates rain might be compelled to journey to a land of sun."

"Can we ever change our references once our lives are in motion?"

"References cannot be changed. An identity with the reference of a predominantly scientific mind will never be *inclined* to take a leap of faith. An identity with a predominantly creative mind *will* be *inclined* to take multiple leaps of faith. If one finds joy in rain, or singing, or studying math, it is unlikely they will ever lose that joy. If one is born with brown eyes, though contact lenses can be applied, the eyes are still brown. A weight problem can be controlled and the quest to handle it results in the fulfillment of an intent, but the weight problem must always be dealt with. If one has the reference that he will go to hell if he doesn't believe a certain way, though that reference can be tweaked, deep down it remains."

"So that belief will always be with him."

He said, "Yes. Unless there is another reference implanted that counters that belief. Then both references would serve to create conflict in the identity toward the end of fulfilling a life intent."

"So, our references influence the beliefs we have."

"Yes. We only know what our references allow us to know. In death or life, each of us is born with references of what life or death is, and those references will be reinforced or countered by our mandates. A person who is sure he will go to hell for not believing a certain way, will have that reference enforced or countered by being born into a religious or non-religious family. Our personalized references such as: physical attributes, intelligence and emotional sensitivity, and likes and dislikes, force us to deal with life in a way that serves the intent. Hence, it would not help us to be able to change them."

"So we are locked into who we are."

"Yes. However, who we are and what our life is really about, is always more than meets the eye. For example: if a woman desires to be a famous actress, but her unconscious life intent is to experience being humble, the desire to be an actress would be a reference that the Being chose for its identity, but maybe not for the purpose one might imagine. Maybe the woman will try for twelve years to be a famous actress but not succeed, and the result is that she is humbled. And in truth then, the woman did not really fail, she succeeded in fulfilling her intent to experience being humble."

"Wow," I said, "failure really is an impossibility."

"Indeed."

The review had really wet my whistle to go to the other side of The Wall. I said eagerly, "Will you show me what else is on the other side of The Wall?"

"Yes, my dear. But for now, bury your cat, and have a day. Mundane life is important too."

"Very well," I said. "I will have my mundane day, but tonight, can I meet you?"

"You know you don't need me for the journey."

"I know, but I feel better when you are there."

"Tonight then, at the Wall of Remembrance." He nodded with a knowing eye, and vanished. Mahler's, *Symphony No.10* ended with haunting tones. *So* beautiful.

I sighed, gathering my resolve to bury my cat. Funny how I can understand death is not an end, yet I will miss the old guy. A tear dripped. I sniffled. Mundane day, here I come.

When evening came, I changed into my soft, dark blue pajamas and fuzzy blues socks. (Yes, I did get out my pajamas that day.) I grabbed my Walkman and headed for my hammock. A night owl hooted, the wind rustled the trees, and I was filled with anticipatory vigor. I crawled into my green-netted hammock and peeked at the stars through the branches. With headphones on ears, I made the hammock rock to calm my nerves. Going beyond The Wall was a bit daunting, even if it was exciting.

As Ludwig van Beethoven's *Symphony No.9* played, I went to the Wall of Remembrance.

As I waited for My Fool, His voice seemed to narrate the music, almost like a prelude to the experience to come on the other side of The Wall.

"As you know, there are multiple identities in your Being like fingers on a hand, or roses on a bush, or protons, neutrons, and electrons in an atom."

He appeared before me, hands in the pockets of His white pants, His head arcing as if perusing the night sky. "Just as one can look all around and see many things—" we both appeared in the center of a wheel, (one of My Fool's favorite teaching illustrations), "—one can also look around the wheel of our Being and see our many selves."

I glanced around the expansive wheel, which was more dimensional than any wheel He'd ever taken me into. I could turn around in place and see a wheel. And I could look to my side, then up, then to my other side, and then down, and see a wheel. No matter what direction I looked, I could see the wheel around me. Looking upon it all at once, I realized it was a sphere.

I shook my head. "Wow! This is complex."

"Yes," He said, "though too complex for the human mind to grasp fully, much insight can yet be gleaned. Now, focus on one angle, and you will view a line of identities, like a meridian that circles the sphere."

I chose an angle to view. I looked to the side of me, then upward, then to the other side, then downward. I saw multiple identities, too many to count.

He said, "As you know, linearly speaking, each meridian of identities lives one at time, experiencing one life, then another, then another, as in reincarnation. However, from here, beyond time, you can see that all identities on every meridian, coexist, and are connected, and therefore interact with each other."

Though He'd shared this concept with me before, I'd never understood it this well. Same subject, I suppose, but a higher course level. Glancing about the wheel, I said, "With thousands of identities existing in a Being, interactions must get complicated."

"No, the interactions are synchronistic. It is very simple even though it seems complex. Each identity at the helm of its ship has a crew of facades. These facades are other the identities in a Being making an appearance."

I gasped in one of those 'ah hah' moments. I got the picture. The facades that I dealt with as Susan, for instance My Nun, were other identities in my Being interacting with me. I said, "So every identity we have ever been, are, or will be, is a part of our personality, and—"

He interrupted, "Yes, however we often suppress the more diametrically opposite identities in our Being, so they seldom appear. In general, the identities we are more familiar with exist on one meridian that circles the sphere. Linearly speaking, these identities trail each other, each experiencing similar lifetimes of one particular angle of a theme, such as oppression. Yet, the personalities of these identities grow and change as the theme is more thoroughly and continually explored. So, a line of identities, such as the nun, the oppressed housewife, the activist bursting out of oppression, and the Russian writer in prison, experience oppression in a similar manner, but deal with it a little differently. While these identities coexist in no time, in the projection of time, one life can build upon another, each life altering the next."

I said, "So, these facades, in psychological terms, are viewed as aspects of a person that everyone possesses, but they are also identities with their own life?"

He nodded. "And you are a facade to them. You are an aspect of them. Your spirit rises in them, sometimes to their joy, and other times to their chagrin."

I shook my head in awe.

He continued, "To regulate this, each identity shuts out the other identities in its Being from its consciousness, so that it can remain the driver of its life. However, unconsciously, the other identities can pop in and influence actions, as is part of the plan."

"Like when My Nun identity pops up, I might start acting like a nun to facilitate part of my story, and then when that is done, I push her out?"

"Basically. Though, regarding her, your current vibration has changed, hence, you do not invite her in as once it did. Therefore, your experience of her would be less. All the identities operate in balance. The facades are not really our enemies, even though we might feel they are at times."

I said, "What happens if we have an experience that changes us, and thus our vibration. Does this invite an identity that we are not so familiar with to emerge in our lives?"

"Yes. Sometimes another identity in our Being inadvertently bleeds through, and people behave out of character. For example, a controlling woman is in a car accident. She is laid up in the hospital with broken legs. Because she is exploring the vibration of control and dependence, the act of temporarily losing control might trigger the experience of one of her other identities living out the life of a paraplegic. The woman might sink into an unexplainable depression, heavier than what would make sense in her current predicament (broken legs). The paraplegic identity in another life has risen as a facade in the woman. Or, as psychologists might say, a dormant aspect in one's personality has come to the forefront."

"I see," I said. "It's like when I was a psychotherapist, so often people came to me thinking they were going crazy. But it was more that one of their identities popped in and took center stage. In psychological circles it is often assumed that our troubles stem from our childhood only, or from events that occurred to us in this current identity, but I suppose it is not always that simple."

"No, it never is. Whether viewed linearly, as in reincarnation, or simultaneously as in 'no time', our other selves are integrally connected to us and life events easily trigger their realities in our own, which for moments, hours, days, or sometimes years, bleed through into our lives. It is all a part of the story, to wrestle with, or be aided by—ourselves."

"Like sometimes we can call upon our facades to help us, like I do My Warrior?"

He nodded. "One's selves can unite and empower an identity, as well as become dominant at times. For instance, the facade of a powerful activist might pop through you one day when you witness an injustice. You might uncharacteristically fight a battle with great success and wonder what got into you. Well, it was yourself—another you, that is another—and yet . . . you."

I said, "Well, in the concept that we have our stories figured out before we live them, I guess there would be a synchronistic timing to when and how our other identities interact with us."

"Let us further explore that incite on the other side of The Wall. Are you ready?"

I nodded eagerly. "Yes."

He threw His arms in the air. "Then let us be off to the other side of The Wall!" He vanished.

My heart sputtered. Okay, I had to concentrate. *Whoever I am, whatever I am—beyond all belief systems—I open to that. Creative Energy dissolves my boundaries in accordance with my well-being.*

I began to feel larger than the identity of Susan. Then I was on the other side of The Wall in a sphere, kind of like the one we were in earlier, but this one seemed more real, and not just an illustration. I felt like I was in the center of a great city, like the kind you see in science fiction. As I looked around, I noticed that instead of viewing identities in my Being, all the identities were me, I mean . . . Susan!

My Fool appeared next to me. He said, "When you were born, one Susan, who is very shy, stayed shy and became a nun. Another shy Susan worked through her shyness with the help of a loving mother who used clever psychology. Another Susan, when she was older, was sexually victimized but recovered, another Susan was sexually victimized and died."

"So, in a sense, it's like there are a thousand me's living out every possible version of the life of Susan?"

"There are more than a thousand you's, but that image will serve you."

"Does each Susan have her own consciousness?"

"Yes and no. Each Susan shares your references with infinitesimal variation. They are all Susan, but each living out a different probability of the way Susan's life will unfold. They are all you—experiencing all possibilities at once. And each Susan in the identity of Susan will contribute to the master story of your Being."

"So," I said, "we are all working toward the same thing."

"Yes." He moved His pointer outward toward a Susan, and then another, and then another.

One Susan was getting into a car with a strange man.

I mumbled, "Don't do that."

She said, "I have to do it."

Another Susan was crying because someone rejected her.

"Don't do that," I whispered.

She replied, "I have to."

Another Susan was so shy she sat by a tree at kindergarten recess and wouldn't play with anyone.

"Oh honey," I mumbled, "don't do that."

"I have to," she replied.

Then simultaneously they said, "We must do what we must do."

And then I realized that we all must do what we must do. We are experimenting in our life adventure, and we are supposed to experiment because experimenting creates new experiences.

Then recalling the time when I was a kid and my mom almost drowned in the ocean, I asked My Fool, "The first time the ocean almost took my mom, did a version of her die, and yet another version remain with me and my siblings? And if so, when my mom died two and a half years ago, is a version of her still alive in a reality with me, my brother, and sister?"

"Yes," He said, "these other versions, in a way, are all condensed in any given identity, and yet living lives of their own."

"So, we are in each other but we emanate different probabilities, like perhaps a sun that shines rays."

"Basically."

"In this version of Susan that I now experience, can I visit myself at different ages?"

"You can. Like a book, you flip from page to page through the times of your life."

"If we remember ourselves at a certain age, is that the same as visiting ourselves?"

"No. We remember what we remember differently at age five than we do at age ten and so on. This is why people often dispute a shared event, because not only do they remember the event differently, but that memory changes as new experiences and perceptions mix into their minds."

I said, "So in a way, if two people insist vehemently that they know the truth of a shared past event, they are both . . . kind of—wrong?"

"Not wrong as much as inaccurate. They each see one piece of an old picture filtered through their individual references. Judgments are made, and reality to them rests in the confines of the beliefs born from those judgments. These beliefs catalyze events critical to the unfolding of their stories, so the *inaccuracy* is meant to be."

"So because our recollections are skewed, we cannot time travel through memory."

"Precisely."

"Well, if not by memory as in recall, how do we visit ourselves in our current identity? How do I visit the ten-year-old Susan? I mean from here, in this sphere?"

"To experience Susan in the so-called past, for instance, 1970, you must leave your current location which is Susan, right now, this moment. Then, without recollection or pre-judgment, re-enter your life in 1970. You can peer in or be in the body of Susan as you were then, not how you remember it. You will be able to see exactly why you made certain choices, or why you reacted a certain way. Then it can be seen that choices made were for a viable reason, and reactions had were understandable. In memory, you cannot see this."

"What about going to the identity of Susan in the future? "

"You can, but it requires immense openness and loosening of your current focus—the judging or interpretive mind cannot go. This is what occurs with psychics who predict the future. Their conscious mind will interpret what they glimpse through the net of their beliefs. To further complicate the matter, given there are numerous versions of Susan in parallel realities, one never knows which Susan is honed in upon. So futures can be visited, but interpretations are subject to error."

He flipped out His hand, and even though we were still in the sphere, I saw a vision of my mother's two women friends, Judy, who is psychic, and Mary who was asking Judy questions. Judy apparently was channeling my deceased mother.

I asked My Fool, "Can it be that a version of my mother is being channeled through Judy?"

"It *can* be," He replied. "However, because channeling is filtered through the belief system of the one channeling, the interpretation can get twisted."

"Yes. I have seen that in psychics who do have ability. That is why I prefer to be my own psychic, although for those who can't, I understand why they reach out. I mean I understand why Mary is calling to my mother through Judy."

He said, "Judy and Mary are getting out of your mother what they need to get out of your mother because that fits into their story. But your mother is experiencing many realities even while people feel she is visiting theirs."

The vision of the two women vanished.

My Fool said, "Open your hand."

I held out my palm.

He placed a visible snowflake in it. "This is the Gem of Multiplicity. In one, we are many. We are original, yet the same. The way that the water molecules interrelate in the snowflake will determine its design, making it an original. Yet every snowflake is still—snow. And the ways that multiple identities interrelate in a Being make the Being an original. Yet all original Beings are still one Creative Energy."

I said, "So, we are different in our sameness, and multiple in our oneness."

His eyes gleamed. "Opposites are always the same. Now, focus on the whole sphere while also going deeper into the center of yourself."

"So I am to focus on moving outward and inward at the same time?"

He nodded.

While envisioning the sphere, I focused on traveling within to my center. Upon that, I seemed to expand and the sphere was a tiny spec within me, and another sphere was all around me. As I gazed upon that sphere, I saw the identities in my Being.

I could not see My Fool, but I heard His voice. "Now while holding focus on the identities in your Being around you, go into the center of yourself again."

While envisioning the sphere of identities in my Being, I traveled within again, focusing on going to my center. And again, I seemed to expand and that sphere was a tiny spec within me and another sphere was all around me. As I gazed upon it, I noticed thousands of Beings.

My Fool said, "Now, while focusing on the sphere of countless Beings all around you, go further into the center of yourself."

And when I did, I seemed to expand and that sphere was a tiny spec within me and another sphere was all around me. As I gazed upon that sphere, I noticed thousands of earths.

"And again," My Fool said.

Repeating the process, I looked around the new sphere and saw thousands of universes.

"Again," My Fool's voice said.

I did it one more time and I seemed to explode into infinite vastness but only for a fraction of a second, and then I was back in my hammock, heart pounding. I was just me, just Susan, just this version of Susan. And I realized how all these millions and trillions of selves and existences were just one existence, one self, one . . . vast experience. I cannot begin to explain how odd it felt to be one in trillions, and at the same time be trillions in one.

Inside felt out, and outside felt in. Everything was nothing. And nothing was everything.

I heard My Fool whisper, "Ain't life great!"

Then I felt my body in the hammock. It was quite some time before my heart calmed, and it was only then I could hear the end of Beethoven's *Symphony No. 9*. I opened my eyes, and glimpsed a shooting star in the night sky. And oddly, I felt like it was me.

Yes, life *was* great.

In the Wizard of Oz, Dorothy clicks her heels and says, "There is no place like home." But what is home? Home is everywhere or anywhere, but basically associated with what feels most familiar to us. And in that, we have a place to root ourselves. But what happens when we follow that root system and experience our complexity? We begin to discover how large we are, and at the same time how small and wonderful and precious we are. We are a rose on a bush, and roses on a bush, and the whole bush, and all the rose bushes in the world.

When you feel small, focus on the great within, on *your* great within. Envision that the inner you is as vast as the outer world and beyond. For it is. The outer world is a *reflection* of the inner world. And as you go inward, focus on the center of yourself, as the center of a circle. In the center, all of life connects. Open to have the experience that is right for you, and so you shall. While embracing your great presence and multiple you's, hold in reverence your current identity that is on an amazing journey to have a story and celebrate life.

The Amazing World of Counter Balance

"Opposites are an illusion; opposites are the same."

Gem #4 DUALITY

I had a book signing trip coming up in London in about a month. Nervous about traveling that far out into the world, I was going through a phase when I just wanted to see flowers and butterflies and all the pretty things in life, the purring kitten, the beautiful stars, and the buttercups out my kitchen window. I did not want to think about the harshness of war, or crime, or even a child falling down and bumping her knee.

I drifted along in my little fairytale world for most of June and some of July, reading poetry, singing songs while playing my guitar, and running through the evergreens celebrating nature.

In my fairytale world, no one died, no one suffered, and everyone smiled all the time.

Of course, I knew that peace and joy only existed against the barometers of chaos and strife. And I knew that people suffered everyday, crime occurred every minute, wars raged somewhere in the world all the time, and people died constantly.

But it's just fun to pretend sometimes, fun to while away the hours in la la land if one is in the situation to do so. Some people call it going on vacation. I just didn't have to go anywhere but my mind, to take mine.

But then I started getting bored, as one would if every single day was uneventful and the same. So that night I decided to pursue an old project involving research on Russian spies for a novel I wanted to write. I clicked on the television, inserted a Russian spy movie, and plopped on my bed to watch the show.

My heart raced as the movie began. I felt compelled to know

more on this subject. How do spies operate in Russia? What are their motives? What state of mind must they possess to do their job?

As the movie played, I began feeling strange, overcome with an empathic reception of a loved one in distress. I clicked off the television so I could focus on the situation at hand. It was like hearing a cry of pain without the voice, and feeling like a spear had gone clean through my heart, only the pain was emotional. I focused on each family member in an attempt to find the owner of the pain, but I sensed no great disturbance.

Then, realizing the pain had arrived while I was watching the spy movie, I determined that this was not an ordinary empathic response. My heartache escalated. Who was I empathing? I laid there in the dark, concentrating on the owner of that pain.

Sinking into a meditative state, I became quiet and still, calm and soft. I released all judgment and conscious knowing, so that I might discover what is beyond judgment and conscious knowing.

I fell within myself, and into the vibration of the person's cry, eager to nurture the ailing one with my mothering heart. Many passageways appeared around me. And though I knew my body was lying on my bed, my ethereal body was on a journey. A magnetic energy pulled me into one of the passageways.

I exited the passageway into the outdoors at night. The scene ahead was a grove of sycamore trees. The source of the heartache emanated from the grove. I walked softly through the trees, moving toward this silent cry like rain to the ground. Moonlight spilling through the leafy canopies cast a ghostly glow, creating all kinds of shadow.

I saw a dark form hunched against a tree trunk. I neared it. And though I was in the grove, because I still knew myself as Susan, I did not feel *completely* there. It was as if I was on the end of a fishing rod cast out to sea, but I was still rooted on land—in my bed, back at home.

As I came upon the dark figure, I realized it was a man in distress. His body was hunched over, head dropped in palms.

I tried to touch his shoulder, but my hand went through it. He lifted his head and I read his thought, even though it seemed to be in a foreign language, *Is someone there?*

I sat before him as only one can do when they are seemingly incorporeal.

His head jerked up, and I wondered if he could see me. But as he looked around a bit, I figured not.

He spoke softly in a foreign language, Russian I think. Though I didn't understand the language, I somehow knew what he was saying. "Oh, my angel, you are here. I can feel you. You always come to me when I yearn for a spark of innocence, a moment of tenderness, and the smallest ray of light to touch my dark, cold world."

I wanted to tell him that I was just a human woman, and that I was no angel, but he continued speaking softly in his language, and I continued to somehow understand. "I had planned to leave the agency. My life grew brighter at that prospect. And now I have been sucked into a case that has pulled me back into the darkest side of human nature, and I don't know if I can get out. There is something in me almost addicted to it—the adrenaline that is. It comes with having a mission and playing a game, and seeking a victory that becomes all encompassing. But all the players in the game are equally addicted and resolved to achieve victory. Cunning, deception, courage, and intense pressure are enlivening at the moment, but they also serve to deplete anything that is good in me, and now I feel my goodness nearly gone."

My heart gushed with compassion. *Unconditional* love flowed from me. The love was not my love; it was pure love that was in and of itself. I imagined the love energy flowing all around him and inside him—because he needed it.

He inhaled deeply, absorbing the love, and he exhaled with quivering breath, feeling some relief.

As I continued to flow the love energy into him, I spoke, but I was not sure he could hear me, even with his inner ear, oh not the physical inner ear, you know, telepathic type hearing. I said, "Release your conscious knowing and just believe in your story.

Just because there is no seeming way out, doesn't mean that you will not find one."

He took a deep breath. His thoughts emitted something like, *Yes, yes. I hope that is the case.*

And then it was strange but I had an urge to move inside him. I didn't know if I could do it, but I decided it wouldn't hurt to try. And so I crawled inside him, assuming his body position.

He started to weep, a weep that was soft, gentle, and barely audible, yet the pain inside the weep was mountain big. His heart had opened to receive me. I sat in him like a flame of medicinal love. But around the flame was darkness. And in that darkness were flashes of bloody bodies, guns, poison, cruel laughter, vacant stares, and much emptiness. It came to me then that he was a spy. And something of his heart accompanied with words, spilled into me, *If my heart dies, it is over for me.*

And as I sat inside him, it occurred to me that I had been taking a deep vacation from the harsher side of reality. And I wondered if this man was an identity in my Being, perhaps one of my many warrior selves, maybe even one who has aided me at some time. Maybe he has dreamt of an ailing woman whom he saved. Maybe that woman was me.

I wondered how often this might happen to all of us. How often did our other selves come to our own rescue, but we deemed them angels, or such? And how many times had we been tormented by our other selves, and viewed them bad, as ghosts or demons?

And maybe what people call angels, ghosts, or spirit guides have tangible three-dimensional lives somewhere. Who is to say that for life to be real, or identities to be real, that they must *appear* as solid and three-dimensional?

What is life? What isn't life—really?

The man's thoughts sounded once more. *Thank you, angel, thank you.* I realized that I'd come out of the man and I was standing before him, probably because I shifted my focus to extracting insights.

The man stood up and walked away. I watched until I could see him no more, imagining what his life must be like. I could never, not ever survive one day, one hour, one minute of his life. I wished I could nurture him right out of that existence. But then, that was *my* nature, and I'd learned long ago that if I could succeed in making everyone's pain disappear, I'd rob them from the best parts of their story, which usually happen after painful ordeals.

Well, the man seemed to feel better and my heart didn't hurt anymore, so I thought of my bed and how comfortable it was and how I felt like lying down. A moment later, I was there in the dark, thinking, *I am an angel to someone.*

Wanting to know more about this experience, I grabbed my Walkman off the dresser, slipped my headphones over my ears, and listened to Shostakovich, *Symphony No.5*. I focused on the Wall of Remembrance thinking of My Fool. Shortly after, I was there. He appeared: gray-white beard and mustache, twinkling eyes, violet sweatshirt, white pants, and jogging shoes with the toe part cut out.

I asked Him, "I am curious about the experience I just had." This was the great thing about My Fool, I didn't have to fill him in on my life events. He somehow knew.

He said, "The man, as you suspected, is an identity in your Being, As you know, the many identities in your Being affect each other all the time, even though they are unaware. As you retreated into a one-sided experience of all things bright and tender, this other identity in your Being retreated further into his dark and dangerous world."

I exclaimed, "I knew identities were connected, but not that connected!"

He said, "As you played in an extreme feminine vibration, he worked in an extreme masculine vibration."

I asked, "So, if he had moved into a brighter way of living, would I have been forced into a darker way of living?"

"It's not like that," said My Fool. "All your identities are experiencing everything simultaneously, even if time periods seem of the past or maybe the future. It only appears that there is first this and then that. As you know, the idea of a timeline is necessary to experience a location and an identity, but synchronicity exists in all of life, in the smallest things, the tiniest thoughts, the most fleeting of emotions, and the most minor of acts. Everything meshes together perfectly."

"So I did *not* cause the spy to fall back into darkness?"

"No, and he did not make you take a vacation into light. It was simultaneous. All your selves are like a team, each member experiencing all the different roles of one play. Each character experiences the play from his or her perspective."

"So, this man was experiencing a different perspective of the same play I am in?"

He continued, "Yes, but this man was not just an identity in your Being, he is your current diametric opposite in the wheel of your Being. In that, you would be keenly aware of him, even if only in the unconscious state."

"My diametric opposite? I never quite thought about that before."

My Fool flopped His wrist out, palm up, as if saying *voila*! A wheel appeared. From the hub, numerous spokes jutted. At the end of each spoke was a small circle. The circles at the top half of the wheel were colored in various shades of gray and black. The circles at the bottom half of the wheel were colored in various shades of white and beige.

In standard form, He held a crystalline pointer.

He pointed to the wheel hub in the center. "This is your Being." He pointed to a circle at the end of the spoke. "The circles at end of the spokes are your counterpart identities."

"So by counterpart identities, do you mean all the identities in the wheel of my Being that counterbalance each other?"

"That is what I mean." He trailed the pointer along the circles on the bottom half of the wheel. "The lighter circles represent the female principle which is basically connection, nurturing, sacrifice, and beginnings." Then He trailed the pointer along the circles at the top part of the wheel. "The darker circles represent the male principal, which is basically repelling, protection, conquering, and endings."

Then He pointed to a dark circle at the top of the wheel and traced along the spoke to the center, going directly through the hub, along the opposite spoke to the end where a light circle resided. He said, "Everything has a counterbalance, an opposite. And every time one's vibratory configuration changes, so does the opposite."

I shook my head. "It's amazing. Though every thing is always changing, it remains balanced with all the energies around it."

"There are many versions of positive and negative polarities. All cultures and religions will have their own spin. But remember, no spin can possibly depict the whole picture. There is always, *always* more than what can be understood."

"Yes," I said, "for example, I have noticed that many cultures attribute the physical to the female and spirit energy to the male, but I always felt there was more to it than that."

He smiled. "There always is. All identities have the male and female principle within them, just in differing degrees. A male can be more feminine than masculine, and a female can be more masculine than feminine. The physical world has both masculine and feminine properties. The spirit world has both masculine and feminine properties."

He dabbed His pointer upon various light circles. "The feminine principle (which is not to say—a woman) in more detail, is associated with union, blending, heart, pacifism, emotional survival, resolution through peace, hearth and home, tranquility, concession, creativity, birthing, imagination, and harmony."

He dabbed His pointer on various dark circles. "The Masculine Principle (which is not to say—a man) in more detail, is associated with resistance, detachment, mind, aggression, physical survival, resolution through war, guarding boundary, competition, destruction, solidification, and conflict."

I said, "That's very interesting, as throughout history, women are usually associated with the dark and the cold, and the men with the sun and the light." The sociologist in me came out, "Those determinations were likely born of ruling men, or male spiritual leaders which, to me, often come off rather degrading to women."

He grinned. "See Susan, you are playing your role in the current social story to help loosen cemented judgments."

I returned the smile. This felt like old times with Him, and I loved it. Refocusing on the wheel, I said, "So, let me guess, the darker the circles—the greater degree of male energy, and the lighter the circles—the higher degree of female energy."

"Excellent!" He exclaimed. Then He pointed to a very light circle. "This is you." His pointer glided across the center to other end where a very dark circle resided. "And this is the man you visited."

I said, "And he is my opposite."

"He is your diametric opposite." He pointed to the top of the wheel. "Radically simplified, the top half of the wheel are identities experiencing predominantly the male principal, whether or not the identities are actually male or female." Pointing to the bottom of the wheel, He said, "The lower half of the wheel consists of identities predominantly experiencing the female principal whether those identities are in a female body or not."

"Zero in on a few spokes so that you can have this experience with limited confusion."

I followed His instructions. The spokes narrowed down to six equally disbursed spokes, and the wheel was stationary. I found it interesting that by shifting the manner in which I focused, I altered what I viewed. I wondered how many other scenes in life viewed one way, might significantly alter if the focus even slightly shifted. The boy stealing a wallet from a stranger's back pocket might be interpreted differently than a boy in the same act only with a visual in his head of his sick mother needing medicine.

And as I thought that, the dark circle on the top left turned into a dark-skinned boy about fourteen years old, living on the streets in a country I could not identify. He was dirty and clever, emanating an 'I don't care' energy. He was tough and frequently got into fights. He stole from and conned others relentlessly. He was a little thug. He looked straight at me. And I was startled. His rich, brown eyes locked into mine, even though I was not physically present in his reality. I was deeply stirred. Then he was snatched by a policeman, and in fast forward time I saw him placed in a children's home.

My focus wandered to the next dark circle at the end of a spoke. It changed into an Irish woman in a long brown dress, around forty years old in what might be judged—the past.

I felt myself projected into this Irish woman. I had a 17-year-old daughter living with me, and five sons who were away fighting in the Irish revolution. I ignored my daughter and praised my boys for fighting. I was cold and tough and very detached in order to survive. For many years my husband was drunk at the tavern, and the aloneness I felt, I passed onto my daughter. I had birthed her all by myself, squatting on the wood-slatted floor of my tiny bedroom. Feeling unloved, she secretly joined the revolution just to feel a sense of belonging. I trailed her to the meeting house in the pouring rain. I feared for her, but I kept the fear inside, for something in me would not let me show her love.

The next morning I searched for my daughter. The sun blared in my eyes. I saw a figure on the top of the hill. I raised the back of my hand over my eyes so I could peek through my fingers and dim the sun. The figure seemed to be a woman lying in a heap. I ran up the hill with my skirt catching between my legs. When I reached the figure, it was my dead daughter, obviously tortured, and with wet face and hair, probably drowned. I gasped. Agony ripped my heart wide open, and I fell upon my daughter and sobbed. I sobbed with such intensity that my once toxic heart was purged and filled with the purest love for my precious daughter. But my precious daughter never knew how much she had been loved! She died thinking her mother did not care about her; she died thinking that her mother only cared for her sons. I did not stop sobbing until there was no liquid left in my body. Still sprawled across my daughter, I grew silent, and I died.

Bringing my focus back to Susan, I felt stunned, like I wasn't Susan, but the woman. To experience such coldness, well, as Susan, I simply never had.

My Fool said, "Look to the next dark circle."

My eyes wandered to the next dark circle at the end of the spoke, at the top half of the wheel.

A man leaned against a sycamore tree. It was the man who called for me, the man whom I believed was a Russian spy.

Looking at the three identities, the Abandoned Boy, the Irish Woman, and the Spy, my heart welled with compassion, and strangely they all jerked a bit as if they had received something.

"Now," My Fool said, "look at the bottom half of the wheel. They will be experiencing an equal transformation."

And then the first light circle at the end of a spoke at the bottom half of the wheel turned into—me! Susan. And my diametric opposite was the spy. The second light circle at the bottom half of the wheel took the shape of a nun leaving the convent. She was merging into the outer world to know human love, but she looked very frightened. Her diametric opposite was the Irish woman. The third light circle at the bottom half of the wheel turned into a kind-hearted teenage boy who had been relentlessly bullied. He was learning how to defend himself. His diametric opposite was the little boy thug who was taken into the children's home.

"You can see," said My Fool, "that just as those you's predominantly experiencing the masculine principle are integrating heart, the you's who are predominantly experiencing the feminine principal (as in Susan), are integrating the sword."

"Why is it," I asked My Fool, "that I can relate so clearly to my selves in the feminine half of the wheel, but not the masculine half? I mean, even though I can empath the lives of those on the top of the wheel, I, as Susan can't imagine ever acting like them."

My Fool replied, "You cannot relate to your opposites because your focus is on Susan. Susan's Focus Experience is to deal with the victimization that comes from giving one's self away, which leads to your demise. The Focus Experience of Susan is to learn how to *fight* for self-respect, which is really an integration of the male principal. So naturally you would relate to the selves that are similar to you, having similar experiences. However, if for example, there are hundreds of you's existing predominantly in the feminine principal, each one will have a slightly different ratio of female energy to male energy. If you, Susan, have seventy percent feminine energy to thirty percent masculine energy, another you would have sixty-nine percent feminine energy to thirty-one percent masculine energy. And so on."

"Oh!" I exclaimed, "I get it! The experiment is to experience everything."

"Always. Come now." His pointer vanished, and He walked a bit and stepped onto what seemed a like a strip of metal, kind of like a sled. I kept wanting to call it a rocket strip. I followed and stepped onto the strip with him.

He said, "Loosen your identity so that we may traverse The Wall."

Traversing The Wall was getting easier and easier, and without much effort, it was done. The rocket strip shot forth through The Wall as if in hyperspace, moving thru blinks of light. Finally, we stopped in a land that looked like the negative of a picture taken from an old-fashioned camera. Then, the negative blinked to a bright picture, and then back to the negative again. Back and forth, blinking.

"Gee," I said, "It's like even whole pictures, scenes and stories have a counter world of some kind."

He said, "For the earth that is dying, there is an earth that is flourishing. For the country at war, that same country in the world of counterbalance is also at peace."

"It is kind of like, all stories are happening at once, and that there really is no this or that, for every scenario of story is happening somewhere."

He nodded. "Everything has an opposite, but the opposite of anything is the *same* thing. A picture negative from a camera will show the lighting in reverse from the actual picture taken. The face of a person cannot exist without the back of the head, nor a coin without two sides. Yet the negative and the picture are the same picture. The back and front of the person's head are one head. The back and front of a coin are but one coin. In this, opposition exists only in the world of perception. In oneness the opposition does not exist. However, humans do live in a world of perceptions, so in that, perception of opposition is necessary."

My Fool said, "Open your hand."

I outstretched my palm.

He placed in it an old fashion scale, like the one representing Libra in astrology. He said, "This is the Gem of Duality. It is as a teeter-totter, one side up, the other down. Opposition is merely about balance. All opposition is about equilibrium. Nothing can ever be out of balance, it only seems so. So all is always well. In the counterbalance . . . all . . . is . . . well."

As the scale absorbed into my palm, I quite suddenly snapped back into my body, lying on my bed at night. My cat had jumped on my stomach from the windowsill with a certain amount of force that almost took the wind out of me. I guess that explained my sudden return. From my bed I sent out a 'thank you My Fool' and decided the cat was part of the great synchronicity.

I clicked the television back on and watched the end of my spy movie, feeling a greater urge to write my spy thriller. My mind fell into daydreams, and my night filled with night dreams exploring this arena. I proceeded in this fashion for a few days, until the night before my book signing trip to London. My nerves felt like they were going through a meat grinder. I feared exposing myself to foreigners all the way across the ocean.

It had taken me a long time to adapt to being seen and noticed as an author and lecturer, as my nun facade held the belief that to be seen and noticed in a positive manner was a sin. In the past, whenever I doubted myself, My Nun facade would take that as her cue to rise up in me. However, because I was aware of that occurrence, I had learned to ignore her and handled the inner workings of my mind in a new way, *my* way, and she was not rearing her pious head now. However, my shy little girl facade—had.

Though over the course of my life, I'd overcome much of my shyness, widening my boundary to include foreign countries invited its return. Given I was to leave in the morning, I desperately needed a meditation to pull myself together. I went out to my green hammock in the beautiful afternoon with my Walkman clipped to my waist, and headphones on ears. I had selected Gustav Mahler's *Symphony No.1*. Rocking myself in the green net, the warm July breeze caressed my face. I surrendered myself to all that is, to the whole of life. I gathered my fear, preparing to purge it.

Interestingly, a forceful energy began building in my solar plexus. It was repressed fear from other times and places when going out it to the world got me snuffed. I began heaving from my solar plexus in violent thrusts, purging fear for several minutes. When the purging was complete, pure energy filled me. It felt wonderful. My body began to vibrate, softly at first, growing, mounting, until it vibrated with the force of a smooth flowing river. It was as if this vibration was of all sounds, all elements, everything.

My hands began to move in repetitive patterns, first one pattern, then another. Sometimes my hands moved in, sometimes out, sometimes in fast circles in a specific direction over different chakras of my body. Sometimes the direction changed. I did not interpret what was happening. I just knew all was well for I had given myself to the whole of creation for a tune up. Therefore, I trusted that whatever was happening was in the name of that.

In the symphony's last movement, I had an epiphany. I began chanting, "I have no face, I have no name. I am not an identity. I am all identities. I am all faces. I am all names." And I felt myself in all the people of the world. And I saw that no matter where I travel, even if it is to London, and that no matter how much I might be seen and noticed in a good way or a so-called bad way, I was a reflection of everyone. And everyone is a reflection of me. I experienced being one collective force, but appearing as millions.

Knowing that we really are all each other, that we really are all the same, deeply calmed me. As the symphony ended, the concept of myself as disconnected from others, had defused. And though I knew myself as Susan, a vehicle to have a journey, I also felt myself as *The All. Polyphonic living*, My Fool called it.

Early the next morning I was on the plane to London. Things seemed to move along smoothly until the following day. I was in the bookstore preparing to do a book reading for my latest book. It was a hot day, and I was coolly dressed in a sleeveless, ice blue, silk blouse, and white pants. My blue pumps were comfortable, and my hair was up in a French twist with light hair wisps edging my forehead and temples.

My eyes embraced a crowd of faces. I thought of the faces as my face. Even though those faces lived in the name of a singular identity and had their very own special story, I reminded myself that on a panoramic level, we all dance the same dance—the dance of the earth.

I read a book excerpt with full heart, pure authenticity, and no mask of identity.

These were my words: "The greatest oppression there is, exists in the belief that we know things. We know we are right. We know we are bad. We know what God is. We have the answers.

"Our consciousness makes conclusions based on our perceptions, mixed with our underlying beliefs. People, insecure about their worth, might perceive a compliment as an insult, unbelieving that anyone would truly deem them worthy. Those people *know* they were insulted, even though they were not. And so it is with all things we think we know. We build our whole reality based on skewed perceptions. It is the way it is supposed to be.

"However, there are times when we are ready to change our realities. We've had enough of whatever scenario we feel trapped in. The fear of change is overridden by the discomfort of the current situation. 'If I must stay in this marriage for the kids, or I will have failed as a mother.' 'I must remain in my current job, even if it is killing me, because I am secured with a good paycheck.' 'If I have an affair to get my needs met, I can save the marriage.'

"Therefore, changing realities is rooted in examining what we *think* we know. The best way to examine, without creating a new skewed perception, is to leave intellect behind and dive into our central self. There, in the quiet, away from outer world chattering and inner world confusion, we can be still and open to sense the deeper *intent* of our life story. We have set down the script we are playing, and journeyed to the writer.

"The deeper intent will feel like a current that springs from the core of our existence, like *I yearn to . . .* This yearning will override surface tendencies to quell pain, such as getting drunk, or having an affair to boost one's ego. These surface yearnings invite us to *cover* our pain. The deeper yearning is about how we can *dissolve* the *source* of our pain. *I yearn to be creative* when acted upon, is a powerful way to dissolve the pain of staleness in one's life. *I yearn to love myself,* when acted upon, is a powerful way to dissolve the pain of needing affirmation from others.

"In sensing our deeper current, even if we can't quite put a finger on it, our 'knowing' changes. We suddenly see things differently. And because we see things differently, we behave differently, and soon after, our life has changed."

I proceeded to speak about personal power and the keys to changing outworn destructive behavior, into behavior that nourishes one's well being.

Then there was a question and answer period, which went quite well. After few hours of signing my books, I was really in the mood to see some sites.

My London coordinator took me to lunch and a few galleries that included paintings of the old masters. The last place was the Dulwarch Picture Gallery.

At that point I really *yearned* to be outside in the quiet and open air, and preferably alone. I needed time to process the contents of my day. I had heard about a forest that was once used by King Henry as a hunting ground. Before that, it belonged to William the Conqueror. And before that, it belonged to King Harold. In other words, it had a lot of history to it. And I loved history, antiquity, and the study of genealogy. I always somehow felt larger than myself when I touched the past—like I was bringing it to the present, and all the people I studied were inside me.

This historic forest was called Hatfield forest. I heard there was a bus that went there. My coordinator dropped me at the bus stop, and bid me goodbye. I waited for my bus to come. I had never done the bus thing before, so I was a bit nervous. I studied the area maps at the stop and determined which bus I was waiting for. I felt very proud and eager to see the forest.

A red double-decker bus stopped. People boarded. So did I—with zing, vim, and vigor.

After twenty minutes I had the sinking suspicion I boarded the wrong bus. I asked the person next to me if the bus went to Hatfield forest. No, was the answer. Wrong bus, realized too late.

I felt panicky and got off at the next stop. Then I was really confused, reminding me of my old college nickname, wrong way Susan, a name given because I always did things backwards.

I was flustered, and suddenly afraid to trust myself. I asked an elderly gentleman sitting on the bus stop bench if the bus coming went to Hatfield Forest.

An attractive man, attractive to me anyway, who leaned on a cement pole near the elderly man, said with a slight Russian accent, "I am going there; you can wait with me." His accent intrigued me a bit since I had been Russian focused of late.

"Thank you." I said politely. I assessed him closely though, as in my past, in the identity of Susan, I tended to be a predator magnet. It hadn't much happened since I'd begun integrating my warrior energy five years ago. I was hoping I had integrated it enough to nix that old broken record—victim again, and again, and again.

The man wore black boots, blue jeans, and a black tee shirt. His dark wavy hair was kind of long, almost to the shoulders. It curled a little around his neck. His deep-set, blue eyes did not look like they would hurt me. He seemed a little despondent, not at all throwing energy at me as many predators had in the past, as if they were trying to capture me in a net. I decided it was okay to trust him.

The red double-decker bus arrived. We boarded on the lower level and wound up sitting together, shoulder to shoulder, the skin on our arms touching. I hated it that I felt attracted to him. For me, attraction generally meant that the guy was my antithesis, a warrior-like, insensitive, power monger, too dominating to be any good for me. Besides, I'd grown most happy being a carefree single woman, and I truly wanted to stay that way.

He gave me a sidelong glance. "I am Dmitri."

His name reminded me of a time I was lost in the forest, and some kind of entity named Nicodemas helped me get home.

"I am Susan," I said in kind.

"By your accent, you are American. What brings you to London?"

I replied, "A book signing. I write metaphysical books and novels."

He smiled. "Metaphysical, hmm." He paused and then said, "I have great interest in such things."

"What brings you to London," I asked, "or do you live here?"

The bus breaks squeaked as it stopped and some people were getting off as he replied, "My life is intense and spending time outdoors helps me much. I am a Russian interpreter for Russian speaking guest lectures at the Chatham house."

"What is Chatham House," I asked.

His voice was low and beautiful and I am almost ashamed to say I got lost in it. And I thought to myself that he must be really sinister for my attraction to be so.

He said, "Chatham House is where high-profile speakers from around the world converge in a heavy programme of events and conferences. The goal is to set agendas and shape policies by encouraging new ideas in international affairs."

"Wow," I said, "That sounds fascinating."

"Oh," he said, "it is all a matter of perspective."

We talked for a while about the meaning of people's life stories, and how everything unfolds in a most magical mystical way, even if we don't notice it at any given time. We talked about Plato, the power of classical music, and how nature is underestimated in bringing sanity to humankind.

I *really* enjoyed talking with him. Other than My Fool, I had never talked so deeply with a man.

Somewhere in there we changed busses, and I was really glad that I was not alone. Getting lost was just a thing I did—my nature and all, even though I'd tried ever so hard to change it.

When we arrived, expansive meadows and forest entwined. We got off the bus. It felt great to step into nature after being in the city. Dmitri and I had bonded quite nicely during our conversation on the ride over, so we decided to walk together. As he had been to Hatfield Park many times, I felt like I had a guide.

I asked, "What draws you to this place? I mean there are a lot of people here and I think with your work you might want more isolation, you know, so that you could be alone."

He answered, "I have places for that too. But my life is high-pressure. Sometimes I just want to go where things are light and playful, where children run in the sun and parents buy them ice cream cones."

I asked, "Is that what your childhood was like?"

"No," he said, "no. It was quite the opposite, but I do not talk of it."

"I'm sorry," I said, "I didn't mean to turn the tone dark for you when you need simple joy, a break from what you do at work."

"And what of you?" he asked, "was your childhood like that?"

"Yes, it was nurturing and joyful—and meant to be, I think, because as a youth I was extremely shy of the world and I did not possess a very strong survival instinct. It always seemed to me that dying would be easier than trying to survive something horrible. And I respect so deeply those that can fight hard to survive—those that can use the metaphorical sword to guard their boundary. I *am* trying."

"Yes," he said, "writing books and lecturing does bring you out into the world. And look, now you are in a foreign country talking with me—a stranger."

I narrowed an eye, hoping so much that my time with this man wouldn't turn out like nearly every encounter I had with strange males, who were never as innocent as I deemed them to be. I needed this man to be different only because it would prove that I had changed my energy enough not to attract the darker sorts anymore.

Then behind us, a ruckus. I turned around and gasped. Two men were yelling at each other. One-man punched the other one in the stomach.

I spun away from the scene, crouching on the ground, holding my stomach, eyes squeezed shut, and whimpered. I hated it when I involuntarily experienced the pain of others as if it were my own. This happened often, but I always pretended like it didn't because I hated drawing attention to myself, not wishing to be spotlighted regarding my differences.

Dmitri squatted next to me. He placed his warm hand on my back. "Are you all right?"

"Not really," I said, teary-eyed. "I feel like I was punched. And I feel the anger of those men. And that hurts more. I am highly empathic. Anger, cruelty, or violence of any kind, even the killing of a fly, deeply, deeply upsets me."

He gently eased me upward to stand. "Come," he said, "let us go look at the fountain." He guided me over to a white stone, square fountain squirting a great column of water at its center. The fountain had a long white stone bench on each side. Between the benches were square beds of purple and yellow petunias. The site was most inviting.

We sat on a bench, cool against the warm air, shoulder to shoulder, our body energy making a connection.

He pointed to the water and said, "Look how it sparkles in the sun. See the light prisms?"

The moving water, interacting with sunlight, looked magical. "Yes, it is most beautiful."

He said kindly, "Feel the life of the water, Susan. Move empathically into that experience."

I was amazed that he could work with me like this. Most men just yelled at me or rolled their eyes when I was being 'sensitive.'

I stared into the water, moving into that reality. I was the liquid in its entirety and yet I could feel myself sucked up into the fountain, rising high and splashing down to the pool below. And I felt myself as the water droplets in the air, filling with sunlight, revealing my prism beauty. I landed in the pool reunited with the body of water that was me, free, exhilarated, content.

He said, "You are the water now, aren't you?"

I looked at him askance, teary-eyed with joy. "Oh, yes, and it feels wonderful." I wiped away a tear, about to roll down my cheek as I looked at him looking at me. "You think I am a bit crazy, don't you?"

He kissed my cheek innocently. "I think you are a bit sweet."

"People usually think I'm weak because I feel so much."

"To experience such emotion without fear—is to be strong."

I smiled. "I've never viewed myself that way before. Thank you." He was right, when it came to emotion, I was fearless. I said, "Well, even so, I've been striving to be less reactive."

He said, "And I—more. I compartmentalize everything. I live only in a small arena of myself that is almost devoid of tenderness. I am cold inside. I can function and do my job, but I feel more empty with each passing day. I wish I could change that, but I don't think I can."

I studied his forlorn face for a moment as he gazed into the moving water of the fountain. He really reminded me of the man hunched against the sycamore tree. But this man was probably just of that vibration.

I said, "I sense why we met. We are opposites in nature, yet I yearn to be more like you, and you yearn to be more like me. We would not have come together if you wanted to remain cold, and I wanted to stay susceptible, because," I sighed, "I don't do that anymore."

He said, "I appreciate your philosophical mind."

I added, "I like exploring beyond the boundaries of mundane focus. I am drawn to what is outside the box, gleaning my own awareness, rather than studying accepted philosophies, even though I might deem them brilliant."

"How do you do this, go outside the box of your reality?" he asked.

"I meditate, not formally per se. It is more a state of mind where I am open to everything, to see the bigger picture while at the same time taking care not to fall into any piece of the picture. In other words I try not to let my beliefs get in the way of what would otherwise be a very pure experience."

"You are most open-minded. I want to be," he sighed, "but I am frozen inside, like ice. I want to flow. I need to flow, but it just doesn't happen."

The top of my head stirred as it does when my consciousness expands. I asked him, "May I place my hand over your heart?"

"Yes," he said curiously.

"And can I put my other hand over your head?"

He nodded.

I turned sideways on the bench, and propped myself up on my knees. I hovered my left palm over his heart, and my right over the top his head. In my mind, I envisioned totality in the form of the Universe, and I sent it through my hands. I let the energy flow purely without any wish or command, for how can I truly know what is right for this man? Maybe there was a reason he couldn't flow and I didn't want to interfere. What if I helped him and circumvented a great experience that could only be had by him learning to flow on his own? So I did not presume any position as healer or as anyone who 'knows.'

My eyes closed. "Dmitri, close your eyes and open your mind and heart for whatever is right for you, beyond what you think is right for you. Whoever you are, whatever you are, whatever is right for you—this moment, so be it. Do not think. Just take a deep breath—and be."

He exhaled heavily, and then became very quiet.

I could see the twists and turns of his inner being, like a black and white maze where at every turn were beatings, guns, blood, cold eyes, hot eyes, dying eyes, and mere splashes of color that promised hope. And the prize at the end of the maze—was . . . himself, glowing and transcendent. And I wondered just what kind of an interpreter had a life like this?

His body began to vibrate gently. He gasped suddenly, and with each of his hands, he gently gripped each of my wrists.

I opened my eyes, withdrawing my hands from his grip, wondering what had happened.

His eyes were open too, and he looked shaken. He said, "I . . . had to stop you. Something intense was occurring, but too fast. It felt like a good thing, but too fast for me, can be a bad thing. But thank you." He sighed with quivering breath. "I must make some changes in my outer world before I am in position to flow like this. But now I know I can. I thought it was too late for me, but it is not," he caught his breath, "it is not too late—for me."

He seemed like he was crying without crying, and I wanted to cry too—for him.

He said, "Your authenticity triggers mine. That is dangerous for me at this time. Your presence is changing me too fast, even though I need to change. I must leave you to your day, and I must return to mine."

"Don't you want your time in the sun to watch the children play and see their parents buy them ice cream cones?"

He smiled faintly. "You have more than filled me with all of that, Susan. But I will buy your books and I will read them to see what you have discovered in the inner and other worlds, and maybe one day I will join you there." He rose. "You can find your way home then?"

"Yes," I said assuredly. "I might get lost, but I always, eventually find my way. I will be okay."

He nodded and walked away.

I was thinking about what I saw inside him during the meditation. On impulse I called, "Dmitri?"

He turned back.

"What you said you do for a living, it's not that . . . really, is it?"

He looked into me.

I said, "It is dangerous, very dangerous, isn't it?"

He nodded, ever so slightly. His eyes were glossy. Mine were too. Then he turned and walked away.

Who was this man? Who was he to me? Who was I to him? When he gasped, it was almost as if he'd been resuscitated.

I watched him head back to where the busses came and went, wishing a little that I'd not decided to abstain from male involvement, and yet I knew it was for my best to do just that. I still did not trust my romantic choices, the same sort over and over. And the story always plays the same, and the story always ends the same. And so for now, I would continue having this wonderful relationship with myself. Maybe one day when I had flowered beyond repeating old patterns, I could be open to communion with a companion. But that was maybe one day, and not at all necessary. For now, my life was complete.

After watching Dmitri disappear onto a bus, I spent hours enjoying the place. When it was time to leave, I decided to forget about the bus, given my propensity to get lost, and took a taxi back to the hotel.

On the ride back, I pushed my thoughts away from Dmitri, from a fantasy that could never be, for it was just a fantasy, not realistic. I always projected what I wanted in a mate onto that mate, making up my own little fiction, as so many of us do in love relationships. And when the one we are in love with does not live up to our standards, we feel betrayed, even though we are the ones that saw the other through rose-colored glasses.

Arriving at my hotel, I hurried upstairs, eager to flop into bed and rest. I opened the door to my room, and went to the queen-sized bed, pulling back the dark green comforter. I crawled upon the soft white sheets, curling up on my side when Dmitri popped into my head again.

I mustn't get diverted by playing old records, repeating old patterns that had simply done me in. I knew where those roads would lead and my feet would not walk them ever again.

I rolled onto my back, hands on stomach. I stared up at the white ceiling. I reminded myself that my story this time around was to come forward as an authentic person and sing my once repressed song purely from my heart without shame or fear. In my mind's eye, I saw myself at the end of my life path, blossomed into my full potential of all that I could be in the story of Susan. And then I saw this me as a composite of all the characters that I'd ever been. And like in my earlier meditation, I felt again that great epiphany. "I have no face. I have no name because I am all faces and I am all names. There is no I, because I is all."

I closed my eyes, feeling myself sliding away from the trap, the trap of falling into the world of another, which would only distract me from moving deeper into the world of myself. I'd made others my reason for living long enough. No more chasing rainbows in the outer world that simply led me to repeat old patterns. I reached to the bed stand for my Walkman and placed the headphones on my ears. I listened to Sergei Rachmaninoff's, *Piano Concerto No. 2*.

As the music played, I realized that it was not as important to project myself in the outer world to be heard, as it was to focus inward and be heard in the community within myself—all the many selves within me, and all the many selves of my Being in this earth journey. I murmured sleepily to my many me's, "I love you all." I felt as if I were speaking to the back of me, like speaking into my rearview mirror.

As I drifted into slumber, held in the bosom of myself, My Fool's lovely voice sounded, as if reading a child to sleep. "It is well to have diverse experiences. Nothing can go off course, for everything has a counterbalance. Duality is ever present. Joy lurks, even when sadness is in the spotlight. Sadness lurks, even when joy is in the spotlight. If we were in joy all the time, it would lose its power to be joy, and sadness would ensue. If we were sad all the time, joy would accumulate on the other side of the scale, until one day, the balance would shift and great joy would be had. It is the counterbalance. And in the counterbalance . . . all . . . is . . . well."

My last thought before sleep was that the checks and balances were always there, always. I whispered, echoing My Fool, "In the counterbalance . . . all is well."

And all is well for you too, everything is always well even when it doesn't' feel like it. Life *is* fair. Everything comes to balance even if you do nothing, for everything is integrally connected, dark and light, hardship and ease, sorrow and laughter. They dance together, weave in and out, always the breath, in and out, always the pulse, one, two, one two, always the night and day, the male and female, the polarities ever and always making music, making stories, creating energy. Sometimes if we step back and back and back, things appear less tragic. From a broader perspective, life seems like a symphony with harmony and dissonance, a climax, and an ending that brings resolution.

And so, if your focus is on a part of the symphony that brings dissonance and you don't feel so good, be the flying bird, and know that the landscape of your life is a beautiful thing when you can experience it from a panoramic view. Everything that has ever happened to you, happened so that a very great story could be had, the meaning of which will live on—forever.

The Chronicles of Life

"We write the story we live, and we live to live the story."

GEM #5 THE STORY

Jet-lagged after my plane ride home from London, I dragged myself through the front door of my Oregon home, just as the sun began to set. I greeted my cats, and seeing that my neighbor had taken great care of them, I tumbled into bed with Walkman in hand and headphones over my ears. Pressing the Walkman's play button, Richard Strauss's *Alpine Suite* sounded. Drifting towards sleep, I sank like a stone, while rising like a helium balloon. Pictures flashed in my head: cells dividing, amebas swimming, water molecules turned to vapor by the sun, fire burning wood, visible breath in cold air, a bullet flying.

On the pictures flashed: volcano erupting, wave crashing to shore, lightning in a rainstorm, bug crawling on a leaf, cat having kittens, eagle soaring in the sky.

So many pictures, more and more and a hundred more: teenage girl getting her first kiss, a little boy showing his report card to his mother, a mother holding an infant in her arms, a man skydiving, a couple getting married, a daughter sitting with her father on his deathbed . . . .

On and on the pictures flashed a hundred fold: of wars, inaugurations, crowds gathered at protests, celebrations, and space launches . . . . On and on and on the pictures flashed: nations, the planet, the solar system, the Universe. Then a hundred more pictures. I tossed. I turned, and a hundred more.

Then quite suddenly I became the taker of the pictures. Or rather the creator of the pictures. I felt myself as energy: expansive and finite, flowing yet still, everything yet nothing. How could this be?

My extreme exhaustion had opened a door into a realm that in normal times is most difficult to locate. Not quite asleep, nor really awake, I stepped into the mystery beyond the door.

My consciousness settled in a sea of energy, and every cell in my body felt charged. I was big and I was small. I was not me, and yet me.

I sensed My Fool in a way as never before. I gasped briskly, not a sudden inhale as gasping is described, but a sudden exhale, so deep and sharp, that for a moment I lost my breath and felt a shock in my heart. With fear leaking in, I felt more small than big. I could not see My Fool.

"Where are you, My Fool?" I asked, feeling smaller.

His voice replied in surround-sound. "I am everywhere."

"Who are you, My Fool?" I asked, feeling smaller still.

Choral voices in surround-sound replied, "I am everyone."

I was daunted by the sheer intensity of experiencing the multiplicity of small scenes and the panorama—simultaneously. I was getting smaller by the moment, and I knew I was about to fall away from the experience.

My Fool's singular voice whispered from inside me, as if I were speaking to myself. The voice crept through my heart, and crawled into my limbs, moving around within me like a warm and comforting wind. "O . . . pen. Re . . . lax. O . . . pen. Re . . . ceive."

I inhaled slowly and deeply with quivering breath, pushing past fear. Fear of the unknown . . . and fear itself. The top of my head tickled in the center. The tickle rose to a sensation of rushing bubbles like the effervescence in soda. Then the sensation mounted to a flower opening at high speed. My body felt porous, expanding into the larger me. Fortified in this mind state, My Fool's surround-sound voice spoke once more. The words multiplied around me, these words I'd heard before, but not like this, *never* like this. Hearing them in this expanded state deepened my insight significantly.

"Creative Energy is all that is. It is the quark, the atom, the molecule. It is you, me, mind, emotion, spirit, and body. It is the earth, the sky, galaxies, universes, inner worlds, outer worlds, and other worlds. Creative Energy is everything blended into one homogenous energy. It is neither finite, nor bound by time."

My body seemed to spread out and lighten in density, until I could not feel it anymore. I almost lost consciousness even within my half-sleep state. I was barely holding on to myself as a 'self.'

The words continued: "Creative Energy, in the act of being creative, has an idea to know itself. So it projects the idea of experiencing separation by configuring energy. When the energy of *all that is* begins to configure in various ways, it appears to become something apart from other things, such as various atoms. These configurations give rise to new possibilities."

I glimpsed a flash of Susan. Then I flashed *into* Susan. Then I flashed into one homogenized Creative Energy. This flashing went back and forth, and it began to feel more like blinking.

The words continued: "This projection of energy configured presents the impression of time and space. The projection exists *simultaneously* with one homogenized Creative Energy."

The blinking continued, and I was actually getting used it. It was like a movie projector flashing frames. The tiny space between frames was the one homogenized Creative Energy, and the frames were the energy configured.

My Fool's surround-sound words continued to flow: "Creative energy configured in countless ways, presents the impression of countless things, micro and macro: atoms, molecules, cells, water, dirt, fire, and air; fish, bugs, animals, and people; planets, stars, variations in light and sound; mental, emotional, and physical energy, and so on. In this, all things configured experience interaction with each other."

It occurred to me then why I'd entered this experience by seeing flashes of picture after picture. They were pictures of interactions.

The words continued: "These interactions create stories. Everything has a story that builds into a greater story. Protons, neutrons, and electrons have a rich experience in themselves and also as an atom. The atom has a rich experience in itself and also as a molecule. The molecule has a rich experience it itself and also as, for instance, a drop of water. The drop of water has a rich experience in itself as well as with rivers, oceans, clouds, and rain. A seed, a root, a leaf, a tree each have separate stories that together make a collective story, all dependent upon interaction with each other: a sperm, an ovum, an embryo; a baby, a child, an adult, each have individual stories that build into group stories by interacting with each other: relationships, families, communities, nations, and humanity itself."

The blinking continued between the parts of the atom and the whole atom, between atom and molecule; water drop and ocean; seed and tree; gametes and human being, human being and the earth.

My Fool's surround-sound voice said: "And to each, the story *it* experiences is *the* story. No story is small. Even the tiniest interactions yield significant energy from having the experience."

The blinking, which kept me from focusing on any one thing, allowed me to see the deep worth in every drama in any story. Our little lives are really big. And each personal story, even ones that seem trite or boring, is a treasure. While these stories ensue, we never leave the one homogenous Creative Energy. We are always blinking into the projection of the story and back to the whole. And the blinking seems to be what keeps the projection going.

My Fool's surround-sound continued: "The blinking occurs everywhere. We blink from moment to moment to moment. In blinking from one thing to another to another, it feels like we are moving. This gives the sensation of time passing."

I could see the blinking even in our personal viewpoints. One person blinks to a small view of a big picture. Another person blinks to a different small view of a big picture. This generates discussion and argument about which view is true. I could see more clearly from here, how all views are true. We just blink on to different parts of the picture, that's all.

The words continued: "In the human world, the whole picture is never seen because it is too big and complex to be viewed in totality. If totality could be seen, it would appear as one homogenized Pure Creative Energy."

And for one prolonged, slow motion blink, I was the one homogenized Creative Energy. Because my focus was on no one thing, no thing, nothing, the projection of separation stopped, and there were no pictures at all. Then the slow motion blink ended, and I was back in the projection. I could see why we, as humans, absolutely had to have different views or 'blink' if were to keep the experience going.

My Fool's surround-sound voice said: "Yes. The blinking keeps alive the impression of separation that stimulates a need for belonging, a quest for love, and a mission for power. All this ensures a story, all stories, *the* story."

I gasped, as a blink of pure beauty consumed me. I was on the other side of the story. All stories begin and end in beauty. I can't explain it. I can explain it no better than that.

My Fool's surround-sound voice said, "It is the way it is supposed to be—to be in the story with limited understanding. We are then motivated to go on adventures, searching for—more. This is what gives the story beauty."

The irony floored me. Pure Creative Energy in its homogenized wholeness grows by experiencing separation and living stories. Humans, who feel separated, grow in their quest to return to the whole, whether it is perceived as God, the Universe, or any variation of that. The two flows, the whole moving into separation, and separation moving into the whole, plow into each other like two streams moving in opposite directions. However, in this convergence they are one stream, even though they seem antithetical.

My Fool continued: "It is the beat of life. Wholeness breathes out in a cosmic exhale. What is breathed out tries to return to its source with a cosmic inhale. Breathing in, breathing out, like waves crashing to the shore and receding. Like the heartbeat, ba boom, ba boom. The pause between the inhaling and exhaling, the moment between the waves ebbing and flowing, and the infinitesimal fraction of space between the beats of a heart—these in-betweens are the one homogenized Creative Energy. In blinking we can experience separation *while* remaining whole."

With that, I finally understood something My Fool had once told me: *We are not a part of Creative Energy, we are each—all total Creative Energy*. While we are always One, the blinking makes us experience things that detract us from experiencing our oneness. This blinking was so vast, with so many multiplicities, it boggled my mind.

My Fool's surround-sound voice said, "Everything blinks, not only between oneness and separation, but in *every* way, all the time. Protons, neutrons, and electrons blink (change focus) back and forth into the whole atom and back to themselves. The atom blinks (changes focus) back and forth into the whole molecule, and then back to itself as an atom. On all levels, we are always blinking, always changing focus, separation and totality, from one part to another, from a part of something, to a bigger part of that something, from one view to the next, from one moment to the next. The blinking also occurs in any life you have seemed to live and between all the identities you seem to be. This blinking extends to parallel worlds, and even multiple earths, with duplicate contents living different versions of the same story."

Memories flashed in my mind. When I was two years old, a dog bit me. Then blink. I remembered when I got married. Blink. A daydream. Blink. A night dream. Blink. A foreign thought. Blink. An abstract feeling, blink, a déjà vu, blink, a seeming fugue, blink, not acting like myself. I could see it then, how we are really never here, nor there, but really always everywhere. And oh, how opposite that is from what humans deem life to be. Life to humans generally means individual bodies living in the everyday life. Anything else is viewed as realms unknown, fantasy, or imagination—not *real* life. Yet, what we term 'real life' is but a projection of the life force. *Everything else* is on the Other Side of what we call—life.

My Fool's surround-sound voice said, "Even so, behind the mask of consciousness, we know we are the whole of creation. Behind the mask we are enlightened, always perfect, always worthy. We are cosmic dust and star shine. We are all that exists, not only in time and space, but beyond time and space."

A wave of appreciation rolled through my heart. What a gift it was to experience time and space, to live amazing stories that we, as Creative Energy—created. And in that, I began to think of my own story, which I'd deemed rather insignificant in the greater scheme of things, and the greater scope of life. Not that I was comparatively insignificant, but rather that the stories we lived were no big deal. My thinking used to be: *who cares, we are all one anyway, so what is the point*? But now, more than ever, I felt that the story, as all stories are, was sacrosanct. And I, for the first time in the life of Susan, held my life in the high regard that a religious person might hold a sacred symbol.

With that I fell out of the pluralistic mind state and found myself at the Wall of Remembrance, still between the awake and dreaming worlds, no longer aware of the blinking. Here at The Wall, I became steeped in my own story, yearning to converse with My Fool as I had known Him. I was feeling a little sad as if I had learned too late how great a story is, any story, Susan's story. I was getting on in years, and for the first time ever, I felt saddled to my age. Fears of aging that I didn't know I had, seized me in an unceremonious fashion.

My Fool's image appeared in The Wall, and then it stepped out and stood before me in violet sweatshirt, white pants, and jogging shoes, cut out at the toes, orange socks peeking through. "Feeling old, are you?" He smiled, as if saying he was ancient and loving it.

I sighed, a bit frustrated. "Now that I covet my life story, I realize my adventurous years are nearly over." I heard the tones of Richard Straus's Alpine Suite through my headphones, even though I was in an ethereal state with My Fool. It was the part of the music that equated with reaching the mountain peak. And it was appropriate, for I now felt myself at the peak of my life expectations, preparing to descend.

My Fool said, "When you knew me, I relished old age. I found joy in the bones and the brain not working as they once did. Climbing up the mountain in youth was exhilarating. Reaching the top was triumphant. However the climb down brought relief. And coming off the mountain altogether was resplendent."

"Really," I said, "but you as The Fool in a human body were most unusual. Perhaps few can experience age they way you did."

"We experience what we want to experience." Sunglasses appeared on His face. In the lenses, I could see a conglomeration of old, decrepit faces, and I almost stepped back from Him.

He continued, "If one removes the sunglasses to aging," the sunglasses disappeared, "much beauty is present. When a story concludes, it is the best part. When my story finished, I gazed out the window while the music played. I watched the story I lived fly by and onward like a bird—without me. Our life stories will live on for others to appreciate. Our life stories never die, even if it seems that we do. Then we will begin another story, and we will live it just as vividly, story upon story. Oh, how grand it is that we can have these adventures with layers and layers of exploration, climaxes and resolutions. It is an honor to be a part of the earth, and to participate as such."

My face warmed. "So going up the mountain of a story is no more exciting than coming down the mountain and concluding the story."

"Indeed," He said, "the elderly often chase after old memories wishing to be young again. That is called growing old. There is always more to experience, even in age. And if we are open to it, we can grow *into* age. It is wonderful to climb the mountain of a story, but what would it be like if we just stayed at the peak forever, and never experienced the richness of descent? How terrible it would be if there are was no climb down, and no next adventure."

I cocked my head. "Yes. The truth of it is, I do feel more content as the years pass. Why would I want to go backward toward youth? Life seemed harder then."

I recalled when as a psychotherapist, my clients twisted about past decisions, wishing they could go back in time and do things over. Yet, who we are at any second is based upon multiple factors: environment, activities of significant others, thoughts and feelings of the moment, and hidden roots that wind through time and space passages. So if we went back in time, all these factors that we have forgotten would be back in place, and we would do everything the same. I said, "I can see how we each live our life exactly as we are supposed to live it. We did not do it wrong. We did not fail. A good thing about aging, I suppose, is that we can see the bigger picture of our lives with the perceived passage of time."

"Bravo Susan," My Fool exclaimed, "the beauty of growing into age is that we can see things we did not see before, a panoramic view of our life, and the opportunity to arrive at new conclusions that better serve our well being; better known as—wisdom."

I said, "I have, so far, never wished to be young again. So far, I have been able to embrace each birthday with joy."

"And that is well, for as each moment seems to pass we are, in perceived time, always changing anyway, if only a little, like a seed that turns into a flower and slowly blossoms—unfolding its story that is not over until the flower falls from the stem and dissolves into the earth."

I interjected, "And dissolving into the earth, that too is a great experience, that will only lead to a new becoming. In a way, we always exist, we always *are*, so aging is an illusion."

"Our essence is ageless, as energy is neither created nor destroyed. Growing into age is to simply allow the boundaries of what we *think we know* to loosen. In that, we open ourselves to new experiences, even as elderly people. If we instead choose to cling to the reflection of who we *were*, then we spend much time reinforcing the old boundaries, like playing an old record even if we are bored with it. This choice is often made as an unconscious attempt to block death."

"Fearing death then can be a road block to receiving the gifts of old age?"

"A road block it may seem, but still a part of that person's story. However, for those whom age is not to be a roadblock to deeper experiences, the wisdom of age will become available. We always 'are' in youth and age, life and death, one focus to another. We cannot *not* exist. The secret of growing into age and moving smoothly through the doors of death is to remain open and in the moment."

I said, "So, the opportunity to experience more is always there. It doesn't have to end because we are old."

"Yes, but even so, if new adventures are blocked because we insist we *know what we know*, and cling to that, then in death, which is the transitioning from one existence to another, the opportunity rises again. Nothing is ever lost, escaped or left behind. One way or another, we deal with everything eventually, because everything is a part of the life experience. Some grow into age in the physical world. Some just grow old."

"So whether we grow into age or just grow old, we are all doing exactly what we are supposed to be doing."

"Yes," He said, "a writer writes, a teacher teaches, and an engineer engineers, and an old warrior just fades away."

I thought about My Fool when He was a human who was dying. He was an old warrior who seemed to fade away. But not from me. No, never from me.

I choked back tears.

"You are thinking of my life as you knew me. Let us talk of your life and these new fears of aging you have that defy your wisdom."

I said, "I think it involves my Russian diametric opposite. He seems about my age. And though I've generally been fine regarding aging, aging in our society seems to take on significance when flirting with romantic interests. The western world generally deems the young more valuable than the old, and throws self-doubt into the mix for many."

He said, "Romantic interests represent a need to be loved—to belong, to be beheld, simulating our oneness with all that is. Because we have forgotten we are One, and live in the illusion of separation, there is a natural compulsion to connect to others. This is also true for all relationships. Your attraction to the Russian is *yourself* trying to connect to—yourself."

I sighed, daydreaming a bit about the Russian: Deep set eyes, blue, so blue. I wanted to swim in them, oh what was wrong with me? I said, "But I really don't want romance or that kind of relationship in my life right now."

My Fool said, "It is okay to live in the small picture (age issues) incited by being attracted to your Russian, while also being aware of the big picture (we are all ageless) and that includes you and your Russian. You can have experiences, Susan. Open to what is right for you beyond conscious conjecture, for only what *is* right for you—can happen."

I said, a bit sheepishly, "Even so, I am really afraid I might replicate my experience at the Minefields of Love when the warriors who were bad for me responded so boldly to my unconscious call."

"That was then. Then, you wanted another to do your work. You wanted to attract a warrior into your life so you would not have to be one yourself. You are currently taking responsibility for that in as much as your nature will allow."

"So, you are saying I will attract different kinds of men than I used to?"

"You no longer are playing that scene of attracting a dominating man who dominates you and you must then escape. Now you are trying to merge with your diametric opposite to become more like each other, to blend into one. So the more balanced you become, so too will be those you attract."

"But I don't want a man in my life, not that I could have him, but knowing him has opened me to those possibilities. I'm really enjoying my life being alone."

He said, "Trust your story, Susan. When it seems that what you have chosen, (to stop the old pattern of seeking relationships with warrior-like men, and instead have one with yourself) is being overridden (feeling attracted to a warrior) you are *not* veering away from your story. You *cannot* veer away from your story. Your story is reinforced by the intent of Susan. Your intent as Susan was created for you—by you, as Creative Energy."

"So, in a sense, I get my marching orders from the life intent I created before I was born."

"Yes. Your intent keeps the vibration of your identity in tune with the story that you have designed for yourself."

"So, you are saying, it might seem like something is overriding the story I wish to have, like being attracted to a man I don't want to be attracted to—but if it is in accordance with fulfilling my intent—it will be, and if it is not, it won't be."

He nodded. "In a way, we are programmed, by ourselves as Creative Energy, to become what we have decided to become. A poppy is programmed to be a poppy before it grows and unfolds. A kitten is programmed to be a cat before it is born. An orange tree will flourish into an orange tree. A child with an aggressive makeup will become an aggressive person. There *is* free will, but only within the guidelines of the story, and only in is as much as it serves our life intent."

"Okay," I said, "so I, Susan, have free will to integrate warrior energy but only as much as my references will allow. To become a black belt in Karate, for instance, is beyond what I can handle given my empathic sensitivities. However, I can learn to repel predators. And this is so because my life intent is not about becoming a full-fledged warrior, but merely to absorb some of that energy so that my personal story, whatever it is, can come into fruition."

He nodded. "That's pretty much it. Our personal references such as genetic, psychological, and mental encoding, influence our perceptions and give direction to our story. You, Susan, have a strong reaction when a fly is killed. You perceive all violence, unbearable. In that, the vibration of your pacifistic energy has attracted either violent people, or people who are non-reactive to violence (cold-hearted), into your life. This has set the scene for you to develop inner strength and to embrace the metaphorical sword, hold it high, and announce, 'No more!' "

I nodded strongly. "That is *so* very true. It is interesting that we are born with inclinations that are beyond the influences of our life. We often have fears and likes that don't seem logical. One might fear trains even when no bad experiences with trains have been had, and yet there is great rhyme and reason to have that reference. Somehow it serves the life story. Then my references attracted the men with whom I chose to have interaction, and those interactions have served my life story."

"That is the way of it. Our references create perceptions that facilitate the fulfillment of our life intent. We are what our references say we are: a poor kid from the slums, a jilted lover, cock of the walk, lord and king, and so on. This is why no one can be converted to our way of thinking unless they have encoded themselves with references to move into that way of thinking. Our understanding of life, born from these references, affects all we see and believe, and hence factors into our actions and reactions. This, along with our mandate (the set up of our birth, location, our parents, siblings, and events that occur) is critical to the unfolding of our story."

"So, we are always becoming who we already are?"

"Yes! Therefore, anything we have ever said or done was not wrong. Anything we ever say or do will not be wrong. Natural law *always* kicks in and brings justice. What we deem wrong, propels us to grapple in the dark until we can find the sun. Who is to say that the man behind bars is not fulfilling an intent?"

I added, "So our judgment of another will always be missing many pieces in the picture that would change that judgment. And since the big picture is seldom seen, our judgments of others, and even ourselves are somewhat distorted."

He said, "Open-mindedness allows us to locate and connect new pieces to the greater picture. More of the greater picture is seen, and in that, perception changes. In the greater panoramic scene, everything and everyone is right and true. However, it is the existence of disagreement born from limited perceptions that is the great gift. It forces everyone to take a personal journey to live a life that is right for them and no other."

"It is hard for humans to wrap their minds around the idea that everything is true because so many concepts seem oppositional, like: There is reincarnation or there isn't. We either have free will or we are fated to predestination. When one has a near death experience she might see a bright light that seems to be calling her. Science might regard that as a hallucination due to a fluid being excreted in the brain. Why can't both sides of all these topics be true?"

He affirmed. "Yes, whatever exists, so does the opposite."

"And yet, most people can argue with commitment and vigor and sometimes fight for their view even to the death, because they absolutely know it is true. And it *is* true. But so is everything else."

"Yes. We know what we know. Hence we have multitudes of experiences that facilitate the unfolding of a trillion stories that are all part of the great earth story. Pain, anger, sorrow, confusion, chaos, and depression generate healing, peace, joy, clarity, harmony, and enthusiasm. Everything has polarities. There can never be complete peace just as there can never be complete chaos. We experience everything based on where our focus lies. When we shift our focus, we can experience the world in accordance to that shift. Ignorance is not good or bad. The wars between people or nations are not good or bad. Life *really* is a great adventure."

I shook my head. "Judgment makes us small."

He said, "Sometimes we have to be small to have a story. And when the story is played, even the small ones, even if the story is but a drama that occurs in a day, we feel our greater self for a bit, and we get enlightened for a while. Then the story becomes another thread in the tapestry of life. Even the smallest stories are great. The little girl who saves her allowance for a month to buy the shoes all her friends are wearing. The woman who feels no one understands her, so she begins painting pictures to express herself. The man who berates his wife, and she glares back rejecting his view of her. These are huge stories, though not often celebrated by the public."

I said, "I suppose, deep down we know when a small thing is a big thing—even if it is not consciously acknowledged."

He added, "And sometimes, humans make small things big things by twisting the truth."

"Yeah, like the guy who accuses his girlfriend, (who is looking out the car window admiring the trees), of daydreaming about other men. Or the woman who isn't acknowledged for her hard work (even though she is a saint) and therefore deems herself a loser."

He said, "Yes, we know what we know even if it is cementing us into a story that we wish to end."

I added, "We are a stubborn bunch!"

"Yes. Our identity is made up of strong non-bending systems held in place by references, such as the system of a warrior with references to guard boundary and conquer territory. Or the system of a villain with references of feeling cheated by the world and the need to cheat the world in return. Or a system of a martyr with references to constantly sacrifice for others. When those systems are no longer called for, as in the warrior who has nothing left to conquer and grows lonely in his or her armor. As in the villain who doesn't want to play the game anymore and just wishes she could get the chip off her shoulder and know peace, or the martyr who is worn out and sinking fast, needing so badly to nourish himself. Most are unable to adjust to the changed state within them, and continue to view life through their old systems that are in dry dock. They often grow depressed because they will not find a new way; they cling to the old way, even though it has expended itself."

"Yes, I can see that in myself," I said. "I lived in the martyr-victim system for decades, even though it was killing me. Deciding to release it was highly uncomfortable, yet I couldn't live that way anymore. When you helped me merge with the warrior energy I had blacklisted, my martyr-victim ways began to diminish. I still have to work on it, but basically I now live in a way that allows me to breathe easier and experience a whole new life in the identity of Susan."

He splayed His palms outward. "Yes, it is the letting go of what seems to make us who we are—that is the hardest. Before I died (changed focus), I slowly released the references that cemented me into a warrior system because there were no more scenes to play out under that banner. And that was the last system for me to dissolve, for I had played out all the others. Like a force of water, I had made my splash and all the droplets of my many selves joined into 'one.' "

"I still get confused sometimes, what 'I' means. 'I' seems to mean three things: an identity, a Being, and *The All*."

"The three I's you mentioned are not different. A drop of water—is also the ocean—and water itself. The particle of anything is not less than its whole. An atom is not more than what is inside it. One person is not less than all people."

Beholding the three 'I's all at once made me feel odd: small, big, and massive; thick, porous, and invisible; a scene, a chapter, and a story. Suddenly, some part of me flew into the cosmic sky and fell through a veil of glistening diamond light. When one falls, it is usually thought to be in the direction of down. But this falling wasn't down, it was across—into something.

On the other side of the veil, I saw a young woman standing in a marsh looking for food in the early morning. Then I was this young woman in a marsh looking for food. I wore a long tattered dress, wet from the grassy water that reached my knees. I had long, red curly hair that tumbled over my chest tangled and matted. My stomach hurt from hunger.

Beyond the marsh there were dense woods where my crazy brother lived. He had been reduced to a rogue; a poor, damaged man assaulted by the tyrant who overthrew and killed my father. My father had been a visionary, a powerful ruler trying to unite five factions in Denmark.

I feared my brother since insanity took him, but I loved him too. I heard pounding hooves. My heart lurched and my throat burned. I knew that sound. It was the tyrant's men, a handful of soldiers sent out to torment me and my brother as an example of what happens to dissenters. The men came a couple times a week, seven of them, and they would rape me.

I gasped. "No!"

My crazy brother ran out of the woods across the marsh shouting for me to come to him, that he would hide me. But . . . too late, the men charged toward me on horseback.

Somewhere inside me, I hid so deeply that I disappeared.

I fell again through the diamond veil, into a stark cell in a monastery. I was a prisoner there, punished for putting notions in the head of women that they had sacred powers as important as a man's. A monk came into my cell. He said in French, "I will purge the Devil from you." And he climbed upon me, pulling up my gown, and he raped me.

I shrank up deep inside myself until I was a dot, until I was nothing.

I fell through another veil and I was a nun in a great French convent where miracles occurred. My sisters were many and our abbey was famous. When I was on the upper floor washing one of the old sisters in a tub, invaders stormed the abbey. They raped me and my sisters, even the old one.

I couldn't breathe. My ears stung with pain. No, no, no. My head thrashed, and I cried out, "No more!"

I shrank again falling into myself.

This pattern occurred several more times: I was held prisoner in a dungeon, naked, and men raped me, one after the other. Another time I was forced into prostitution. Another time my stepfather kept molesting me.

I began screaming trying to wake myself up from these nightmares. Had I fallen asleep? I felt like I was trying to break out of a tube that kept transporting me to similar lifetimes. With sheer will, I commanded, "I *will* return to My Fool." Suddenly, I dropped downward, falling fast. My fall was broken by arms. Someone caught me. I was horizontal, held like baby. I looked into the face that was holding me. It was My Fool.

"I don't like these stories!" I started crying. I mean boo hoo sobbing, even though these things had not happened to the identity of Susan, I felt them as surely as they had. But since I was connected to all the selves I ever was, or . . . am; what they experience, I experience whether consciously remembered, or not. Those were not dreams I had, not ordinary dreams. I had been to other places, visiting myself.

My Fool was patient, letting me cry, letting me feel, letting me be human. And after the crying was done, he set me on my feet.

I looked at Him gratefully, but I still needed to process the experience. I said, "I experienced the same story over and over, like when I so-called 'past-life regress' someone multiple times, they experience a similar theme, reflecting their current life pattern, thus illuminating self-understanding. But this . . . this repetition seemed never ending and too much to bear!"

He said, "You also have other kinds of experiences involving your antithetical counterpart identities, but tapping those times would just cloud your understanding of the current pattern you are exploring."

I exhaled briskly, wanting be done with those stupid lives that brought so much pain. It was then I became aware that we seemed to be standing on clouds, or in clouds. Then the clouds cleared and before us was a great tunnel. It reminded me of the ones that you drive your car through on the interstate somewhere. It was huge. Then we were at the tunnel's entrance. Embedded in the circumference of the tunnel were parallel lines the spanned its seemingly endless length.

My Fool walked inside and bade me follow.

Walking alongside Him, He said, "This is the tunnel of your Being. The tunnel is as the center of the wheel. From here you can look all around and see the ribbed lines stretching along the length of the tunnel. Each line represents an identity in your Being. Each identity, as you know, carries with it similar lifetime experiences with variations, as you just lived in being sexually victimized over and over, in life, after seeming life. Until that experience is complete, the focus will remain no matter what body you are in."

I said, "So, it isn't that we repeat the experience until we 'get it right.'

"No," He said. "We know before we live each life (in the concept of linear time) what the storyline will be. We are well enlightened before the life experience is had. We forget what we know so that we may fully explore the experience. Through experiencing a long procession of trailing identities, you have explored female degradation and sought to find ways to survive it. Since it was men who seemed to keep taking your honor away, you kept trying to get them to give it back. Even your nun identities sought approval from a male God. When you stopped trying to get your honor from men, you learned how to get it from yourself. When you gave honor to yourself, you no longer needed to continue that line of martyr-victim experiences. Now you are making peace with male energy and integrating it into the identity of Susan."

"So does that mean I am about to finish this particular line of exploration?"

"Yes."

"What happens then?"

"You shift focus to a new line of exploration. For instance," He pointed to a rib, "shifting focus from the counterpart identity you have been exploring," and then He pointed to another parallel rib, "to perhaps, that counterpart identity. All the counterpart identities in your Being are currently experiencing different versions of the same story."

"So if I switch focus to a new rib (line of experiences) to another counterpart identity in my Being, I would live out a different side of the same story."

"Yes. And yet, all the stories continue playing; and you are always all the identities in your Being, ever shifting focus to continue experiencing various facets of life. Blinking here, blinking there, until eventually you blink everywhere."

I shook my head, trying to absorb the insight. Everything was always much more complex, it seemed, than we could ever, ever, as humans, understand.

As we journeyed deeper into the tunnel, He said, "It can never all be understood, however, much can happen when insights are gleaned."

The tunnel suddenly seemed to spin, and I was dizzy. "What is this?" I exclaimed, standing still so I wouldn't fall.

He stood next to me, and placed a warm hand on my back. "This tunnel is as the spoke of another wheel spinning in the concept of time. This spoke is a Being. Another spoke is another Being. All the Beings make a wheel. And that wheel is within another and another."

I said, "Wow. Imagining that, I can glimpse the incredible intricacies and synchronicity in Creative Energy's projection of the story."

He said, "Yes. That is so because the story was not created with a beginning, then middle, then end. The whole story was created at once. As we explore various stories within the story, and various parts of a story, we ever feel as if we are moving in time, and in one sort of identity or another. But really, we are all the characters, and we all are exploring each and every particle of every story. We explore all thoughts, feelings, and physical sensations. We explore the rich wonderland of all that is and all that can be. Our experiences create energy. Even after a flower seemingly dies, its experiences as a flower remain as new energy that was not there before the flower lived. Every experience we have manifests new energy. This is the prize, that we, as Creative Energy, seek. It is newness born from oldness. What can be . . . is born from what is."

I said, "So, it is the interaction then that seemingly generates new energy?"

"Yes," My Fool replied. "Everything has a vibration: even numbers, letters, colors, and musical notes. All of these vibrations in various configurations give rise to seeming differences. Various configurations of notes make different songs. Various configurations of letters make different words. Various configurations of words make different sentences and so on. And when configurations come together as a group, the group manifests differently together than the individuals in the group would manifest by standing alone. A family unit, a group of people, will create their own identity as if they were one a person. Another group will create a different identity. These many groups might come together and manifest something else in the world such as a political party, a religion, or a nation."

"So," I said, "When all these groups are blended together all over the earth, that too is an identity of its own—a vibration of its own."

He nodded. "We are all creating this story together, and it is not just people. Places have vibrations. Things have vibrations. Everything has a vibration. And everything has 'a calling.' Sometimes the calling can change. When we feel vibrant, we are in focus of our calling. If we lose that focus, as in losing interest in our work, we feel numbed and not very present in our lives. When a new focus is found, such as a new line of work, we feel reborn and alive once more. Our calling has changed."

"So everything, the story, the characters, the interactions, and the focus shifts are all part of the great synchronistic adventure. Then really, embracing one's story means to accept what comes before us, and know it is a gift we give ourselves."

"And now I want to give you a gift. Open your hand."

I outstretched my palm. He placed in it a tiny book. It resembled the giant blue book of my Being's lives that He'd once summoned to drop from the sky. Then, it sank into the earth. But now, but now . . . I held it in my hand. I held my story.

He said, "This is the Gem of Story."

I looked up at Him teary-eyed. "I am holding my story. I am finally ready to let it—be."

"Now . . . go . . . . live it." He threw His arms in the air. "Ain't life great!"

I opened my physical eyes, lying in bed. It was morning, and there it was, the Wizard of Oz Poster on my ceiling. My long-haired black and white cat was on my stomach, kneading his paws the way cats do when they are happy, purring like a motor-boat.

Old insights had renewed and brightened as if they were fresh insights: life was about having experiences, not getting them over with. Even if I could have disappeared back into Pure Creative Energy, undone and homogenized, what good would it have done? Creative Energy is always there, and we are always of it, in it—it. And we are here to have adventures and to experience all configurations of earth, air, water, fire, love and hate, sadness and joy, fear and faith, cruelty and compassion. We are here to experience the process of intelligence and wisdom, insight and ignorance, of losing and winning, oppression and freedom, individuality and the collective.

We are here in this play, playing at being individuals. What a miracle it now seemed to me to have the opportunity to live a life, to see what it is like to experience the configuration of an entity, of individualization, of a story, of the collective earth story, a great story, the experience of time and space created from what is outside time and space.

And yet we were all together, together because we can't be apart, because there really is no apart—that is just an illusion. We are the configuration of various atoms in a living, breathing, panorama ever connected, ever dancing together as one Creative Energy.

I sighed, feeling bountiful within and at great peace. We are okay. We are all okay. Life is okay. We are all the same, even in our differences. We are what is beyond the story, even as we live the story. We need no merciful creator to forgive us or guide us. There is nothing to forgive, and nowhere to go. The thrust of life is more about feeling the pulse of a story trying to flower from a seed. We decompress from what starts as, that grows into a great tale.

A tear dripped from my eye. And my cat, Baxter caught it with his tongue as it rolled down my cheek.

We are the Creator. We, as one, *are* the Creator.

I got out of bed to start my mundane day, my beautiful mundane day.

Behold your story. It is your turn to embrace who you are. Place your palms on your heart, one over the other. Close your eyes, take a deep breath and exhale. Let the energy of self-acceptance flow from your hands into your heart, charged with the power of the Universe and the miracle of a seed.

Behold your story. It is your turn to stop judging yourself. Whether you are in a young man's focus, or the old woman's world, or the martyr suffering, or a warrior in conquest—behold your story. Whether you are a drug addict or recovering, a victim or perpetrator of a crime—behold your story. If your children don't like you, or you don't like them, if your home is foreclosed and your bank account empty, if your lover cheated on you or you cheated on your lover, if you didn't get the job or got fired, if you feel lost and can't find your way, or are on a path to nowhere—behold your story!

Behold your story with palms over heart in deep self-acceptance. And now, open to the gifts at hand, the gifts your story is trying to give you. As we are all that exists, to diminish any one thing, even yourself—diminishes everything. Every story begins and ends in beauty, even yours. Behold YOUR story.

The Unfolding of a Story: The Blossoming of Memories

"The seed decompresses; the story is the seed."

GEM #6 COMPRESSION

I was at the ocean this rather cold September day, thinking about my life adventures—the great ones, the painful ones, and the quiet times in-between. As I lay, stomach side down, propped up on elbows in blue jeans and a midnight-blue turtleneck sweater, I observed the foamy waves. With my brown hiking boots and socks off my feet next to me, I swished my naked toes in the cool sand.

A gentle chill breeze blew light brown bang tendrils over my eyelashes. Through the strings of hair, I watched the incoming tide, deep in thought. Each wave brings a new adventure. We can freak out as it crashes over our heads taking us topsy-turvy to the beach. Or, we can ride it in and have an adventure. Or, we can duck under the overwhelming body of rolling water and choose not to react. However, the waves will come, for they, along with everything else, are a line of music in life's rhythm, ever so significant in the Great Earth Story.

The sound of moving water soothed me so, as if saying, *all is as it should be*. Waves crashed to shore, covering dry sand, making it succulent wet. And waves receded to the ocean, bountiful with sea creatures that stun the imagination.

I sighed with exhilaration and looked down at the sand granules between my hands, sometimes dry, sometimes wet, sometimes windswept or stepped upon. We were as the millions of granules, all together in the same boat, in the same story, even though within that story we have grand stories of our own.

I rolled on my back and looked up at the gray sky.

Blue skies, gray skies, cloudy days, rainy days, sunny days. Would we really like it if the sky was exactly the same every day for all of our life? Oh, how I loved a changing sky!

A seagull flew over me. I loved seagulls. How pleasant it must be to live and play at the sea! With my eyes on the bird's belly and soaring wings, I sat up with knees in the air, to follow the winged creature's line of flight.

My hand flew over my heart with a gasp. I was staring at the navy blue shirt-covered chest of a man who stood before me. I forced my eyes upward to view the face.

Dmitri! His dark, wavy hair was beauteous against the backdrop of gray sky. My hand drifted down from my heart. I was relieved and somewhat excited. "It's you, Dmitri; what are you doing here?"

He squatted to my level, and smiled. "I didn't mean to scare you."

"Oh," I said, "I startle easily; it's a sensitivity thing."

He said something but I didn't hear him too well because I was busy absorbing his striking presence. He looked fine in his black boots, blue jeans, and navy blue, short-sleeved tee shirt. His dark brown, shiny soft hair was a bit wind blown, and I liked it that way very much. I asked, "How did you know I was here?"

He said, "Locating people is not so hard for me." He shrugged his shoulders lightly. "I read all your books with interest, but there is more I'd like to understand. I have little time, but I hoped to talk with you. May we?"

I nodded.

Noticing his bare arms, I said, "Aren't you cold?

"No," he said, "where I come from, this would not be considered cold."

I said, "I want to know more about where you come from, about you."

"Not today," he said, "I am moving away from that and so I would rather talk about what I am heading into. Tell me more,

Susan, about the story of life, about endings and beginnings, about letting go of small thinking."

I pointed to the brown rocky part of the shore where protruding rock cliffs beautified the scene. "Shall we walk?"

"Yes," he said. He reached for my brown hiking boots stuffed with a brown sock each, parked next to my hip.

"I can do that," I said shyly, as I brushed sand out of my long, loose hair, shaking my head a bit.

"No," he said, "allow me."

He brushed sand off my feet, and I am sure my face was red. He carefully slipped my socks over my bare skin, one by one, not seductively, but respectfully. Then he slipped on my boots, one by one, and tied them carefully. When he was done, he rose, and reached down his hand to me.

I took it. His fingers seemed strong, his palm secure against mine. He pulled me to stand, and then released me. We headed a bit closer to the waves and walked, still well upon dry land.

He asked, "What is life beyond our human existence?"

I said, "I am working on that book now. I will share with you what I am writing, but just remember everything I say is but a radical simplification of the insights I've had beyond mundane reality. Whatever I say, it's just what 'I' have discovered."

"I understand," he said, "you are just sharing."

I said, "All right. Life as we know it, and life beyond human existence—is energy. Pure Creative Energy is all that is. Humans and all other life forms are projections of that energy configured, thus giving the impression of separation, time and space, and hence numerous stories to live."

Dmitri asked, "So, do we create our stories, or are they created before we live them?"

"Both. We, as Creative Energy, configured energy in a flash. I am using a past tense, but Creative Energy is actually beyond time. The whole projection occurred at once, without beginning or end. These configurations created countless possibilities of interaction, and thus trillions of stories all at once."

"Ah," Dmitri said, "in the greater depth of things there is no before or after, no you or me."

"Yes. The idea of a 'you' and a 'me,' are Creative Energy's projections of itself into Beings with many identities. Beings devise characters or identities to experience the stories. Remember, the Beings, and identities within the Beings, *are* Creative Energy, and not lesser than Creative Energy."

"Yes," he said, "I very much like that concept."

I continued, "Each of a Being's numerous identities are one of a kind, assembled with a vast amount of references that make each identity what it is. These references support the story the identity wishes to have. If for instance, an identity wants to experience being a scientist, she will be born with a scientific mind. If an identity wants to explore individuality, he might be born an identical twin."

Dmitri said, "So if my identity wanted to explore my line of work, it would make sense that I might not only be born into it, but possess the abilities required?"

"Yes. Beings and their numerous identities have chosen stories to experience. These stories are perfect unto themselves, complex and multi-layered, with stories within stories within stories. And all the stories, like pages in a book, create a bigger story. And all those books create a bigger book, and a bigger one, and so on. One such story is the Earth Story. And two sub stories in the Earth Story, are yours and mine. In the projection of time and space, the story and the sub stories unfold."

He said, "So, these stories unfold like seeds that grow into something else, like the story of an evergreen, unfolding from a seed, to sapling, to tree, sprouting acorns, and so on."

"Yes, a story is like that. Life is not about the story though. It is about what *would happen if* we lived the story. What would it be like to experience this or that story?"

"So, when a life story ends," he looked at me with a kind of knowing like he was trying to tell me something, "what dictates the next experience?"

I said, "We are getting into territory I am still exploring. Since you seem to have crossed over into something inside yourself, maybe you could come with me on this psycho spiritual journey that I came here today to experience. On these journeys, I meet the essence of a mentor who shares things with me. I call him My Fool.

"Ah, I remember, you have written about him."

"Yes, would you like to meet him?"

"You mean, meet a spirit form from another world?"

I nodded, "I guess you could call it that."

"I would," he replied, "I don't know if I can do it, but I want to try."

"I have never taken another person with me to My Fool before. This will be very nice."

I led Dmitri up a rock cliff with relative ease. We sat on a flat space, our legs dangling over the cliff's edge, overlooking the raucous surf. And though my headphones weren't on, I could hear Mahler's, *Symphony No. 3* rise from the scene.

I led him into deep meditation, guiding him to The Wall, and he arrived without any seeming effort.

There, in an altered state, we had moved into an ethereal world as real as the one seen with physical eyes.

My Fool was there, as if waiting for our arrival. He grinned at me in that whimsical way of His. "You have brought your diametric opposite, the one you went to in spirit form to the sycamore tree to comfort."

Dmitri and I looked at each other and said simultaneously, "That was you?"

My Fool's face beamed. "Well, so it seems that two identities in the same Being have found each other in the everyday world."

I gasped, and so did Dmitri, although my gasp was more audible.

Dmitri said to My Fool, "Ah, perhaps that is why I am so drawn to Susan."

My Fool said, "Yes Dmitri, and in your dreams, you have come to Susan, and given her strength. Identities within a self are always interacting."

Dmitri and I smiled at each other, kind of like long lost family reuniting.

I looked to My Fool. "Dmitri and I are open for more insight." I looked to Dmitri, "Ask Him your question."

Dmitri asked Him, "When a life story ends, what dictates what the next adventure will be?"

My Fool replied, "Well, that answer is complex because it hinges on what is happening in the story. There is the overall story of a Being, the stories of counterpart identities, trailing identities, and the story of one identity in one lifetime. So, an identity's next adventure would depend on all the other stories."

Dmitri said, "So, just because a life story ends, it doesn't necessarily mean that the story is over?"

"That is right," My Fool said. "A story is not always complete in one perceived lifetime, and sometimes more than one story unfolds in a perceived lifetime. And the completion of a story does not always mean the end of a life or rather the defocusing of a life. It can simply mean the end of a pattern within that identity's awareness. Sometimes we have several stories, one after the other, unfold and conclude in one lifetime. For example, in my life as The Fool, my first story was a businessman. My second story was a guru. My third story was to have no story and to finish earth."

"About that—" I said.

"Sometimes—" He gave me a strange little smile and looked to Dmitri. "Sometimes our life story involves one long story, like yours, Dmitri. You were born to a father who groomed you from birth to be a secret agent. This one story has been decompressing over the course of your life."

Dmitri nodded lightly.

My Fool looked at me. "And then some identities have overlapping stories occurring all the time. For instance, Susan, while you were heavy in the story of finding and maintaining your power within your marriage, you also had a story going on with your son, and another with your daughter. You had stories going on with the facades within you, such as the nun. You had a story going on with warrior energy. And you had a story going on with adventuring into unseen worlds. These stories overlapped and intertwined."

I nodded lightly.

My Fool looked at us both. "All these sub-stories support the greater story of the Being."

Dmitri, with great consternation asked, "So, if a life story ends before the greater story is finished, then the identity that dies (or changes focus) will move into another identity to trail the story?"

"That is right," said My Fool. "And when one identity in a Being finishes the greater story, so do all other identities in the Being. Hence, when any identity in the circle of a Being changes, they all change."

I said, "So, Dmitri and I are changing together."

"You are," My Fool affirmed. "Eventually, in the concept of time, the counterbalance identities in a Being become more and more alike, merging the boundaries and becoming one. Dmitri and Susan, you are winding up to that point, although not quite there. You are both ending your respective patterns with your trailing identities, as are each of your counterbalance identities."

"And when we finish?" asked Dmitri.

My Fool replied, "Then your Being might wish to experience another theme, another large story. If so, then all the identities in your Being will reconfigure and do it all again. The Being's identities will each explore a different angle of a theme, such as (this is a simplification) dictatorship and slavery. And then each identity will have a succession of trailing identities, to in as sense, develop one angle of the larger story of the Being."

Dmitri cocked his head slightly. "What happens when a Being finishes experiencing the Earth Story as you have?"

My Fool replied, "The Being can remain as a watcher (to view earth life but not get involved), or move into other vibrations beyond earth, or refocus into the one homogenized Creative Energy."

I furrowed my brow, addressing My Fool. "But, you don't seem to fit into any of those choices. Who . . . or what are *you*?"

His eyes twinkled. "Let the mystery unfold my dear, let it unfold."

I sighed. "Well, can you at least share what occurred after *you* so-called died?"

My Fool replied, "I can. When I came to the sea of conclusion in the earth experience, all the references I used to assemble my identities were given back at the portal of Highway Eleven where we enter and exit earth. These references were left for others to reassemble into identities for earth adventures. From there I have come to experience multiple focuses all at once, in all planes of existence. This keeps me from concretizing into any one focus, even though it might appear to you that I am."

Ah ha, at least He shared a bit more than He did at the beach. I was pleased.

Dmitri said, "Are you what might be termed, an old soul?"

My Fool replied, "There are no old souls, for we are all the same age, or ageless."

Dmitri nodded. "That makes sense."

I asked My Fool, "If you are in all focuses at once, how is it that I can relate with you on the other side of The Wall?"

He answered, "The reason you can touch me on the other side of The Wall, has nothing to do with my state of being, but yours. You move into altered states that allow it. And you allow it because you are ending a pattern, hence it is time for enlightenment."

He looked to Dmitri, "You Dmitri will also be able to touch me beyond The Wall because your life story is almost fully decompressed, and so for you too, it is time for enlightenment."

My heart lurched a little. Was He saying that Dmitri was preparing to die?

My Fool's glimmering eyes caught mine, and He whispered in my brain, *What is death*? I shook my head, trying to integrate the human me with my inner sage.

Dmitri said, "So if I were to move on now—die, and Susan did not, we are still one Being living out a larger story?"

"Yes," My Fool replied, "the concept of death is really just leaving behind an old set of memories and moving into a new set of memories yet to be experienced."

Dmitri sighed, confused, "What do you mean by this, a new set of memories?"

My Fool said, "For that insight, you must come to other side of The Wall."

I looked upon Dmitri's ethereal form. "Do you want to go deeper?"

He looked back at me sincerely, with an almost gentle sense of urgency. "I do."

With that, I guided Dmitri into the necessary state of mind, which he easily sailed into, perhaps because he was going to die soon.

There on the other side of The Wall, we met My Fool as a sparkling energy form, more porous here, and features less visible. And if I didn't hold the focus, the features kept changing.

My Fool said, "Stories are made up of memories that haven't happened yet."

Dmitri raised a brow. "Hmm?"

My Fool said, "The events that will happen in stories have already been created by us as Pure Creative Energy when energy was configured."

"Ah," exclaimed Dmitri, "Energy configured gives way to interaction and hence many stories. If the stories are already written, the memories that the identity will experience are already written."

"Bravo!" exclaimed My Fool. "You can see then how memories would come first. True memories are the blueprints of what the identity will experience in their chosen life."

I said, "So memories are the story written, but not yet experienced."

"Indeed," said My Fool. "Once the memories are experienced, then there is an imprint of what happened. These imprints are what humans usually refer to as memory—but the imprints are more like recollections. As we age, each time we recall something, it will change a little or a lot in accordance with how much we have changed. As we change, our perceptions change; as our perceptions change so do our recollections. Hence, these recollections are subject to much editing, embellishing, and skewed analysis. So what we remember is really less of a memory than a reflection of how we have processed something."

I said, "So true memory is pure and does not involve recollection."

"Yes," My Fool said. "A true memory is created outside time before the experience occurs." My Fool's hand dipped to His heart and glided outward in a gesture of presentation. "The tapestry is woven, but not yet beheld."

He repeated the motion as I added, "The story is already written but not yet read."

And He repeated the motion again when Dmitri added, "The symphony comes together, but is not yet played."

My Fool said, "Yes, yes. For example: a man is hiking. He slips, and his wallet falls out of his pocket down the side of a mountain. As he tries to get it, he tumbles further down the mountain and sprains his ankle badly. After three days on the mountain, he is found. Because of this event, he reevaluates his life, and decides to make important changes. He will remember the event with a perspective in alignment with the personalized references embedded in his identity. However, the pure memory, without being personalized by the identity's references, was created outside time, existing before the event occurred. This memory will be borrowed by many others, but experienced differently."

Dmitri chimed in, "So many others will live that same memory created outside time, the same memory of hiking, slipping, wallet falling out, and in retrieving it—fall down the mountain, sprain an ankle, and be found three days later. But each will experience that memory or event differently, even though the pure memories, created outside time—remain the same."

I added, "And we experience the same memory differently, because our references are different."

"Yes," My Fool said. "If a hundred people get lost in the woods for days and then are found, that memory will have various meanings to each and yield varying experiences to support each identity's particular story. One identity from that experience might hide away from life for a period of time. That same experience happening to another identity might elicit a great life change from a boring career to a tantalizing one. Another identity with the same experience might pay more attention to their family, and another might decide to travel more."

I said, "So the memories, in a way are borrowed by, for lack of better words, a big memory bank and experienced by numerous identities."

My Fool nodded. "Indeed. However, the memory, or event itself is *highly* significant. These memories lived—ensure the fulfillment of our life intent."

I said, "They are like gifts that we lovingly give to ourselves."

Dmitri added, "These gifts ensure rich explorations of life."

"Yes," My Fool chortled. "It is most amusing to work with two identities in the same Being, for since you are both in alignment to each other's transformations, you are in harmony when you speak."

Dmitri and I glanced at each other with deep affection.

My Fool continued, "The memories, or preconceived stories, might be for exact moments, (like picking a flower), days (like a week long vacation), weeks (like the two week visit from your in-law) months, (like summer break) or years (like the years of raising children)."

Dmitri asked, "Are *all* memories lived? I mean can one die, or shift focus to another identity before all the memories are lived?"

My Fool answered, "Death does not rid memory. One cannot 'beat the system' by dying. Whatever our greater consciousness has chosen to experience—it will, whether in this focus, or the next focus, or the next. So, all memories that serve a life intent will be lived."

Dmitri asked, "So when a story ends, and these memories have played out, do we have some sort of a consciousness shift?"

"Yes," said My Fool. "Imagine that your Being lives in a pressure chamber, and a dial controls how much flow enters the chamber. What enters is Creative Energy. If very little Creative Energy is in the chamber, the identities of the Being will feel very separated from each other. They will have forgotten almost completely what it feels like to be connected to not only each other, but totality as well. In this, they can experience individuality and have great adventures."

"I get it," I said, "to launch a story, to feel a sense of individual reality, very little Creative Energy is in the chamber of the Being."

"Yes," My Fool affirmed. "As the story moves into its climax and tension mounts, the identity on some level calls for an increase of Creative Energy to enter the chamber. This increase invites enlightenment."

Dmitri said, "So when we are ready for a story to end, we get wise."

My Fool nodded. "It is then that the identities will, what humans call 'soul search'. They might do it through praying to their idea of a God or Goddess. Or they might seek a guru, or increase meditation. They might take a risk and do something they have never done before to help break the pattern that they no longer wish to continue. Or sometimes, even the unconscious self, calling for relief, will incite an event to force a story to end."

Dmitri said, "So one way or another, the 'light' comes in, and the identities in the Being simultaneously begin to remember what they have forgotten."

"Yes," My Fool said. "Those preparing to finish their story, whether that involves so-called death or not, will somehow begin to feel more deeply connected to the life force, irregardless of what they perceive that life force to be. Relief is finally felt, and the long hard road finally ends."

"Yes," Dmitri nodded, as if thinking of his own life, "yes."

My Fool looked at him with a knowing eye and nodded in acknowledgement. "Sometimes we call people to us who are meant to help us through the transition of ending a story and beginning a new one."

Dmitri looked at me warmly. "Yes."

I smiled gently at Dmitri in his ethereal form, finding it so great we could be here together this way with My Fool.

My Fool said, "However, the times we live in the dark and forget our connection to totality, are no less important than the times when we remember, for it is in the forgetting that we even have a story."

A wheel appeared around us, and Dmitri seemed a bit startled.

I said, "Don't worry, He does this all the time."

Dmitri nodded with a gentle smile and then examined the wheel around us.

My Fool said, "This is the wheel of your Being. Think of it as the pressure chamber. Spokes emanate from the hub where we are now. At the end of each spoke are your various counterbalance identities. Let's click back the dial a notch so that we can see what these identities are experiencing with less Creative Energy in the chamber of the Being. Since this wheel belongs to you both," My Fool pointed upward to the left. "Let us focus on the identity of the homeless boy living on the street in a criminal manner, *before* he is put in a children's home."

Dmitri and I looked to the boy. Dmitri asked me. "He is one of us?"

I nodded. "Yes, he is."

My Fool said, "Take the dial back a notch more, and the boy is abandoned by his mother, living with his uncle who beat him."

I said, "So the less Creative Energy that is in the chamber the more traumatizing the story seems?"

My Fool replied, "In this case, yes. For others with little Creative Energy in the chamber, life might just seem boring. Turning the dial back the other way, allowing more Creative Energy to enter the chamber, and we see the boy *after* he is taken into the children's home. Here we see that he is beginning to form valuable relationships with other children. Turning the dial further up, allowing even more Creative Energy to enter, and the boy is a man who now helps other children in the very place that rescued him."

Dmitri said, "So, one can view any part of their story by turning the dial one way or another, because outside time and space, the story is already written."

My Fool nodded. "The story is already written, however the way one *experiences* the story—is not."

Dmitri said, "So we experience these stories in our own way because we are each a one of a kind identity?"

"Indeed," My Fool replied.

Dmitri continued, "And everything needed for the story to unfold is already encoded into the identity by virtue of individual references?"

"Yes," said My Fool. "Each identity has all the references necessary to have the chosen story. For instance, the boy who lived on the streets may have had a reference of a strong survival instinct. He might also have the reference of wanting a sense of family that he wasn't born with. These references might enable a story such as, when the boy grows up, he will want to stay in the children's home that took him in to help other children. Hence, he creates a sense of family, not only for himself, but for all of many who had none."

I said, "So free will isn't as much about directing a story as it is about living the story we have chosen."

"Yes," My Fool said, "the struggle and glory in life for each identity is the decompression of a seed growing into a flower. There is the trial and error to find the right nutrients to help the bud to grow, as in people trying this or that to feel better. We search high and low to find a way to open and be a part of life. And when we find it—we flower."

"Oh," I gasped. "This must be why we are so drawn to find a mate. Aside from nature making sure we reproduce, we also find comfort in connecting with one who makes us feel special and loved. And this connection helps us flower."

My Fool added, "But the most powerful flowering occurs when one connects with, feeling very special to, and very loved by—one's self. However, inter relating with others to experience that connection is the way it is supposed to be. We do not want that Creative Energy (enlightenment) pouring into us *before* our story unfolds. If we discover it too soon, we are cheated from living the story."

Dmitri said, "This differs from what I have heard in most spiritual circles, which seems to advocate skipping the story altogether and strive to reach a transcended state of being."

I added, "That is almost like saying that other than enlightenment, the rest is garbage. But if our only goal was to achieve enlightenment, there would be no unfolding of the story."

My Fool said, "Yes. What is a story without the parts that make it? What are the stars without the black of outer space? What would it be like to have never known hate or anger or pain? How can a finished product be without the ingredients necessary to make it?"

I said, "So, a woman who goes emotionally crazy and sets off a sequence of events that create a story is no less valuable than the guru who espouses the wisdom of oneness."

"Indeed," My Fool said. "Even if enlightenment (ending a story) is sought, it cannot happen until the story is finished. The story cannot finish until the intent for the story is fulfilled."

Dmitri said, "So our struggles are a gift, and seeming mistakes are actually meant to be so that the story can be experienced. And in that, as the stories unfold, we eventually find the prize at the end."

"Yes," My Fool said, and then He looked at Dmitri, "You Dmitri, were groomed to live a life that drove you so far away from your heart, that now heart is all that you care about."

Dmitri nodded.

Then My Fool looked at me. "Susan, you struggled with your ex-husband for years, yet it all led to you becoming stronger in yourself and flowering in ways you never imagined."

"That is exactly right," I said. "I guess we all have a story that is right for us, even if it doesn't seem so, or if it fails to look like the prototype of what we *think* it should be."

My Fool nodded. "Now, gaze upon the wheel once more and see it is a pressure chamber. This time what surrounds you, Susan, are different versions of Susan. And Dmitri, you will see that what surrounds you are different versions of Dmitri. Each version simultaneously decompresses the memory of its story, just as various counterbalance identities do."

"Each Susan and each Dmitri in this wheel, in this pressure chamber, is experiencing a *different* probability in the *same* story. Picture a thousand parallel realities of Susan." Then he looked to Dmitri. "Picture a thousand parallel realities of Dmitri. Now, turn the dial back on the pressure chamber, letting very little Creative Energy in, and all of the identities in the wheel of your Being are adapting to the life circumstances into which they were born. Turning the dial forward, allows more Creative Energy to filter into the chamber, and all the Susan's in their parallel realities, and all the Dmitri's in theirs, are all figuring out who they are and what they must do to complete the story."

I said, "So it is not just the identities in a being completing a story, it is also all the versions of one identity in parallel realities, completing a story."

"Yes," My Fool said, "yes."

I said, "So somewhere, Dmitri and I are living out a different version of the story with each other than this one?"

My Fool said, "You are living out every version of the story with each other."

Then the three of us seemed to move deeper into the center of the wheel and the landscape changed. My Fool took us like the ghost of Christmas present, or is it the past, or is it the future, into what I can best term as the land where stories are made.

The landscape appeared as a conglomerate of moving energy changing shape, forming into something that could not yet be detected or defined by the human eye.

My Fool said, "What you see are thoughts conjuring, emotions building, and dreams forming, readying to manifest. This is where energy is before it is turned into something else."

"Can we walk through it?" I asked

He replied, "There are no limits, no boundaries."

I said, "So, we can."

He said, "Walk into it and see."

"How?" I inquired.

He said, "Focus on the wellspring of Susan before she became Susan. Dmitri, focus on the well spring of Dmitri before he became Dmitri. Think of that as you walk through the energy."

Dmitri and I, in ethereal form, held hands and slowly walked into the moving blobs of pale colors blending into each other and sometimes standing out on their own. But everything was always changing. Nothing was static.

Then I felt a strange motion all around me. It reminded me of when I was pregnant and I could feel my baby moving inside me. But now it seemed as if I were in the womb. Dmitri had disappeared and I felt strongly that he was experiencing something similar.

As I continued walking, I could feel a consistency of energy moving around me in response to my movement. I murmured, "Who am I? Who am I really? What am I? What am I really?" Suddenly I felt swallowed into a blob of energy. I felt like I was zooming through a wormhole, even though I knew if I realistically was, it would probably destroy me.

Then it seemed I was in an actual woman's womb. Maybe because I was thinking about the womb, I was taken there.

From a distance and yet close-up, I heard My Fool answer in my head, "Yes."

And I had a sense of knowing my intent. I had a sense of a story that wanted to unfold. My story was almost like something that had already happened but had not yet fully manifested, like a flower whose genetics are determined before it exists. Then when the seed has manifested and is planted, it decompresses its story and blossoms into the creation that was designed before it was born. And yet, its experiences are new.

Again from a distance, yet close-up in my head, I heard My Fool answer, "Yes."

Then it seemed that the globules of energy all around me began moving into me. I realized these globules were the stories of my trailing identities, all sharing a particular thread of similar experiences. The globules absorbed into me. They were adding to the references that the identity of Susan would possess. So, although I would be a new identity born from the womb, I would also be all the trailing identities that I'd ever been, and continue a story that's been going on for sometime . . . in the concept of time.

I could see then that the overall story of a Being is ever decompressing from its point of inception. And all the identities in the Being are as scenes in each other's stories, characters in each other's play, which is one great play; all simultaneously decompressing. It is like one of those giant fireworks that explode in the sky with a bunch of smaller fireworks emerging from it.

And then I felt as if I were been being born and for a while, I forgot about all the things I had just said. I did not want to come out of the womb. I was afraid. I had forgotten about the references of my trailing identities that had absorbed into me.

My mother was in labor with me—Susan. And though I was not aware of it, I was born with all the references from my trailing identities, references that made no sense in the life of Susan. I grew up in a nonreligious family, but I adored nuns. And though my home environment was pleasant and nurturing, I felt guilty enjoying food, or having a bad thought, and felt like I'd sinned if I felt anger. I felt like I must suffer to prove my worth, and give my whole being in service to a greater power.

Then I thought about people and their strange idiosyncrasies that make no psychological sense. My daughter, growing up, was terrified of the water, and yet she had not, in this life, experienced danger in water. My son, as a young child, had a philosophical tongue. He shared surprising insights that even got *me*, the deep thinker—thinking.

My Fool's voice filtered in: "When we shift focus to a new identity, what is out of focus—remains. There is usually little or no memory of the old focus (the old life). These old experiences serve as additional references in the new identity. If, Susan, who is modest, dies or shifts to a new identity, that modesty will remain. If, for example, she has experiences in her new identity of flaunting herself, then she will carry both the references of modesty and flaunting into a new Focus Identity. In the new Focus Identity there might be events that bring out the modesty, which was an old reference two identities ago (in linear time) or the flaunting, which was an old reference one identity ago (in linear time). When modesty is triggered, it will bring forth the identity or all the identities that Susan has been where modesty was in the forefront. This conglomeration of similar identities makes the energy of facades. The facade of modest Susan is comprised of *all* the nun's or abused women who had experiences to create modesty."

My insight about facades deepened. For the first time I realized that a facade was seldom just an identity we have been that is triggered and rises to the surface, but more a comprisal of those types of identities that emerge as one."

"Yes," My Fool's voice said, "it is about vibration. The warrior vibration is the warrior facade. The sacrificial vibration is the nun facade, and so on. And this not only happens to people, but —every thing."

Suddenly, I zoomed inward and I felt quite small. I tried to relax so that I could benefit from whatever was happening to me. As I relaxed, I beheld myself as a seed. I moved further inside myself the way I do when I meditate.

Okay, it seemed I was the seed of a . . . pumpkin plant! And I was planted in a garden. Everything that I was to be was already encoded in me. Not encoded . . . was the *experience* I would have in being a pumpkin. I became aware of my genetic makeup. And beyond physical genetics, I moved into another kind of genetics, a kind of psychic genetics or the psyche of the plant, meaning that it was more than a biological organism. It possessed a kind of mind, and a kind of emotional world, not like humans, very different, but there none-the-less. And I could feel the makeup of all the pumpkins that would sprout from me as a plant; each had their own story to experience.

In a time-lapse way, I became a sprout and pushed through the ground. Leaves formed, then flowers, then pumpkins began to grow from me. It was laborious in one way, but quite exciting in another. Interesting, I had fear responses when a foot might step on me, and drowning feelings when I was overly watered. An oddly enough, I felt deeply enriched when I was admired by a human. I could feel bugs crawling over me, and unless they wanted to eat me, the sensation was nice.

A child picked one of my pumpkins before it was mature and threw it at another boy. I felt myself as the plant, but also as the pumpkin. Each pumpkin on my plant had its own genetic code derived from mine.

When my pumpkins grew ripe, a mother picked one, and I again felt I was that pumpkin, though I was still the plant. This must be what it is like for a Being with its counterbalance identities. A Being is the whole plant, and the pumpkins are identities having a variety of different experiences. One of my identities as a pumpkin was taken into the house and carved and put out for Halloween. I experienced that too, all the reactions that people had toward me, and the dog that peed on me, I felt that too. It stung me a bit, but that was not so bad.

Another pumpkin that was me was made into a pie. I felt myself slide down several throats and experienced being digested, transforming into something else. A part of me fed bodies and other parts of me were expelled into a bowl that took me through pipes until I finally settled back down into the earth.

Another pumpkin of mine got gnawed upon by a groundhog. And another became a decoration for a little girl in her bedroom for months. And another rotted on the vine. All these stories in one pumpkin plant. One Being. Finally, I could relate to how the Being experienced everything that its identities experienced!

Then I was back in the center of the wheel with Dmitri and My Fool.

Dmitri said, "That was amazing." And I knew we had indeed experienced the same or similar thing.

Then we all three seemed to be spinning with no solid ground beneath our feet. And I didn't feel sick as I usually do when spinning is involved. As we spun, I felt like we were creating something. All around us, scenes of our many lives together, (My Fool, Dmitri, and me) appeared. We began to spin so fast the scenes around us blurred giving the illusion of one connected circular rim. As our velocity had changed, so had our perception. It was like for a moment we were disengaging from the frames of our time together that we might experience them differently. I became aware then of how people's pace in life would affect their take on reality. Maybe if we changed our pace once in awhile, we'd see life around us another way.

We stopped spinning. We were in the center of a flower. The scenes of our joint lives together had condensed into flower petals unfolding around us to a full bloom. It seemed our story together, (My Fool, Dmitri, and me), had blossomed.

Then it was as if we three were waist deep in clear, sunlit water that sparkled all the colors in existence. A tone sounded. It seemed to encompass all tones in existence, like hearing every musical composition at once. It was all so strikingly beautiful, I felt like I was dissolving into it.

"It is beautiful," I said, "the sound and the sight."

"It is," said Dmitri.

My Fool said, "All energy is held here, every play is playing simultaneously; from ugly to beautiful, from chaos to peace, from a grain of sand to an exploding star. Whatever we view in our daily lives, whatever beliefs we have, are all born from experiencing a tiny part of this collective wholeness."

I became aware of my physical body in the life of Susan, even though I was currently in an ethereal form. I was perfectly still listening to my heartbeat. I inhaled slowly, deeply. I exhaled slowly, deeply. I breathed in and out. In and out. And I heard Dmitri doing the same.

I whispered, "Here I am."

Dmitri whispered, "Here am I."

My Fool whispered, "It is I. It is I. It is I. Don't you know who I am?"

Suddenly, I felt who I was. And I felt who Dmitri was, and My Fool too. I felt who everyone was. And we were all the same.

My Fool said, "Open your hand, Susan."

I opened my ethereal hand.

My Fool dropped a white ethereal seed in my palm. He said, "This is the Gem of Compression. It is a seed, a compressed story, packed with all the mysteries of life. Like a present, it unfolds into something more than it was, a sprig, a sapling, a tree."

With that, the seed absorbed into my hand, My Fool faded away, and Dmitri and I were on the cliff in our physical bodies.

We opened our eyes. Night had fallen. Looking at each other, we drew our legs off the side of the cliff and sat cross-legged, facing each other with shared awe.

He said, "I have never known anything like that. I am more sure than ever that I am finally becoming free of my old life."

I said, "I am glad for you, Dmitri."

He said, "I must be off, my plane leaves at midnight."

I was disappointed he must leave, but I suppose the story would play on as it was meant to, as we had designed it to.

Dmitri helped me down the moonlit cliff with respectful care. Then as we walked along the dark beach toward my car in the parking lot, we had the most delightful philosophical recap, as if we were two as one. Well, I guess we were.

He said, "I find it interesting that sometimes we act in ways so uncharacteristic of our nature. Like me, being here with you, having a night like this. My peers would never understand, and in fact, advise against it. But we will do what we must, and so will everyone else. "

"Yes," I affirmed, "we are often given advice, maybe even good advice that we just cannot seem to take, or bad advice that we *do* take, because we want to, because on some level we *need* to, though we haven't a clue why."

He said, "Yes, we as humans, often judge others for their decisions, and deem them wrong or right based on our advice. But I can see now, it is never about wrong and right. It is about living out a finely tuned storyline designed just for us, by us, as Creative Energy."

I smiled at him as we walked, delighting in our philosophical diatribe. "We plant references, like seeds, along the path of our journey before we take it. Interesting things pop up in the course of our lives, things that will generate new ideas or inspire us to behave differently. A woman determined to save the world, gets depleted, and realizes she must save herself. So she goes within, learns to meditate, and becomes a writer."

Dmitri added, "Or a depressed man might remain in his dark world for days, or months, maybe years, and suddenly feel he must go sit by a sycamore tree. An angel arrives and something washes over him, and quite suddenly he isn't depressed anymore and he doesn't know why."

My heart warmed. I slipped my hand in his. "In both these cases our journey is designed to give us the experiences that we need beyond conscious understanding. The woman who changed her goal from saving the world to knowing herself might have a life intent to develop in her what would help her break a tortuous pattern."

Dmitri said, "The depressed man who changed his goal from racing faster on the fast track to getting off the track all together, might have a life intent to release in him what has proven to be tortuous to others."

Our hand hold tightened. The sound of the waves serenaded us, and the moonlit beach was beautiful, and our words tumbled forth like a song.

I said, "All that happens is a part of our story."

He added, "Knowing everything that has happened, or will happen is a part of our unfolding story, to me, is most comforting."

Against the sound of the surf, I felt lighter as we walked, kind of elated. I said, "Yes. Everything we do or do not do, everything we think and feel is on a timeline. We are never bad, wrong, or make a mistake. We are just having experiences that always carry natural consequences that bring equilibrium to our story. And in the process, we discover 'what would happen if?' A grumpy person will find he loses most if not all of his family and friends. A chronically complaining woman will find people beginning to avoid her. A person who gives all the time will get drained. A person who has to be in control all the time will attract people who don't want responsibility."

He almost choked when he said, "No one gets away with anything—ever, even if it seems so." I somehow felt he was thinking of the dark deeds he'd performed.

I added, "And everyone is behaving just as they should, including us. We are *all* okay. Everyone is a giant and at the helm of their own story, whether it seems so or not." I looked up at him. "I could never judge you, Dmitri."

"But you do not know what I have done."

I sighed, trembling a bit. "I think, I do. I cannot say that what you have done was or was not right for you, I can only judge what is right or not right for me, because whatever we feel is right or not right for us, is just a rudder to give direction to our story."

"Yes," he affirmed, "the only sense we can have of what is right or not right for anyone is for ourselves. I had long felt I was serving my country by all that my job required, but more and more it became a dark game. I was not serving the greater good as first I had thought, but exploring a world of nightmares. And when the nightmares didn't affect me any more, I knew I needed to change."

I said, "And that is where we find power in our lives; not by trying to change others, but by us having the courage to change ourselves. If I had known you years ago, and given you advice to quit your work, you wouldn't have. And if when I was in the save the world stage, and you had tried to get me to take up arms and create boundaries, I wouldn't have."

"Not only can we have confidence that we are living our chosen story, but also that others are living theirs. And though we might play a part in the story of others as in a helping hand or someone we need to—"

I had a feeling he was going to say, punish, but he said . . .

"—push away, we each are the star, the hero, the heroine of our own play."

I added, "And sometimes the darker moments can yield great beauty. When, as a therapist, my clients would sink to the depths of their pain, they might cry or scream—or their face might express suffering . . . but in that moment of pain, it was the authentic self that had surfaced. The image that they projected not only to others but might have even believed themselves to be—was gone."

Dmitri said, "In that moment of reckoning, they were pure."

I smiled, so happy he understood. "Yes, and in the purging of that pain, what remained was incredible beauty." I looked at him, feeling like he was working hard to shed a mask of shame. I stopped us walking, and faced him, taking his other hand in mine also. "The human journey is noble for all. For *all.*"

"I don't know. I suppose I believe it, but I don't feel so noble in my life deeds."

"You are, Dmitri, you are."

He slipped one hand away and started us walking again, as if he weren't quite ready to forgive himself.

He asked, "Do you suppose it is the same for non humans? That they too have a noble journey?"

"The journey of every animal carries the same magic as humans. The journey of trees, and water, and dirt, the same. Every molecule, every atom is *The All.* We, as Creative Energy, are experiencing ourselves as projected images becoming more than we are."

"Yes, I can see that life is an ongoing adventure, the mystery ever unfolding, ebbing, flowing, rising, falling . . . presenting the unexpected, from the smallest pleasantries to the grandest occurrences, and from minor inconveniences to heart rending tragedies. The sacrifices. The Gains. The Story."

I half laughed. "We so often fear the unknown, even though status quo can be boring. And we often walk into trouble, just to appease some deep down yearning, which is there for a purpose. There really are no 'would have, could have, should haves. Those are just paths we did not take. Paths we were not supposed to take."

He said, "And yet the torment of paths not taken, or guilt for the paths that were, *are* part of the story. Our life intent is born in realms beyond our conscious knowing. Sometimes we just must trust it."

"Yes," I said squeezing his hand, "sometimes we must just live the mystery and trust that our subjective world, though naïve in the scope of broader wisdom, is simply a part of our story. There are always signposts to the pathway that is our own: an inner yearning, an outer event, a seeming accidental interaction with a stranger, or a simple event like witnessing a butterfly land on a flower, and in so doing changes our mood. And as we move along in our story, when it is time for change, then we will yearn for that change, and, we will seek a new direction, yet unfolding a new chapter in the great adventure of our lives."

He said, "One might experience loneliness because he fears connecting to others. Who is to say that experiencing loneliness is not valid? And when he is ready to overcome the fear of connection, it will be done, and not one moment before."

I added, "And a person who goes from one romantic interest to another, never looking at herself to assess why the relationships fail, will not do so until the time is right, no matter how much coaxing might come from others."

He said, "Sometimes certain social circles offer 'keys to salvation' by inciting fear. *Stay with us, or else. Do things our way, or else.* For those who accept the threat, that is part of their story, what they need to experience. In this, our effort to change people to our way of thinking, one way or another, is merely an attempt to divert them from their own personal path, and get them to walk with us. Why do we do that?"

I said, "Mostly, we don't want to walk alone. If another walks with us, we somehow feel secured that our path is the 'right path' and hence, we feel less afraid. Oh what a gift we have in knowing fear, such a great contributor to the story, even when we decide to give it up. Having known such darkness, we can see the stars."

"That is true, Susan," he said looking inward, "very true."

I said, "Anger is another emotion that incites our story. Anger stems from somehow feeling assaulted, or from empathically bonding with others whom we have been assaulted. This unpleasant knock in the head sets forth a stream of events in the outer world and in our body too, heart pumping, adrenaline flowing. Repressed anger can cause mental and physical illness. So, we try this and that to deal with our anger. Oh the excitement! Oh the drama! We might find a healthy way to deal with our anger by letting in love and temperance, or we might move into escapist behaviors such as drugs or alcohol, yet, that too is part of the story. And we can only change it when the next chapter in our story is due to arrive."

He said, "And I suppose our individual dramas interlace with each other, creating world drama."

I added, "And world drama is just *our* drama."

He added, "And our drama, becomes the worlds."

I added, "And we find pathways to peace when we are ready to end a story."

Dmitri said softly, "I must have the courage to end my story, to live the mystery, to expel the fear and anger, and let in love and temperance."

I squeezed his hand affectionately. Even with all my wisdom, I did not want to think of his demise in this life. With that, we arrived at my car. His dark car was parked next to mine, a rental I presumed. Neither one of us could say goodbye.

He kissed my forehead, and helped me into my blue Impala. "Lock the doors," he said affectionately.

As I put on my seatbelt, he got into his car. He waited for me to drive away first. And as I did, I tried not to think about him too much. It was bittersweet. But I did think about him all the way home. And I dreamed about him for days. All a part of my story—and so, without resisting, I let it be.

And so can you. Release judgment of yourself and others. Know that everyone, including you, is doing the best they can with the story meant to be lived. Celebrate the decompression of memories that you as Creative Energy gave yourself. Chips on shoulders are imaginary. The evils of the world are fiction. Our stories are things we made up to have experiences. We are okay. You are okay.

Go out under the night sky for a minute, at least a minute. Open your left palm to the sky, and your right palm down to the earth. Envision the energy from the sky flowing through your open hand, through your body and out your right hand into the earth. Repeat aloud or silently to yourself, "Creative Life Energy is flowing through me; I feel it now." Connect. Breathe deeply and slowly, feeling your home in totality, in your body, and in the earth. Wherever you are, you are always home. Whoever you are, you are always with yourself. Whatever your story, behold its gift. Live the Mystery. Live with Gusto. Be.

Nightmares, Ghosts, and Hobgoblins

"Shadows are seen with light; light is seen with dark."

GEM #7 FEAR

I opened my eyes in the morning light, cat purring on my chest, his face almost touching mine. "Good morning, Baxter." Baxter squinted his eyes embedded in his white fur mask against long black hair. I loved the little black spot on his pink nose. I pet him for a few minutes.

Thinking of getting to the computer to write, I sighed. "Okay Baxter, got to write." Multiple ideas ever gathered in my sleep, bunching up against my consciousness to be first in line for expression, and I was compelled to record them.

I edged Baxter off me, and climbed out of bed in my soft, light pink pajamas patterned with dark pink snowflakes. I flipped on the computer, brushed my teeth, made my morning coffee, and settled in to do my morning writing, still in my pj's.

With the strong aroma of coffee wafting from the cup by my computer monitor, I gathered my thoughts. I'd been pondering what people might term occult, scary incidents. Since connecting with Dmitri so deeply with My Fool at the beach, bits and pieces of his violent life had been seeping into my dreams. Or maybe I'd been caught in the net of *his* dreams.

I had a sense that dark entities were gathered all around him as well as the people with whom he had associations. I can't say exactly what dark entities means, other than energy forms who feed off pain, cruelty, and violence. And having been tuned into Dmitri, I was beginning to feel haunted myself. Though I had become adept at dealing with such things, the old fears had returned.

Thus, the subject of dark entities spotlighted my morning writing. I began typing.

'Scary books and movies cannot be written or played without tapping the furthermost reaches of fear. Supernatural events are often the most frightening of all because most people don't understand them, and therefore feel powerless to take control of those situations.

'Due to this fear, people often discount strange experiences. Others adhere to such experiences as some sort of psychic attack. However, in any circumstance, we do not experience anything that we have not, on some conscious or unconscious level *called for*. Calling for help to angels, for instance, will yield some form of help: maybe an old friend calls bringing inspiration, or a stranger miraculously appears from out of nowhere in the nick of time and offers relief; or perhaps an energy entity in the form of an angel or spirit guide might arrive, or maybe a mystical experience is had that can't be explained, but uplifts and enlightens.

'The same is true for those who emanate excessive sorrow, fear, rage, or guilt. Without a healthy release, these emotions compound. Compounded emotions are like beacons.

'Unresolved, prolonged sorrow, for instance, can mount into a desperate cry for anything that can ease the pain. This can attract dark energy forms to explore the situation.

'Fear, for instance, can attract dark energy forms that haunt in dreams, or kind of ride around with the fearful, planting in their minds excessive doubt and extreme paranoid thinking. This in turn can attract human predators, or in the case of mental illness, influence 'the haunted' to become predacious.

'Unresolved hatred also attracts dark energy forms that add fuel to the fire that can result in cruel acts toward self or others. Unresolved guilt often elicits the saboteur in ourselves, resulting in the proverbial toe stubbing, a night of drinking, or setting one's self up for some type of punishment. If unresolved guilt is strong enough, it can attract dark energy forms that mentally and emotionally torture the one harboring the guilt.

'Also capable of attracting dark energy forms are empaths. Deeply sensitive empaths, while able to feel a drop of positive energy anywhere in anything, can also sense, with their built-in radar, negative energy, miniscule and vast, near and far, even when they'd rather forfeit that experience. Hence, they sometimes become sponges, absorbing energies that really have nothing to do with them. The woman who can't shake the feeling she acquired while hearing about a murder on the news. She tosses and turns all night tapping into the energy of murderers all over the world. The man who feels so sorry for a sad woman, he drains himself dry trying to make her smile, because he can't feel better until she feels better. The girl who faints when a sociopath passes her in the grocery store. The boy who hasn't had a drink, but feels drunk because across the way, a man is intoxicated.

In this, empaths not only experience the realities of those with whom they have made a connection, but also with any dark energy forms that have latched onto those with whom they have made a connection. Or sometimes, dark energy forms are attracted to those empaths whose negative emotions have become magnified by their abilities to feel not only their own pain, but the pain of the world.

'Empathic or not, when unsavory mergers are made, the solution is to disconnect and strengthen our own sense of identity. When too focused on the dark energy of others, or on dark energy forms, we have inadvertently strayed from our own center, and, in a sense, the inhabitants of negative energy posses us. If we but say our name aloud, followed by words such as, *I empower myself from the center of me,* we can come back to our own center and restore a sense of well-being.

'If we do not disengage from another's negativity or cease generating our own, we might continue to attract unseen energy forms that play mischievous games, and feed off our negative energy. When negative feelings *are* resolved, or at least minimized, or in the case of an empath, rejected, the dark 'thing' physical or incorporeal, goes away.

'It is ironic really that the strongest weapon we have to repel something so-called 'dark' is to love and have faith in ourselves. By pouring love into ourselves, our vibration changes, emanating what does not attract dark things, and even repels dark things.

'A religious person might call upon a Supreme Being or such to help them, but really that is the same as the caller deciding they are worth being loved and therefore helped. Whether the belief is that a Supreme Being or an angel must save you, or that by loving yourself—you can be saved, it works the same. *Love is love no matter where it comes from.*

'The actual belief in a devil feeds the energy of darker type entities. The belief in evil empowers dark energy forms. The easiest way to repel such forms is to know that they can't hurt us unless we believe they can. And if we believe they can, they couldn't unless some part of us deep inside agrees upon that. If that is the case then a simple meditation to instill a sense of centeredness will ward away the offender. The entity cannot remain when we are balanced within. If we do *not* give it attention, it will not in our reality—exist.

'This is why the mentally ill (as in schizophrenia) have a hard time with this. Medical professions adhere to the idea that voices in one's head or seeing entities invisible to the average human, are hallucinations—not real. Given that paradigm, it becomes difficult to help the one experiencing such things to understand how to repel what taunts them. Just because we cannot see what the person is hallucinating does not mean it is not, in some reality—real.

'As a therapist I could often feel when a dark energy form had latched onto mentally ill clients, feeding them lies and stirring confusion. In this, the dark energy form can feed off these people and consume more power. I would fix this by helping those clients deeply embrace themselves with love. Then they could begin to work out the garbage in their lives because they felt they deserved well-being. The dark energy forms could not remain, for those people had changed their vibration.

'This is *not* to say that a chemical imbalance is not present. It is to say that the imbalance might enable people to see and experience what others cannot. This is *not* to say that drugs aren't appropriate for mental illness. It is to say that those who experience so-called hallucinations might not be as crazy as we deem them to be.

I continued to pour out my feelings when my computer made a little ding indicating someone had written me an email. I usually don't interrupt my writing for an email, but I felt deeply moved to do so now.

I went to my business inbox. My eyes caught upon the name Dmitri.

I opened the email. It read *Susan, will be in Portland to hear your lecture Oct 17. Can we talk afterward?*

Dmitri.

Given that my recent haunted feelings were likely because I'd been empathing Dmitri, I knew the solution was to disconnect from him. But due to our special circumstance, I just couldn't. My attraction for him was deep and getting deeper everyday. The connection frightened me greatly. I took a deep breath. *Oh well, live the mystery.*

I answered the email, short and sweet, trying hard not to become *too* involved, though some part of me wanted to crawl right inside him. *Yes, Dmitri, I will meet with you after the lecture. Until then . . . .* I hit the send button.

I went to sleep that night soaked in trepidation, for Dmitri's world touching mine seemed to elicit dark experiences. Given this, what might happen when I met him after the lecture? Deeper connection? Scarier experiences? I feared closer engagement with him, even if he was, well—me.

I awoke around 2:00 a.m. with an odd sensation to my right. I had been dreaming of warriors, not the more bright warriors I'd come to know, but the cold variety through and through, the kind that feigned virtue but had none.

"I am here, Susan," a voice sounded in my ear. "You have called for me, and I have come."

The voice belonged to a warrior entity. You'd think I would have been happily intrigued with this occurrence, but instead, I felt sickened. This reaction was always a signpost of deception, whether by a dark energy form or human. This warrior did not feel like a true rescuer like the one who aided me in the riptide, or the one who helped me gain balance when I time traveled to find my mother. However, he did intrigue me, though not happily. I know this sounds hokey, even to me, but he had a dragon-like essence from somewhere 'out there' in the celestial sky.

He said, "I will teach you about destruction, how it works, and why people call for it."

Huh?

He said, "Then I will take you away from the harsh earth to my world where I can protect you forever."

Huh?

I half discounted the experience. *Half* discounted it, because the presence of entities was not new to me, and sometimes I attracted things I did not want hanging around. I'd had enough experience to know what was what.

I'd learned, as I'd written on my computer that morning, the best way to rid unwelcome ghostly guests was to disregard them. But this one was hard to turn away, as he was disguised in a persona that appealed to me.

After several days, he'd become a companion that traveled around with me in an incorporeal form explaining why human predators do what they do. Yes, that is unsavory, but as an ex psychotherapist, I was interested to better understand that side of human nature.

I learned a lot, and I even put it on tape, hoping to use it in my writing one day. Then the entity revisited the topic about me going away with him. He said I could leave my body and he would make sure another spirit filled it to finish out my life and no one would even know I had left.

I didn't want to leave my life. I liked my life, so why had I drawn this dark entity to me? Upon examination, I realized that empathing Dmitri had overwhelmed me with the harsh side of earth energies, and a part of me wanted to escape the planet. At any rate, I told the dark entity, no.

It was then that he tried to force his way inside my mind.

As a pro at surviving such things, I knew the next step was to further locate inside me what was attracting him. And then I realized it. My nun facade was at play. Given I was attracted to convent style life, it was not so unbelievable that I'd attracted an energy form who'd offer me sanctuary from the outside world. And given my nun facade believed it sinful to receive attention for writing and lecturing, she was agreeable to me permanently exiting my body. She hadn't much been a part of my life in a long time, so I wasn't expecting her to be activated.

In realizing what had happened, I reclaimed my right to live my human life and to, as My Fool would say, 'live it with gusto!' And just like that, the dark entity disappeared.

After shaking that off, I decided to start jogging again, you know, get healthy, feel my body, but most of all to calm my nerves. I'd gotten so busy that I'd not jogged in over a month, but oh how I needed it now! Between my anticipation of meeting Dmitri again, and continuing to empath the darkness he touched, nightmares were frequent and I had to meditate daily to shake them off. Even though Dmitri was me, and we were going through something together, I had to detach somewhat just to survive.

So, in my gray sweats, I went outside into the crisp October morning. I jogged toward the forest trail in the woods near my home. I had my headphones on my ears and the Walkman clipped to the waist of my jogging pants. I was listening to Richard Wagner's, "The Ring." It was the version that had compiled the instrumental parts.

It was a beautiful day as my feet padded along the dirt trail that paralleled a creek for most of the run. As I jogged, I slipped into meditation. The vibration of the music soaked medicinally into subterranean psychological wounds. The experience was so overwhelmingly beautiful that I had to stop and sit by the creek. There amongst the trees, I cried with pure joy. Since the music was still playing in my ears, I did not hear the approaching hikers. But I did hear a faint voice. "Are you okay?"

When I opened my eyes, I viewed two men. The man in jeans and a blue sweatshirt felt bright, and I felt safe with him. The other man in tan cargo pants and a red flannel shirt had a goofy grin on his face, and he scared me.

I removed my headphones. "I'm fine," I said.

They nodded and walked on up the trail. I wiped away my tears. My once tears of joy had shifted to curiosity about the man who spooked me. Later, I learned that the man who he had been hiking with was just a neighbor whom he'd run into while hiking. It made more sense then why the two did not seem like they would be together.

Later that night, I could not get the creepy guy out of my mind. I had fallen into the energy current that he emanated. How did I let this happen? Why did I choose to shift from my ecstatic Wagner meditation . . . to this? It was as if I had a choice to heal, but something in me was not quite ready. I had just dealt with the nun facade. Was she at it again, or was this something else?

Laboring to keep my internal balance, I meditated each day morning before I jogged. But within minutes, my fear would set in. I kept falling out of what My Fool called—The Zone, and I ran into this creepy guy again and again, no matter what time of day I went jogging and no matter which trail in the woods I chose. He would always somehow pop up with that goofy grin and make comments that sounded like nothing, but the vibration in those comments was invasive. The really spooky thing was that I felt like he'd never broken contact with me since the moment he came upon me crying in the woods.

This continued for several weeks. I had nightmares of this man committing gruesome murders. He seemed to whisper to me why he was doing what he was doing, and it was really freaking me out. I couldn't tell if I was tuning into his current life, a past life, another of his identities, or another version of himself. All I knew is that I had to fight to keep his goofy energy from invading me.

And I had other nightmares too. They all involved emotional and sexual victimization by males. I never felt rested and I was constantly on edge. Finally I could not run in the woods anymore. I felt like I had to get out of this current into which I had fallen. And as My Fool had always told me, the answer to escaping dark experiences was simply to shift my focus. To do that, I needed to stay out of the woods for a while, and give myself over to a series of 'breaking away from spooky things' mediations. Then perhaps, I could escape the current of this disturbing event.

Refraining from the woods for a week, I meditated daily. On the seventh day, I meditated to Mahler's *Symphony No. 2* in my living room, and had one of the most empowering meditations ever. And I learned another way of dealing with dark energies. Concentrating on Pure Creative Energy, I gave permission for anything to happen that needed to happen, no matter what that might be, even if it changed me or my life forever. I would be brave. I walked into purity, naked of image, with an authentic heart. My small self merged with the great self. Small scenes became the larger picture. Separate parts became the whole. All people were the many faces of me. Nothing could hurt me if I claimed the identity of that predacious entity or person as a part of the greater me. I could see that if my vibration changed from the fear that attracted the dark thing, to a cohesive soul-bonding energy, I would, ironically, repel the dark thing.

It was then I learned that dark things can't behave in dark ways unless they feel there is something to conquer. To conquer something there must be a sense that what is being conquered is *separate* from the conqueror. If there is no separation, there is nothing to conquer! With this epiphany, in the meditation, I felt myself as a radiant essence walking right through the essence of the creepy guy. He disappeared. When the meditation ended, I felt deeply safe. I resumed jogging in the woods, and I never saw the man again.

So apparently, to rid one's self of a dark entity, one can disengage . . . or engulf it with Pure Creative Energy. I was pretty proud of my new discovery.

Even so, my qualms regarding Dmitri had not ceased, so I decided to visit My Fool to gain further insight into the dastardly emotion—fear. I went outside in my forested yard with my 32-inch broadsword. The sword represented my willingness to integrate the male principal. Since the Dmitri thing seemed to be about me deepening that integration, the sword was appropriate for my meditation.

With sword in hand, Walkman clipped to the waist of my jeans, and headphones on ears sounding Ottorino Respighi's, *Pines of Rome*, I journeyed into my yard. I sat cross-legged in the grass under blue sky, sword across my lap.

I went into mediation and arrived at The Wall of Remembrance. My Fool was there with a plastic drugstore monster mask on His face. He looked funny, and I had to giggle.

He slipped the mask off His head, and offered it to me.

I shook my head and hugged my stomach. "I don't want the damn thing."

As it disappeared from His hand, I noticed, a two-inch-long shadow of a person on the shoulder of His violet sweatshirt. It walked down his torso and down the leg of His white pants, onto His white jogging shoe. It leapt onto His orange-socked big toe that peeked out from the cut opening, and jumped up and down.

My Fool said, "We tend to fear the shadow, but look at it now. It just wants attention. It wants confirmation that it exists. *Fear* is a merely a reflection of ourselves feeling disconnected from our source."

I said, "Do you mean our fear is born from feeling alone?" As I said that, the shadow raced around the heel of My Fool's shoe, as if it were hiding.

My Fool replied, "Yes. Because we are born into the illusion that we are separate from each other . . . and having forgotten our oneness, we fear many things: hunger, illness, discomfort, and pain. We fear forces of nature, unsavory events, certain insects or animals, other people, and sometimes even ourselves. We fear being alone, being misunderstood, and being unloved. But most of all—we fear death."

"Interesting that fear of death can incite so much."

"In dealing with fear of death, most humans live their lives in accordance with their beliefs of what happens *after* death. 'You only go around once, so take a chance.' 'Live it up now, cause when you're dead, you're dead.' 'What can I do to be remembered in death?' 'I'd better solve my problems, so if I'm reincarnated, I will be reborn into a good life.' 'I best prove myself worthy, so that the Supreme Being will send me to heaven instead of hell.' "

I added, “In some cultures and religions, fear of death is so strong that securing a pleasant afterlife seems to take precedent over living free, full lives in the present.”

“Yes,” He said. “However, fear of death also catalyzes positive attitudes such as protecting our children, eating well and exercising, and avoiding dangerous situations. Without fear of death, or fear itself, we would be unmotivated to live. Fear catalyzes meaningful adventures the world over, unfolding magnificent stories.”

"So fear plays its part to bring us into beauty."

The shadow peeked from around My Fool’s heel and nodded.

My Fool added, “In an attempt to quell our fears, we discover individuality and union, humility and confidence, hate and love.”

I exhaled with quivering breath. “But sometimes fear can be daunting, like fear of dark energy forms: mischievous ghosts, demon, or vampire-like entities, whether attached to humans or acting on their own.”

He laughed. “What is a mischievous ghost? Sometimes it is the lingering essence of a dead person. Sometimes it is a bleed through of an identity from another time and place. Or it can be an identity in your own Being visiting you. Aside from ghost’s seeming invisibility, they are no different than the many people around us.”

Thinking of my ghost experiences, I nodded. “Yes, I suppose that is the gist of a ghost. No big deal, really.”

He continued, “What is a demon? Anyone or anything perceived as having mal-intent with an aim to serve themselves, whether embodied or not. It doesn’t matter where the entity comes from, what it looks like, or what mode of operation it uses to usurp power from others. The vibration is the same. The solution to warding them off, as you know, is the same. Disregard them, love and respect yourself, and know that you cannot be hurt unless you agree to it.”

That was true. Whenever I empowered myself with love and respect, I repelled ‘demons.’

He continued, “What is a vampire? It is any person or entity that feeds off others to survive. The act of a vampire is not always intentional, but the need to feed off the energy of others is paramount. It can be as simple as people who *excessively* manipulate others to give them love, attention, or any kind of energy. Vampires put the needs of the targets beneath their own. Their needs *must* be met no matter who gets hurt, smothered, or siphoned. This does not mean that people who behave as vampires are bad, or even cognizant that they suck upon others, draining their life forces. However, in all cases, there is an attempt to steal energy, and in all cases, energy cannot be stolen; it must be given. Sometimes we give it because we have a problem saying, no. Sometimes we give it because we feel sorry for the energy stealer, or because we feel there is a prize in it for us."

I added, "So, it's just that the vampire-like people or entities are so needy, and when they get away with robbing victims of their energy, they are reinforced to continue sucking upon others to feed themselves. When the bites are continuous, those who allow the biting become more depleted and get either angry or depressed."

"Yes, yes," My Fool said, "but just as you have discovered, it always takes two to play the game. There are really no victims, no villains, only the parts we play and experiences we have chosen to fulfill our individual intents for living. So mischievous ghosts, and demon or vampire like entities or people, can only play their game, *if* we play along."

"And if we choose to play along and experience the fear, then that is okay too?"

"Of course, my dear. We experience fear for a purpose. And when we have fulfilled that purpose, whether it is in having an adventure or opting out because that pattern has been outgrown, the fear dissipates."

"I suppose, since our story will be what it will be, we needn't fear the unknown."

He said, "All things are known, just not consciously. All things exist whether we view them or not."

"So," I asked My Fool, "not that I want to return to that dark vibration, but was I just crazy or was that creepy guy in the woods really dangerous?"

"That physical man resonates to the vibration of your darkest counterpart identity in the wheel of your Being. He is darker than your diametric opposite, Dmitri. Just as you have your opposites, the creepy guy has his, and you resonate to a vibration close to his opposite on the wheel of *his* Being."

I said, "So, you are saying then that we can be attracted to the vibration of those who are *synonymous* with the opposites on the wheel of our own Being?"

"Yes, these attractions occur as an unconscious attempt to make contact with ourselves. Cold, insensitive people fear tenderness because tenderness makes them vulnerable. So they repress their sensitivity as if it does not exist. Yet, because their sensitivity is repressed, they are attracted to others who beam sensitivity. Once contact is made, they have a compulsion to repress the sensitive person in the same manner that they have repressed the sensitive parts of themselves."

"Yes," I said, "I have seen that so clearly, even in couple's relationships. The sensitive one usually plays the peacekeeper because conflict goes against their nurturing nature."

He said, "Highly sensitive people fear conflict because conflict affects them more deeply than most. Thus, they bury their anger, their sword, so to speak, as if it does not exist. Consequently, they have a strong attraction to those who express anger and use the metaphorical sword. A passive person will almost assuredly be attracted to a dominating person, and vice versa. A person with a victim nature will almost assuredly be attracted to a predator, and vice versa. Attracting those with the vibration opposite ours creates an adventure for both."

"I really feel done with victim adventures. I *want* to be done. Do you think my days with the predator vibration are over?"

"Trust your story, Susan," He said. "Don't write history before it arrives. If you don't like a current you are in, shift your focus. If you resist shifting focus, it is only because some part of you is not ready to leave behind the current experience. Not until you are truly done with that sub-story will you succeed in a focus shift."

I said, "It's like when others reject our coaxing to better their lives. If they listened to us and their lives improved, we might be cheating them of the greatest story ever. By walking through adversity, so much is stirred up and brought to the surface. So much is discovered and explored, and great creations are born from chaos."

"Indeed," He said. "And so it has been with your predator experiences, human and otherwise."

"So my predator experiences are not a failing in me, but rather an exploration of myself?"

"Yes, you attracted them because you needed them to spur development in yourself."

"That is so true. I've known many who have experienced great adversity; and yet these same people blossomed into rewarding realities."

He added, "However, sometimes the safe, boring lives carry a great inner pain that no one else can see. Sometimes when things look good on the outside, people don't understand why they are so unhappy on the inside. This is about living life as if one were trying to match a picture on the wall, instead of dynamically flowing and expressing individuality, following inner joy and doing what makes one want to get up in the morning. What feels truly healing and joyful to one might not necessarily feel healing or joyful to others."

I said, "So if I am true to myself and I follow my joy, I needn't fear what tomorrow will hold, because I am blossoming into my intent for living the life of Susan, and the intent of the one homogenized Creative Energy to know itself."

"Yes," He said, smiling.

I said, "We needn't fear, because no matter what happens, it is the way it is supposed to happen. Life brings everything to balance."

"Life brings everything unto itself, because everything is One. If all energy is One, then any thing, any illusion, any story, is a creation of Creative Energy. Can our feet be wrong for walking us along the path that leads to adventure? Even if that adventure seems unsavory to others, it might be what we need to lead us to something beautiful."

I smiled warmly. "There is purpose in treading the unsavory parts of our path."

He said, "There are all kinds of hell on earth. And there are all kinds of heaven on earth. It is about currents. And if you calm yourself down and go so deep within that you cannot hear all the chattering voices, of not only the outside world, but your various selves chattering what is true for *their* vibration, (such as the critical self criticizing you or others); and instead focus on totality, then thinking, feeling and acting in ways that facilitate the unfolding of your story will occur minus fear, panic, depression, or confusion."

"Yes," I concurred, "fear diminishes when viewing life's big picture."

"Though some of the threads we weave in life's tapestry might seem ugly, when seen from the overview, these ugly threads are what make the tapestry so beautiful."

I realized then that my 'dark' experiences were just energies, threads in the tapestry. I was now in a broader flow. I felt done with those who would feed off me. These perpetrators, human or otherwise, did what they were supposed to do. They catalyzed me to survive. To survive, I had to love and respect myself. To love and respect myself, I had to kick and scream and fight and hatch out of my pacifistic shell.

Reading my mind, My Fool said, "And thus, you have."

I said, "When I first realized I must fight to defend myself, I screamed desperately, 'No!' as if saying, *Please don't hurt me.* Then, after a while, I commanded firmly, 'No,' as if saying, *You will not hurt me.* And then, eventually, with confidence, I quietly shook my head, no, as if saying, *I cannot be hurt.* Now, I do believe I can detach from any who attempt to demean me. I will guard my boundaries with sword held high, and sing my little song, the song of Susan. I will sing my song like a fool, a fool on the hill, despite acceptance or rejection." I felt teary recalling a story My Fool once to me. "You told me that when my heart grows larger than my body, no one can hurt me. Poison arrows shot at me turn to paper. Harsh energies cannot touch me. Authenticity empowers."

His form sparkled for a moment, as if responding to my state of mind.

I sighed, feeling a bit of joy. "I have come far in living authentically. And in that, I am currently quite happy in my little corner of the world, just—being me. I am lessening my need for approval from others, and instead, I fill myself up from within. In this, I have removed myself from much trauma. Not that there's anything wrong with trauma. As you have told me, it gives a story. But I currently prefer being once removed from the intensity of hysteria. I like being a human who can experience things without being taken by them. I want to be done with that. At least I do today, at this moment—now."

He added, "Those who express, as you are, not from image, but from their quintessential self, are as a volcano erupting what was once unseen, hence they are often feared. But when the new land generated, solidifies and supports fresh life, it is appreciated. In time, newness, change—is appreciated. To be brave and allow ourselves to change is a noble act indeed. To risk being abandoned, to risk being alone, can be frightening. But when, through meditation of some kind, we feel connected to totality, and experience ourselves as a giant rather than a small person, it is not so hard. Horrible insecure feelings can be met head on. The inner churning is quieted with the awareness that what is being feared is an illusion, a trauma that we created by how we perceive the world, those in our lives, and ourselves."

I nodded, "That is so true. Drama thrives on the small picture. When we tire of the drama, widening the view always brings peace. When we traverse the conscious mind and release what we think we know—"

He interjected, "—remaining open, quiet, and still, while diving deep into ourselves—"

I finished, "—yields *in*sight to the bigger picture which beautifies what might appear ugly in the binocular view. A car accident is generally viewed as a bad thing. However, if for example, the car accident triggers a life change that takes us off the fast-track and slows us down enough to meet a great friend who becomes a lover and lifetime mate—was the car accident really a bad thing? We have the ability to view tumultuous incidents in the larger picture, and find a way to live with them and even appreciate them, even though they were most difficult to endure."

"Yes," He confirmed. "It's as they say, the only thing to fear is fear itself.'

I heard giggling. On My Fool's orange-socked big toe, the tiny shadow person was crouched bobbing up and down with laughter, with little hand over mouth. It murmured in-between chortles, "Fear itself, fear itself."

My Fool reached down with one hand and scooped up the shadow. "Open your hand."

I outstretched my palm. My Fool dropped the shadow in it. It stood in my palm, facing me.

The shadow said, "It is just me. I am you."

It was then I noticed that the shadow was *my* shadow.

My Fool said, "This is the Gem of Fear. We fear when we glimpse the shadows, but the shadows are nothing more than a reflection of what is light. When we fear, we, in truth . . . fear ourselves. When we find peace within ourselves, and *with* ourselves, fear diminishes."

A bright little me leapt out of my heart, and took the shadow me's hands. The two danced in circles on my palm, and then both shot back into my heart. I suddenly felt quite at peace with myself, myself of dark and light, of conflict and peace, fear and faith."

My Fool smiled. "You are embracing your fear, for really, the only thing that we fear more than fear—is our self. Nothing can happen without our compliance on some level, and if we do comply, there *is* a valid reason."

The shadow seemed to become one with me, no longer something out there chasing me around. And with that, I felt myself sitting cross-legged on the grass again in the afternoon sunshine, with sword on my lap. A little bluebird landed on the tip of the blade jerking its head about here and there, with a tiny grasshopper in its beak. Then it flew away.

And that is the law of life, I suppose, prey and predator are one. Self and shadow are one. Fear and faith go together. Mundane life is the stage upon which we dance with ourselves, and everything on the other side of life supports the dance. What we call death is what lurks in the shadows beyond conscious reach. And there was so much energy in these mystical realms in which we so often push away because fear takes the lead.

I reverently stroked the blade of my sword, over the runes I had etched in it: warrior, strength, protection, gateway, wholeness. I gripped the hilt, and rose. Armed with my Walkman and sword, I walked across my yard confidently. I'd cower no more from what I feared. It was time to *dance* in the shadows.

Take heart when scary things go bump in the night; what you fear is just you looking at a reflection of your doubts and insecurities in the small picture. When you shift focus from fear to faith in yourself and your story and life, you will also see the refection of life's beauty: the baby smiling, the flower blowing in the wind, the squirrel scampering from tree to tree, the child reaching for a hug, value in even whom you dislike, and the struggle in your own eyes, so worthy of compassion.

Fear diminishes when we recognize we are all that is—including fear. We are of that energy too. What part do you consign fear to play in your story so that you can discover beauty? And when that beauty is discovered, you are embracing life's synchronicity, the overview, Pure Creative Energy. In these moments, there is nothing to fear, not even death, for we are all *always* whole, always waiting to be discovered—by ourselves.

Angels, Spirit Guides, and Entities of the Natural World

"Releasing what we think we know, is to know beyond what we think."

GEM # 8 FAITH

That morning, as usual, I made haste to my computer. Having dealt with a bout of fear, my focus was now on faith. Wiggling my toes and stretching my arms, my fingers touched the keyboard ready to write what had risen during sleep.

'We often trap ourselves in a tidy little box comprised of our knowledge and beliefs. This box makes the infinite—finite, pure vision—filtered vision, and opportunities for expansion—four surrounding walls that we call truth. This often works well until depression or anxiety set in. It is then that the walls of our box begin dissolving.

'The dissolving is evident when we lose faith in our situations such as work or living arrangements, our religion, our relationships, or sometimes even ourselves. The most common response is to find a new box within which to live: a new job, a new home, a new religion, a new relationship, or perhaps a physical makeover to appear 'new.' In this, we can renew our faith.

These transitional periods, in the quest to renew faith, are when the spiritually or metaphysically minded might glimpse a religious icon, angel, spirit guide, or an entity in or of the natural world. If they cannot succeed at this alone, they might seek someone who can. Communicating with a wise being of some kind gives us hope to find an answer to our current dilemma, or to cure unsavory moods. Faith is generally renewed by communicating with spiritual identities or entities outside themselves.

‘Then there are the scientific types who refer to faith as the F word. However, they seem to have faith in logic and reason to help them through life transitions. Or in their quest for proof for what can’t be seen, they might not even notice their life transitions, focused instead on the thrill of discovery, perhaps in research or chasing unidentified flying objects or exploring areas where strange, mythical or hypothetical creatures are thought to dwell. Living a bit outside themselves, not having faith beyond logic and reason seems to drive their story.

‘And then there are those who make transitions in a very practical manner. These are the die-hard cynics that live simply with an ABC belief system. “I am born into this world. I eat, sleep, work, play, and die. And that is life. Faith lies in the concrete world. They have faith in what they can see. This usually works pretty well until they grow into their elderly years when fear and panic rise triggering a midlife crisis that continues for decades, sometimes until death. However, sometimes, faith in something beyond the concrete world creeps in to quell the fear of death.

‘Then there are those philosophical adventurers who have faith in life itself and make transitions using insight. They read between the lines and delve into abstraction, seeking the bigger reality beyond all boxes. They wish to remove the glasses, rose-colored or gray, that alter perception, and dissolve the boundaries of limitation. In this broadband view, they discover mind sates to smoothly assimilate the events of their lives.

‘Yet, all types of people are *equally* evolved in their sense of faith and have life experiences that are imperative for their own ‘becoming.’

‘And in that spirit, I cannot say what is true—ever. I can only share insights like puzzle pieces that I have experienced by releasing what I think I know. And as I am of the metaphysical and philosophical persuasion, regarding faith, my discoveries are rendered in that light. In this, I am led to disclose my insights regarding, angles, spirits and entities of the natural world.

‘In the concept that everything is one homogenized Creative Energy, there really is no distinction in anything, only a perceived difference, from slight to vast. Hence, what we perceive as a religious icon, angel, spirit guide, or an entity of the natural world *is* valid. However, there is more to these positive energy forms than meets the tutored eye. Tutored, meaning preconceived notions about energy forms such as these. Examples are: Believing that an animal can be the personification of a deceased loved one. Believing that angels come to us in our time of need. Believing that spirit guides can help us more than we can help ourselves.

'While these beliefs have merit, and are true to some degree, there is always more to the picture. *There are no falsehoods, only limited understanding*.

'So, for instance, experiencing something like . . . the spirit of trees or mountains, or perhaps even something like flower fairies, will be filtered through our consciousness and our underlying belief system. A person who believes in a Supreme Being and a Devil will view positive entities as connected to, or the actual presence of—the Supreme Being. A negative type entity would be viewed as 'of the Devil,' or at least to some degree—evil.

'The laws of attraction that connect us to darker type entities also connect us to the more positive ones. But again, as all these entities are really—us . . . as the one homogenized Creative Energy. We attract what we perceive as entities to be players in our story, just as we attract people to be players in our story. Hundreds of thousands of life forms exist in many worlds. They are all around us all the time. Sometimes the worlds touch or bleed through into each other.

'We have numerous other-worldly experiences in which we are consciously unaware. In dreams and meditations, in alcohol or drug induced states, and in mentally ill conditions, our consciousness is altered and we can see into realms that are invisible to the average human eye.

'So if one chooses to believe that a spirit guide helps them, yes a spirit guide helps them, but still that guide's advice is filtered through the consciousness of the person listening to the guide. Hence, the person parroting what the guide says will be swayed by their underlying beliefs. For instance, a spirit guide might convey that a sacred event will unfold. The person interpreting what the spirit guide said might be of a pagan religion, and thus interpret a *sacred event* as 'the goddess will bring you a gift.' If that same person, however, is a strong believer of God as a He who lives in heaven, the interpretation of the *sacred event* might come out as 'God will guide you through your troubles.'

'However, if we leave conscious interpretation behind and move into the overview, we might get the sense that all entities are rooted in one homogenized energy. Thus, it is ourselves having an experience with ourselves. Ourselves meaning that we are multi-faceted and infinite. Anyone we talk to, or relate to, embodied or not—is us. We are each other. We are everything. But for purposes of having a story, it is perfectly acceptable to embrace *un* embodied energies as religious icons, angels, spirit guides, or nature entities. They *are* these things, but *more*.'

I wrote for most of the day, and retired early to bed.

Thinking of the vibration of entities that seem to bring us hope and comfort, I fell into a dream.

In the first scene, I was in what looked like a religious version of heaven, pearly gates and all. I was in a long white gown walking through moving mist. The mist cleared, and a figure sat on a throne. The scene seemed like a manifested belief of God as a Man in the Sky. But the figure at the throne was My Fool in long white robes. His voice boomed, "Divinity takes many forms."

Then the scene changed, and I was a medieval warrior at a feast in some world like Valhalla in Norse Mythology. The table had freshly cooked wild boar, loaves of steaming bread, and tankards of ail. The men talked of the great tournaments to follow, where they could fight each other and never die. To me, as a medieval warrior in Valhalla, it seemed heaven was a place where men could be men forever. The great god Odin sat at the head of the table. But when I looked closer, Odin's face was the face of My Fool. He said, "Divinity takes many forms."

Then the scene changed. I was in a green flowing gown dancing in a meadow of little yellow flowers, when I noticed a ground hog peaking up at me from a hole. The groundhog's face was My Fool's. It said in a high voice, "Divinity takes many forms."

I experienced many scenes like this. I saw My Fool as an angel, wings and all, soaring over houses dropping energy feathers of love into all the open-hearted sleeping, as He sang, "Divinity takes many forms."

I saw My Fool as a red devil with horns. I wasn't too shocked, having long ago learned that chaos has merit. The red devil cackled, "Divinity takes many forms."

I saw My Fool as the tree, as the wind, as my daughter, as my son, as other people I loved, and even as people I did not like. I saw My Fool as a cat, a caterpillar, and an ameba. And in every scene My Fool would say, "Divinity takes many forms."

And then behind me, My Fool spoke, "Turn around, Susan."

I used to fear turning around, afraid of what I might see, but My Fool had taught me that when I face things, I am usually pleasantly surprised. So I turned around and saw My Fool as I knew Him in His violet sweatshirt and white pants. He said, "Divinity takes many forms. What is *not* Divine? What is *not* sacred?"

I answered. "Everything is sacred. Everything is divine."

"Open your hand," He said.

I held my opened palm toward Him. In it He placed a golden flame. "This is the Gem of Faith. Faith in that which is beyond tangible reality. Faith in the Life Force beyond conscious knowing. What we need, we *always* receive." His voice turned to a drawn out whisper as He said, "F a i t h." And then He vanished.

I woke up with a start. "Reeeeeer." A cat screech had erupted in the night outside my window. I scanned my cat beds. Two cat heads were perked up toward the noise outdoors. The screech did not belong to my cats. And though I know better than to try and save everything, it was my nature to in some degree lend a hand when I could do so without hurting myself. So I rose to my knees on my bed and stared out my window, scanning the territory. I couldn't see anything except darkness and moonlight filtering through the evergreen trees in my backyard.

I slipped into blue jeans, a blue sweater, and black jogging shoes. I grabbed a small flashlight and went outside into the cool night and cried, "Kitty kitty, are you okay?" A breeze blew over my face, kicking back my hair over my shoulders. It felt lovely. I didn't hear any more screeching and I couldn't see a cat anywhere, however, I had an urge to walk into the forest up the road from my house.

And so I did. The moon was bright enough that I only needed my flashlight to get through the dark spots. My sneakers padded along the trail I usually ran in daylight. Celestial light bathed the sycamore trees, splashing patches of luminosity along the dirt trail. A cry in the wild caught my attention. I moved toward the cry, not of coyote, not of owl, or of anything with a red beating heart. It was more like a moan from the trees that rose into a string of discernible words. "We . . . want . . . you . . . to know . . . the intelligence . . . of the trees." Were the trees speaking to me? The moan intensified and elongated, repeating, "We waaaant you to know the intelligeeeence of the treeees." I'd never experienced what I might interpret 'the trees speaking to me,' and I never imagined that I would. And I tried not to definitively proclaim they were doing so now. My goal was to absorb what I needed from the experience with an open mind, so that I'd neither distort nor miss out on all the experience had to offer.

So, for whatever it was worth, I opened myself to receive the intelligence of the trees, wholeheartedly committing to bond with whatever aspect of life that was communicating with me.

I tiptoed past campers across the creek, my heart thudding rather hard. Humans frightened me more than bears, wolves, or even ghosts. The orange red fires were inviting. The men laughing at jokes and swilling beer, were not. Oh, inviting to many maybe, and innocuous enough, but my empathic abilities, as always, rendered me hyper-sensitive to life's baser energies.

I climbed gradually higher up the canyon trail, driven by a sense of adventure. The trail was pinching off. What was this force driving me to forge a path into the unknown? I told myself, *Don't interpret, Susan, just experience*. The trail was gone, but on I climbed.

Sycamore trees intermingled with cedar. The campgrounds were now far away. Against the sound of moaning trees, a whispery voice came through the woods toward me. "Will you receive, 'The Ancient?' "

The Ancient, I wondered, *the ancient what?*

"Will you receive it?" the whispery voice asked again.

"Yes," I whispered. I did not blindly trust the unseen worlds, but as long as I didn't have a bad feeling, I was often brave.

The earth seemed to tremble, though, surely it wasn't. I had a vision. Beneath our physical earth, I saw an etheric earth. They were connected by a chord. This etheric earth, like a placenta, sent energy into our earth, keeping it in a manifested state. Or another way of saying it, it kept our earth alive.

A thread-like stream of power rose from the etheric earth into the physical earth, into my feet, and expanded in my body. I cried out because the purity of the power shocked me. I began vibrating intensely. I dropped my flashlight and heard it roll into the creek. My knees buckled. My back arched and came down slowly over a large, flat boulder. My whole body was quaking so hard and I could barely breathe.

I told myself, *hold steady, stay focused, allow this to happen.* Energy poured in, condensing within me to pack in more. A compacted sphere shot into my mind. I murmured, "Timeless wisdom." I don't know why I murmured that, but I did. The energy intensified. I could not contain it. The run off of energy had me screaming into my palms. I did not want strangers to hear, but I could *not* refrain from screaming.

The energy began to dissipate. And then all was quiet, all was still—even me.

The whispery voice said, "You have received The Ancient."

"What is it?" I asked, my voice raspy.

"You cannot comprehend it," the whispery voice said. "It is enough that you have received it."

I cleared my throat and sat up, panting, with tears around the corners of my eyes. I felt the trees across the creek calling to me.

"Oh," I whimpered. Had I not experienced enough for one evening? I guess not. Trusting in life's synchronicity, I would finish what I had started.

With each step crossing the creek, wet to my ankles, I moved increasingly slower. Upon reaching the other side, I moved with slow motion fluidity amongst cedar trees like a sensuous cat. One tree in particular seemed to call to me. I placed my palms against the cedar bark, and inadvertently brought my face close, inhaling the sweet scent, as if I were inhaling the essence of the tree. The tree seemed to say, "Fall into me."

I allowed my essence to fall into the tree; I fell in with all my heart, with pure intentions, open and brave.

"There, there," the tree seemed to say, "give us your buried pain from wounds so deep."

I said, "But I am afraid it will hurt you."

The tree seemed to say, "One tree is of all trees. We are conscious of our connection, unlike humans. We are vast, and we can absorb your pain, and it will not hurt us. We will transform it into nourishing energy, in a manner similar to the way we help clean the air around us."

Confident that I wouldn't hurt the tree, I summoned buried pain from other times and places, as well as pain that I might not even be aware of hidden in my Focus Life. The pain gushed from my solar plexus, into my heart, through my hands, and into the tree. And when I had given it all I could, I experienced the oddest relief, as if I had thrown out toxic garbage. I felt buoyant, free, and uplifted. Then, the energy rolled back into me from the tree, but now, it was not of pain; it was pure energy. And I felt strong. It was like I had gone through emotional dialysis.

I felt bathed in a mellow gold light that like medicine, shined into all the dark corners of myself that I had not yet discovered. I inhaled a jagged breath, and the experience seemed over.

I rose, looking to return home by a different path, since I'd misplaced my flashlight. I walked past the shadowy trees into the moonlit meadow that led to the main road. Gold meadow grasses appeared strangely luminescent as my feet crushed the blades. I was altered in some beautiful way. Somehow, it seemed that the trees were in me, of me, and my world was bigger now.

From then on, nothing would seem quite the same, least of all, me. The confidence and calm I had needed to help me deal with my fears of emerging into the outer world, and the Dmitri thing, came to me in a fashion in which I'd be open to receive. Being a nature person, I am most sensitive to the energies that reside in the natural world, therefore, the medium chosen—was trees.

I basked joyfully in my new mind state of what I might term 'tree fortification,' for several weeks. Then came a morning that sickened me with dread. I was resting on my living room floor in my grey sweats after my morning jog when I received a telephone call from my daughter in Arizona. My son had been in an ATV accident. She said he was in a lot of pain, and the doctors didn't know yet how bad it was. I made airline reservations to fly out to Arizona that afternoon. Though my outward persona looked calm, a part of me was hysterical within. Oh, the ties that bind mother to child! Whenever our loved ones are hurting, it truly tests our inner resolve and the strength we *think* we have.

In that moment, I felt the colossal scope of reality, and much of it was not wonderful. In fact, much of reality was quite painful. In the face of traumatic incidence, I generally preferred to go into denial. If I denied, I felt safe in a twisted way. But this traumatic incident involved my son, so in order to be strong for him, I decided to face my fear in advance and deal with the any possible fate he might have to endure—now.

Time to meditate. While gathering my Walkman and selecting music for the meditation, I thought of my son in pain. Then I felt millions of people in pain. I groaned. I wished I could ease their suffering! I shook my head, realizing I'd spun off into the old martyr thing. I commanded myself to push past this old way and continue discovering what existed beyond it.

I sat on my living room floor, barefooted, in a half-lotus with Walkman clipped to my pant's waist, and headphones on ears. I had chosen *Mahler's Symphony No.2* to bring my inner strength to the forefront. As the music played, I moved into meditation. I whispered, "Whoever I am, whatever I am, so be it. I have the courage to embrace the unfolding of my story. I choose to transcend fear. With faith, I step into the unknown."

My physical body started vibrating gently. This intensified as I gave myself over to the one homogenized Creative Energy, knowing that Creative Energy is me beyond the illusion of my separate identity, which was currently freaked out.

My charged hands started moving over my chakras without conscious direction, mostly over my solar plexus. A pressure in my solar plexus mounted. And just as one might throw up with the exit being the mouth, my solar plexus began convulsing, (similar to what happened in my meditation before the London trip). I was heaving the last remnants of fear that held me back in life. It was time, I suppose. Though these fears had been references needed to catalyze my story, my son's accident was triggering a marker to catalyze a new direction in my life, which was also a part of my story.

And my son had his story too, the accident. It was meant to be. It was how his story was unfolding. It was relevant to his 'becoming.'

As the solar plexus heaving continued, I absorbed the vibration of the music reverberating in my body. I exhaled my sacrificial ways over and over, seeing clearly that any attempt to rob others of their pain, including my son, merely inhibits the unfolding of their stories.

Then the expulsion of energy from my solar plexus stopped. My body vibrated gently and I had a vision. Thousands of people in a natural disaster were screaming because the masks they wore, (their self-image) were being ripped off their faces. And they were so out of touch with who they really were, with who they were on the inside, that they were frightened because they did not recognize themselves.

And while all was well in the greater scheme of things, they experienced disaster, for they felt lost without the masks that gave them surface security in the absence of deep down security.

I felt bad for them because I, like the natural disaster, emanated an energy that melted masks. However, I also knew that I'd be repelled by those who, from the unconscious level, wanted their masks in place. But if I repressed this energy, I would be chained in an old world that I could no longer bear. So I reaffirmed my commitment to be myself without a mask in as much as possible.

Then I had an epiphany. The masks that were ripped off the people were the masks I was ripping off myself, my selves, and, the many facades within me, that we could better blend.

Then I saw a cosmic sky, and I moved into pure beauty that is unexplainable. My body, absorbing this beauty, vibrated more and more intensely, more than my muscles could handle. Tears streamed from my eyes, *the beauty . . . the beauty.* It was the beauty of life in perfect synchronicity. *All is well.* Somehow, someway, I experienced that *all, is always well, everywhere.*

I was physically worn out, and slumped forward in a heap in the yoga position of 'mother and child' face to the floor. At this point, the music was culminating toward the end of the symphony. I opened the small self to receive the large self—the one homogenized Creative Energy.

I heard a choir of voices in song. This song was sung with great compassion. The voices were not physical. It was a tonal vibration that I did not hear with my outer ear, but rather my psychic ear. The voices sounded off to my right. I felt the gathering presence of many.

I sat back on my knees and looked around. To my right where the voices sang in my living room, I saw a circle of illuminated energy forms, in white, gold, and pink. Their song of compassion soaked into me, and I felt *so* loved. I cried with joy.

Thinking of my son in pain, my heart hurt. My human love as a mother synergized with the compassion flowing into me, and without thinking, I sent the compassion onward to my son.

Against the choir, I heard my son's voice from the hospital. "It is all right, mom, I know what I am doing." And with face in palms, I sobbed. It was as if my son's spirit was telling me that the accident was part of his plan to unfold his story.

I began to calm down where my son was concerned. These beings had helped me, just as the trees had. And I sensed it then as I still do today, that we are *never* alone, none of us, no matter how it might seem.

And then the meditation was over.

I suppose those with certain spiritual orientations might presume the illuminated energy forms were angels, or in some spiritual orientations, perhaps devils, but as always, I did not grab onto any particular notion. While I was opened to the idea that these energy forms seemed kind of angel-like, there was probably more to it than I would ever understand. Hence, I remained open-minded that I may break new ground.

I leaned back, and lay flat on the floor with a heavy sigh, pleased that I seemed to be able to break new ground in the mystical world on a constant basis. Breaking new ground always requires a certain amount of bravery, because the people around us, including those in professional communities, often get afraid, so they endeavor to push us back into the little box that has been collectively accepted as normal. They command, 'Don't be like that, be like this,' 'You don't see what you see, or know what you know. This is what you should see. This is what you should know.' Or, at the very least, 'It's all in your imagination.' If we accept their small-minded perceptions, we go back into the box and forfeit exploration. We so often do not believe in ourselves, even though absolutely *no one* can have a better sense of what is right or wrong for us, of what we need to do or not do—than ourselves.

The next morning I flew to my son, whom though in pain, after a lot of physical therapy, would return to a fairly normal life. I had a lovely reunion with my children in Arizona. And lo and behold, only months later did I realize that my son's accident had led him to a whole new life, to a woman he loved, and into college. Yes, he had come to me in meditation, and said, "Don't worry mom, I know what I am doing." And so he did. And all our children do, whether we think so or not. This is not to say that we shouldn't ever intervene upon their choice, for that too can be part of their story. However, it often helps to have a little faith that our loved ones are giants in their own right, just living their stories the way they are supposed to be lived, whether we see eye to eye with them or not.

Tragedies will occur, and are imperative for a story, but they are never the whole story. It is like the dissonant moments in a symphony, but the beauty ever follows, somehow, someway, in some part of ourselves, on some level, in some world. And ever there to nourish us, and aid us in our darkest moments, or even seemingly save our lives, are the cat, dog, the sea turtle, the dolphin; the entities of mountain, tree, and babbling brook; the unexpected human, the incorporeal being, and what sometimes feels like divine intervention. These so-called sacred happenings are just Pure Creative Energy touching itself, reuniting for a moment to remind us that we are never, never alone, for we were never really separated.

And now it is your turn to invite pure nourishing energy into you too. Place a hand over your solar plexus and the other over your heart, and say. "Whoever I am, whatever I am, whatever I need beyond my conscious knowing, I open to this." Allow Pure Creative Energy to move through your hands into your heart, knowing, that without asking for specifics, you are getting what you need. Do not hope you are getting what you need. Know that you are getting it. And instantly or in the coming days, you will experience the manifestation of this small act.

This occurs because when we open with pure heart to *what is beyond all beliefs,* then the box that we live in grows less dense, and gives way to the vast sky of insight and regenerative energy.

And when the needed experience arrives, and it will, in its own way, and its own time, the way and time that is truly right for you, refrain from interpretation. You simply received what you needed beyond what you consciously understood.

The true power of faith is not to have it in any particular thing, or ideology, but rather having faith in life itself, whatever it is, beyond interpretation.

Live the Mystery.

The Land Before Time

"We make the dream and live it; we are the living dream."

GEM #9 DREAMING

Today was the day I would give my lecture on dreaming at a metaphysical seminar at the college. And today was the day I would meet Dmitri again. I was far more nervous about that.

I felt like wearing a long flowing gown or a pixie costume, for I certainly felt too mystically connected to wear the usual lecture get-up. But I did. Besides, dressing conventionally would help me reign in my feelings for Dmitri, even if he was an identity in my Being. Can you fall in love with yourself? I guess so. Knowing that he was preparing to die made it worse.

I dressed smartly in black pants and a midnight blue dress shirt. I pulled my hair into a bun, held in place by a blue glittering clip. Looking at myself in the mirror, I decided I was emanating a studious facade because I was afraid. Not that there is anything wrong with being afraid, but I was aspiring to be my authentic self, so I let my hair down and left it long and flowing, brave to be me.

Well, if I were really to be me, I'd be wearing the long flowing gown. However, while aspiring to being an authentic person, I also realized that people fear the strange, so I also sought to make my audience comfortable. People are curious, but when uncertainty creeps in, they often shut down.

At 6:30 p.m. I slipped on my black pumps, bid my cats goodbye, and drove to the college in my dark blue Impala. Driving into the parking lot, the sun was setting, not only in Portland, but inside me. As I pulled into a parking space, my stomach gurgled nervously. I sat there a moment to gain my resolve.

Tonight I would present My Fool's insights, combined with my own, on Dreaming, not just dreams that we have at night, but the constant state of dreaming we are always in. I would speak about how life is the dream. Yeah, I know, big topic, but . . . .

I always had big things to say, but since I wasn't parroting an ideology, philosophy, or doctrine from other psychological, metaphysical, or spiritual leaders, it was a daunting task. Imparting my ever flowing and always deepening insights from outside 'the box,' put me at greater risk for rejection. And in a thick netting of all the latest trends in mind power and spiritual doctrine, it was difficult to introduce a somewhat fresh and almost 'over the top' abstract perspective. But Dmitri seemed to understand it. Dmitri seemed to care.

I pressed my palm over my heart, trying to still its rapid beating. Dmitri seemed to sense the authentic me . . . that my work was not about the quest for fame or fortune, although there was nothing wrong with that. Something from my core being was crying to get out. When I let it out, I felt in tune with the Universe, the fool singing her song, even if no one listened. No matter. The song was the thing. What came of it would be okay, even if that meant rejection. *Rejection is never personal.* Those doing the rejecting are merely exacting what they *must* to move along in their *own* life adventure.

I sighed hard, summoning confidence. I got out of my car and headed toward the lecture hall. *I have no face. I have no name. I have all faces. I am all names.* The entrance doors were open. People were going inside and taking seats. When I walked in, a middle-aged woman in a royal blue pantsuit greeted me, and led me backstage.

I sat there in a metal chair taking time to center myself. With one palm turned up to the sky, and the other parallel the ground, I thought the words: *Creative Life Energy is flowing through me; I feel it now.* After a while, I heard the woman in the blue pantsuit speaking at the podium in front of azure curtain. She was introducing me. I walked out onto the stage. People clapped. *I have no face; I have no name.* When I arrived, the woman moved off stage. My hands rested on the soft, dark wood of the old podium. *I am all faces; I am all names.* I eyed the crowd of several hundred, delighted to see so many brave adventurers. I scanned the audience for Dmitri, but could not spot him at first glance. Maybe he did not make it. No matter, or it kind of did, but I pretended that it didn't.

I hoped the words I was about to speak would calm me. And to my relief, I felt pleasantly energized when my voice emerged.

"Good evening ladies and gentlemen. Tonight's topic is Dreaming. By focusing on what is beyond my finite conscious self, I have journeyed into states of being that have yielded insights that are almost beyond words. But I shall endeavor to share them."

I cleared my throat. "What is dreaming? The earth is a product of dreaming. We are a product of dreaming. And when we sleep, we dip into the dreaming worlds that manifested physical reality. Sleep dreaming and daily life go hand in glove.

"In sleep, we tap the whole life force and connect with everything that exists. We gather what we need to help us along in our daily lives. How often have we awakened perceiving or feeling differently? Sometimes we awaken feeling agitated with a sense there is something we must do. Sometimes we awaken with a sense of calm, seeing things more clearly than before we went to sleep. Without sleep, our everyday life cannot move along.

"Most sleep dreams are not remembered and yet they continue to reaffirm and facilitate the fulfillment of our life purpose, which is different for each one of us, and usually far beyond our comprehension, even though we might have a clue. And a side note, when I refer to life purpose, I am inferring a purpose for living that serves *you*, not others. A martyr might think they were born to die for a cause. But the true purpose is to experience what it is like to a martyr. We are all already One—so the notion that we can save each other is an illusion, even though our efforts are definitely integral to the story.

"Sometimes lack of remembering our dreams is meant to be. For example, we might not remember a dream that signals danger in our daily life because we are meant to have a dangerous experience that will help us fulfill our life intent. Or we might not remember because remembering might detour us from a wonderful upcoming event. It can also work the opposite way. We might remember a dream because it will help steer us away from a dark occurrence or in a direction critical to fulfilling our life intent. So, whether you do or do not remember your dreams—trust that.

"In dreams, our conscious mind seems to go to sleep and our dreams feel like real life. And when our conscious minds awaken, real life feels like the mundane day ahead. In physical death we seem to leave our bodies and move on to other realities. Yet, when sleeping, the process is similar in that we leave our bodies and assemble in the meeting ground of countless worlds beyond our everyday existence.

"In this meeting ground of sleep dreams, our daily life experiences fuel the dream world, like wood thrown on a fire. In the creative fires of dreaming, our daily life experiences are processed and converted into renewed energy. This renewed energy scripts the play that will be performed that day upon awakening. And the script *always* serves to fulfill our life intent.

"Further, in sleep dreams, we move into alternate worlds and communicate with each other, the identities in our Being, other versions of ourselves in parallel worlds, and with various energy forms in multiple realities. We tap and commune with all that we need in order to attune our vibration in such a way that it stabilizes the boundaries of our storyline. If, for example, the storyline is that after age thirty you will never be assaulted again, then the dream worlds will attune you to a vibration that will free you from assault and facilitate the rest of the story.

"Even when we are so-called awake in the mundane world, the dream continues. We have merely shifted focus from the many dream worlds to the singular everyday life. The mundane world is the manifestation of 'the dream,' the dream of life, the dream of life on earth, and sometimes beyond. Hence, our sleep experiences can be quite extraordinary.

"Deep level sleep experiences are often difficult to bring back into conscious awareness, and if they are retrieved, they are almost beyond words to explain. In these experiences, boundaries have dropped away, and we are not defined by our identity. In that freedom, we touch the world and all other worlds as they are *before* they were manifested. These deep level dreams are like a ride on the winds where all perceptions exist, and everything can be explored."

A hand raised in the far back of the room. I called upon the person to ask the question. He rose. It was Dmitri! He wore a light blue dress shirt, and black pants, kind of matching me. His hair was pulled back in a ponytail.

My heart pounded and I was embarrassed, but outwardly, I kept my cool.

Dmitri asked, "What is the relationship between the one homogenized Creative Energy and the dreaming that takes place on earth?"

He sat down to let me answer the question. I missed his face. I didn't want to, but I did.

I cleared my throat and concentrated on the question. "Creative Energy has an idea to know itself, so it projects a dream of configured energy that creates an enormous story where infinite possibilities can be explored in various settings with numerous characters. There is only *one* dream. Earth, like everything else, is a manifestation of that dream. In fact, even when we sleep, we are all having the same dream. We experience the dream differently because we each have personalized references. If one of my references is that I fear tigers, and one of yours is that you bond with tigers, the way we experience tigers in our dreams will be quite different. Hence, the dream might seem different, though it is the same.

"Without the dream, there is no projection of Creative Energy configured, hence, no world, no life as we know it—only the one homogenized Creative Energy."

A woman in the front row raised her hand.

I pointed to her. "Yes?"

She rose and asked, "There seems to be a lot of chaotic interplay in this one great dream. How does synchronicity fit into it?"

As she sat down, I replied, "Chaotic interplay is how we explore the dream, and in fact, it is what makes the dream so exciting. But since this dream was projected all at once, even in all its complexity and infinite possibility for interaction, synchronicity is a given. This is why, in linear time, everything seems to happen for a reason. For example: The cat delays you getting into your car, and that delay saved you from a car accident. You are thinking of a friend. The phone rings, and it is your friend. You meet a stranger in the grocery store who connects you to a great new job. Every event, from the tiniest to the biggest, creates a seeming chain reaction that seemingly weaves life's tapestry.

"But since the tapestry was already created from outside time and space, and all the threads of seeming futures are already woven and in place, how could their not be synchronicity? Moving our focus from this thread to that thread gives the illusion of time, but really . . . there is no time.

"The tapestry is the dream, already created, but not yet experienced. And this is the beauty of the dream—to experience it. These experiences generate an energy that enriches the life force. The energy produced—is the gift. The energy is the result of . . . we, as Creative Energy, experiencing our self."

Two hours passed as I spoke and answered questions. Finally, the lecture was over. As I stepped off the podium, Dmitri approached. He looked more beautiful than I remembered.

He reached his hand to me. And as I took it, I inadvertently nodded my head, and closed my eyes. Tears gathered.

"I know," he said, "I know," and he pulled me into his arms. I felt like I was in a Hollywood movie that wasn't real, and yet it felt so very real. He just held me as if time had stopped and the outer world did not exist.

His heart pounded in my ear like the rhythm of time unfolding. He stepped back slightly to look down upon me. I looked up, and our eyes locked. For a moment I spun through time. Did he? Tragic scenes of love lost flashed as if in memory of what we'd experienced together on the time line.

Then, he put his arm around me and started us walking. "Where can we go to talk and . . . just be."

I said, "We can go to my house. Did you drive here?"

"No," he said, "I took a taxi."

I steered us outside to my car in the dark parking lot. The sun had set at last, and I felt better now in the dark where I could be more free.

Interesting that no one approached us. It was as if our combined energy had created a vibration that would not allow it.

My hand was shaking when I tried to unlock my car door. "Would you mind driving?"

"I will drive." He took the key. "Come on," he said, going around to the passenger side.

I followed. Normally, I'd say, *Thanks, but I can open my own door*, but this was different. He was showing me respect and it came from no personal motive to manipulate me.

He opened the door. As I slipped inside, I said, "We can talk in my forested yard. It is very pretty."

"That sounds nice." He walked around to the driver's side of the car and slipped into the seat. "I'd like to be outside with you. It is better for us to be free of boundary."

I loved the way he talked to me. I just *loved* it.

As we drove home on the highway, we passed all the beautiful scenes of Portland at night, like the city lights glistening on the dark waters of Waterfront Park. Rows and clusters of evergreens lined the road. The moon rose over treetops splashing over the land as if some magic had been bequeathed upon us. All the cars drove in unison as if everyone agreed to sing a little song together.

Dmitri and I were quiet. We were quiet because a sort of energy was roaring in the car. We were so immersed in making this physical connection that it seemed to speak for itself. The drive felt three seconds long and yet strangely eternal.

When we pulled into my driveway and the car stopped, we looked at each other in dark shadow and paused.

"Susan," he said with a bit of accent.

"Dmitri," I said with a catch in my throat.

He said, "It is amazing to me that you were the angel that came to me that night when I lamented at the sycamore tree."

I said, "And it amazes me that you have come to me in spirit form, and helped me just the same."

He said, "We are two identities in the same Being."

I said, "We are diametric opposites in the same Being, slowly coming into balance with each other."

He said, "Yes, but our time like this will be brief, for I am soon to spin out of this reality."

He meant, die. Even though death was just a change of focus, to me, this moment, the word die described it more. I felt sad. Even though I believed in my story, and in his story, and our joint story, I felt sad.

He said, "Let us not talk in this car. Let us be in the trees as you suggested."

I nodded and we got out of the car. I offered food, and water. He denied both. I did get a warm blanket though. October nights could get chilly.

We went into the yard bypassing lawn chairs, and sat on the grass in a clearing where the stars shined. With the blanket wrapped around us, our words flowed.

He opened up and shared his life story, the details of how he'd come from a long line of agents over the ages, and had been groomed for the position of international spy, and it was no calm thing. He shared the terrible things that he'd done and terrible things that were done to him. He shared these things with me like he was in confession with a priest. He had connived, and killed, and had done so many things that took a piece of his soul, until he could barely feel himself anymore.

He ended his story softly, "That is when I met you as an angel."

I said, "I wasn't an angel."

He said, "What is an angel anyway, if not our self touching our self?"

"Like now," I said, "like now."

"And so, I have come here tonight, Susan, to say goodbye."

I sighed, and though I knew death wasn't really death, I just didn't want to accept it. "Can't you get asylum in another country?"

"I am in too deep, more so than you could ever imagine. I will be found, and I will be—"

I put my fingers to his lips. "Don't say it."

So odd it was, that I was aware of the synchronistic panorama that encompassed the small picture, yet here I was living out a little drama that I knew was a little drama (in the scope of totality), but if felt *so* big. However, experiencing the drama *is* the thing, and it was okay to have this drama that loomed so all encompassing in me and over me like a hungry grizzly bear that targeted me for food.

He slipped his arm around my back and said, "Let us gaze upon the night sky, which we are all of, and let us remember that there really is no separation or death, or parting."

Staring at the stars, I felt myself move into them. And I felt Dmitri move into them. And there we were together.

Then I jolted. My mind had flashed upon a horrible scene, another tragic ending for me and Dmitri, already written but not yet played. I saw him dead in Russia in an alley, laying flat on garbage, face up to the night sky.

My cheeks welled and my lips trembled. I did not want to see what I saw, but I did, as if telling myself to accept what lay ahead. But I would not tell him of the vision, for I think he already knew.

He said, "You will hold my sword for me?"

I almost burst out crying. I had gone through something like that with My Fool when he so-called, died, and going through it again was almost too much to bear. I knew I wasn't really being left behind, but it sure felt like it.

We talked all night, oh not about Russia or of the concrete world, but of all the odd experiences we'd ever had, like pulling out numerous puzzle pieces and putting them together showing us a bigger picture.

He would say things like, "Once when I had to kill, I went outside my body and saw myself and couldn't believe it was me doing this thing."

And I would say, "Once when I was thrown across a room by a man, I went outside my body, and I couldn't believe I was the one who had been thrown."

And finally he said, "And for all I did to feel power, I can do no longer."

And I said, "And for all the things I endured in the name of sacrifice, I can do no longer."

"And so here we are," he said.

"Here we are," said I.

Then we climbed into the hammock and snuggled close together under the warm blanket, and we slept under the stars. It's funny how in the movies great loves usually involve sexual communion, but our connection was so deep and so pure, we bypassed that altogether. After all, the urge for sex, beyond obvious physical rewards, was about getting closer, as close as one could be. However, we were already closer than that.

When morning came, he took a shower, and we had omelets, toast, and coffee at the kitchen table. Baxter and Angel nudged his ankles with a grand welcome, or perhaps a goodbye. When he was finished, he took his dishes to the sink and said, "I must get to the airport."

I drove him there, quietly, holding on to the moments. His solitude was just as deep. When we arrived, we went to the airport locker where he retrieved a brown leather carry on. He'd done his flight check in on my computer, so we headed toward security. He carried his bag in one hand, and with the other, he held mine.

We walked along, holding hands, skin on skin, body heat mingling—not in a clinging way, but more of a sacred way. We passed through seas of airport people masked in their dramas. Some faces shined secret joy. Others drooped with unknown sorrow. And some expressions were posed in dark contemplation in search of illusive answers. The knowing and not knowing, the fear and excitement, permeated the crowds—each person steeped in their own rich world of being.

We reached security and then the drama was mine.

Dmitri faced me, and though his body stance appeared secure, his hand was shaking when he stroked my cheek. But when I cupped my hand over his, the shaking stopped.

I said, "You can't stay here?"

Our hands transformed to a gentle interlocking of fingers over my heart. He leaned into my ear and whispered, "Innocent people would get hurt. You, for instance."

My mouth quivered. "I will never see you again, will I?"

He drew back his head and looked at me. "Not in this life."

I said, "I know we can never really die, and we, in the concept of time, will have future connections in other time-space locations, but still, this moment is hard to release."

"Then do not release it, Susan. This moment is always happening, remember?"

He embraced me one last time. I felt his heart beating against mine. And though I no longer had any notions about a cold hand of death bringing an end to our mortal lives, it was the human touch of those I loved on the threshold of leaving *my* life—that stirred me so. I was, after all, human with all my references.

And when his body drew back from mine and turned away, a part of me went with him, perhaps another version of myself that I could not see. And the version that was currently my Focus Self, remained. My chest cracked with a sharp pain. I watched Dmitri head into the security section, his hair in a ponytail, over his blue dress shirt. His stride was sad and noble and beautiful in its own way, like the knights who die on the battlefield for country and king.

He put his black boots on the security belt, and gave me one last look that shot through space and time. And his blue eyes said, *be strong*. Carry the sword for me.

Then he moved through security, and vanished in the crowd. Sorrow rose in me from the depths of somewhere, superseding the current situation. I made a mad dash for a bathroom stall, before uncontrollable sobbing could claim me.

And there, crouched down in the bathroom stall, with face in hands, my sorrow erupted in the loudest silent crying I had ever experienced. Breathy screams that had no voice shattered the airport bathroom with an energy that could not be seen or heard, but I was oh so certain it could be felt by any who shared that space with me.

Even as I was in my drama, another part of me felt it was all so stupid. Dmitri and I had barely grazed each other in this life. But then again, if we were of the same Being, then the clicking of the wheel turn—selves shifting focus would intensely affect all the members of that unit. How many times have we been elated or devastated for no apparent reason? How many times has this happened to me? When the mood passes, we often forget about it because we have no tangible reason to pin it on.

I wiped my eyes and pushed myself out of the stall. I went to a sink and washed my hands, splashing water on my face. A woman in dark green skirt suit with short blonde curly hair, asked, "Are you all right?"

I half joked, "Oh, we all go through everything eventually and great gifts are to be had in the hard times, so . . . yes."

She looked at me strangely, with a silent, 'O-kay.'

I suppose I could have just said, *Yes, thank you.*

But as I am me, philosophically natured answers were always falling out of my mouth.

I exited the bathroom and found my car. I cried all the way home, trying to be strong, trying to be strong for him, he that was me. He was fulfilling his life intent to move out of the coldness and to feel warmth. And he had received it, received the warm touch of Creative Energy's communal hand, the hand of the all, the hand of us all. Oh, how precious it must be for him to be touched by totality, the power of the Universe, the magic of the heartbeat, and the gentle whispering of the silent gentle things that go mostly unseen by the populous. And I had what I needed: my freedom. I could remain married to myself, which had made me very joyful thus far.

That night I journeyed to my hammock with Walkman and headphones. I listened to Richard Strauss's, *Death and Transfiguration* while I called for My Fool, crying and crying, and crying.

And though He came, I could not go through The Wall to get new information. I was only in a place to be reminded of the old wisdom He'd already told me. I couldn't even see Him. But at least I could hear Him against the beautiful music.

"Susan. Susan," His voice was warm. "This day of days, after a night of nights, the markers in the brain of the Focus Identity, Susan, and the Focus Identity known as Dmitri, have been triggered, unleashing a reference you both share, 'living and dying for freedom.' Different spins on the same story."

I nodded, tears dripping around my headphones, seeping into my ears.

His voice continued to soak deeply into my brain, and even more so my aching heart. "These markers that trigger emotions create defining moments. They arise at the crossroads in our stories as pinnacle transitions, as climaxes in our life experience.

"At these times, the mundane and deeper dreaming worlds merge. You and Dmitri, as two identities in the same Being, have physically touched. But remember, this Being, or any Being, or all Being, is merely one pure energy configured. Coming and going is an illusion, separation and communion, an illusion. Outside time, we are homogenized eternal infinity."

I cried, "That is what I want to experience, not this feeling of separation that I will lose Dmitri!"

He said, "But that is part of the great experiment my dear, to see what would happen if? The illusion of separation is essential, as well as the various connections made within the illusion."

I cried out like a two year old, "I don't want Dmitri to die!"

"Then feel that. Cry and grieve. It's part of the human experience. One way or the other, we have all recently died from something. Can we actually tell if we are awake, asleep, dead, in transit, or never really made it this far? Not really. We believe. We accept. We know. But we really don't."

"I know I don't know, what I think I know," I blubbered. His words with the music were having a deep healing affect on me, even though I was still in trauma. *Sometimes trauma must be lived before it can be released.*

He said, "This memory, written outside time before you were born . . . this memory that you now play out, seems welcome or unwelcome, or both, depending on how you perceive it. No memory written outside time is ever positive or negative, it is just given a label that befits our judgment of the experience. We feel blessed or cursed, but no matter which, we are brighter for having had the experience. Experience breeds energy that always takes us into something new in the reality of linear time. Then life is perception, like winning and losing. Whatever you lose you win; whatever you win you lose. You will lose Dmitri but you have won his heart. And if he were to remain here with you, you would win him, but lose him, for the reality of embedding another in your physical life right now, ironically, would thwart your life intent to experience 'freedom' in the form of being married to yourself."

I knew that. I did. I stopped crying, bleary eyed, and peeked at the trees overhead, leaves fluttering in the breeze. Three seagulls flew over my yard. And I felt a bit more accepting of the situation. My eyes slid shut from exhaustion. "Still," I asked, "will I see him again?"

He said, "Wait and see, Susan. Open your mind, open wide, forget what you know, trust in synchronicity. Birthing and dying are just perceptions. Shake it off and live with gusto. It is not necessary to understand the complexity of the inner worlds, but even so, deep beyond the mask of mundane reality is the face of pure energy where we find peace with our nature and our situation. This is what Dmitri has found."

I said, "Do you mean, he has seen beyond his persona of the role he has played, realizing that his references and memories facilitated a story that was meant to be?"

"Yes, he sees the overview of his mandate in life, and he is fulfilling his intent. He realizes he is not the story, or the character, not really, but that he is totality. He has learned to meditate, to be in that state of mind. He has deeply reflected the meaning of the earth story and the reason why his particular identity was assembled. He has embraced his chosen identity as well as his totality, as well as what is outside time and space. He beholds the seed of the intent of his personalized story as well as the greater collective story of earth. And as the human heart cries out for help, help arrives. And the help is I—"

A dramatic calm overcame me. I whispered, "It is I. I is I, It is I, don't you know who I am?"

"Don't you know who I am?" He repeated with an air of peace that held everything. "Then slowly, very slowly that question will have meaning beyond religion and science, beyond one's knowing. When deeply imbedded in certain symphonies and forces of nature that vibrate the unexplainable, there can be that brief escape of time and space. And there in that in-between of inhaling and exhaling, Dmitri now resides. In this vibration, he is attuned to *The All*. He is touched by what others might term 'the hand of God'—but not the God most envision, but rather the other side of god, the god beyond all belief systems, the god the encompasses all and is everything that exists without separation."

I said, "You mean then, that he has been touched by—himself as the creator of his own dream."

"Yes, then everything for that moment blends into one. Everything in that moment is okay. He has stepped out of the story and into the dreaming before the story was created."

I smiled, tired and worn in my hammock with the beautiful notes of Strauss's music swelling in my ears. And finally, I could see My Fool at the Wall of Remembrance. Ethereally, I stood before Him. He said, "Open your hand."

I outstretched my palm.

He placed a wispy, cosmic cloud in it. "This is the Gem of Dreaming. The dreaming comes from the one homogenized Creative Energy outside time and space, and gives us the experience of time and space."

The wispy cloud absorbed into my palm. For a moment, I blended into the One. For that moment everything was okay. I was okay.

And then I fell asleep in my hammock, and despite the Dmitri trauma, I was at peace.

And whenever you need peace, it is there for you if you allow yourself to fall into it. When you are done grieving, whatever your grief might entail: loss, rejection, or loneliness—sink into your deeper self, like a feather drifting down from the skies reminding you where you come from. You *are* okay. You are always okay, whether you can fathom it or not.

The one great dream was projected in perfect symmetry. Each and every event in your life story has value. Living your life is like exploring the integral workings of a snowflake. Whether you understand it or not, you are very beautiful.

The one great dream is a gift. Dreaming, or exploring the dream is an opportunity. You, the explorer of the dream are the star of the show. Behold yourself and your life in this manner: whether you are yelling at someone, or they—you; whether you are lonely or feeling crowded, whether you are bored to tears or so passionate you feel you will burst. You are dreaming the synchronous dream, and in that, no matter what it might seem, the dream is perfect as it is, and you are perfect as you are.

While we aspire to find value in the dream of life and value in ourselves—it is there whether we find it our not. Exploration is the thing. We are becoming more than we are by exploring the dream.

And so I say to you, happy dreams, or I mean, sweet dreams, or rather thrilling dreams, or maybe poignant dreams. Such a countless panorama to explore! So, I guess what I really mean to say is . . . dream on!'

In the Land of Time

"Inside the box we incubate; outside the box we soar."

GEM #10 IMAGINATION

I was having a bad day. Everyone has them, even the wise. And as bad days always held a gift, I tried to keep that focus.

I was stuck in the airport waiting for my delayed plane to arrive while snow storms loomed and receded outside. My destination was Arizona to spend Christmas with my daughter and son. Christmas to me was about fairy tale things, Santa Claus, elves, pretty lights, and all that. I loved letting my imagination soar.

However, after ten hours of waiting for my rescheduled flight from this morning's cancellation, I felt stifled. I was bored, tired, and feeling very blah, especially when thoughts of Dmitri's demise prevailed in my mind. I presumed I might feel the event of his death, though I wasn't sure.

Anyway, seeing my children would help a lot. But as it was, I'd been trying to leave Oregon for four days in the midst of a series of uncharacteristically harsh snowstorms, and it was already Christmas Eve.

Portland airport had a television propped up above the heads of the milling and despondent crowd. I was sitting on the floor in my blue jeans, red sweater, and black boots, leaning against a post with my carry on bag at my side. I was watching a show on how cats are birthed. Swimming sperm were fighting their way through obstacles inside the cat's womb on this great adventure, encountering colorful challenges on their mission to join with an egg to eventually become an embryo.

It seemed people were just the same, like sperm, even after

they were born, trying so hard to attain something before they die. And it didn't seem so very odd a thought that neither as sperm nor people do we truly understand what we are trying to achieve.

People are bombarded with conscious programming such as 'get a good education,' 'get a good job,' 'make money,' 'pick the right mate,' 'raise your children well,' and for many, 'prepare yourself for a rewarding afterlife.' And the sperm might experience something like, 'get through the membrane' 'compete with fellow sperm' 'be patient while substances mature for landing.' And as five or six sperm make it into the cat's eggs, they might view themselves as the winners.

An announcement over the airport intercom informed me that my plane was delayed—again, so I stuffed my carry on bag behind my back and slid down until I was pretty much laying on the floor. It was kind of yucky, but all the seats were taken.

Listening to the rest of the cat story on the television, I dozed, thinking of the fight to 'become,' and I was feeling a bit mad at all the drama we are all faced to go through, even though I clearly understood the wisdom of it. Again, I was having a bad day. Oh the drama! Dmitri's drama, my drama, the drama of everyone I loved, and . . . well—everyone's drama. Stop the drama! Enough drama! No more suffering! And a bit of the old peacemaker rose in me, just wanting everyone to smile, and I was mad that they weren't able. Well, once in a while, being more human than sage was just meant to be.

Then I fell asleep.

I was in a land that could be considered anything but 'la la.' You know, la la land. There was no drama. The world was gray. And the people wore simple gray shirts and pants and shoes and never any makeup. And we lived in houses with no style. People did not have new ideas. They had collaborated to live a very simple life.

I was a mother of three children who never smiled because they never cried. School was to teach them how to be like everyone else and get along because if they were different they would upset the harmony of the community. The best way to get everyone to agree with everything all the time was to not present anything new, basically—to avoid change.

A rather grotesque looking man who wore lots of color would appear on a hill every morning, juggling balls. The people of the community ignored him, as did I. No change, for change would disturb the harmony of the community. Who was this man? *Go away,* we thought. *You are ugly.*

Sometimes the children would be interested to watch the grotesque man juggle, so we would call them away from him, and tell them to go inside and study the rules of society. And they did.

Our children's hair was always neat, their faces clean, and their teeth were very white. They aspired to appear as expected and to play their role for the benefit of the community. Nothing else mattered.

Everyone quit aging once they reached their prime at about thirty, yet they could live on into the hundreds for disease was rare and accidents few. And if death came calling, people were happy, because life was so boring.

And though I was this mother of three, I was also aware of my identity as Susan inside this mother. I felt cooped up being in a land I was not familiar with in a body so bland, forced to act like all the others—forced to pretend that I was the same. How could they live like this, with no imagination? My head felt like it was swarming with bees, and I wished I was a bee so that I could fly freely in the sky. I was so desperate that I went outside to watch the grotesque juggler.

But when I saw him on the hill in his colorful clothes, juggling colorful balls, he didn't look grotesque anymore. I found myself walking toward him, mesmerized, like he was my hope for salvation. I knew what I was risking: peace, harmony, unsettling the community, and not being loved anymore, but at this point, I would be willing to endure some drama if only to feel alive inside!

The nearer I got to the juggler, the more beautiful he appeared. Closer, closer. C . . l . .o . . s . . e . .r. And when I got really close, the face of the juggler was My Fool. The face smiled, and I cried, and laughed, and frowned. And I loved it. And then the face on the juggler became mine.

I woke up hearing that my flight was boarding. I jumped up, grabbed my luggage, and boarded the plane, strangely appreciating the drama. Would the plane get off the ground, or would a snowstorm stop it? Would I get to Arizona for Christmas, or would I be spending Christmas with my cats?

I made it onto the plane, but they had to de-ice it, but could they de-ice it in time? Another storm was coming. And I heard somewhere that the flights after mine were cancelled. Sitting in my seat, I waited, heart pounding. Would we ever take off?

Finally, the plane ascended into the night sky through moving mist—into ethereal splendor! And I loved this hunk of metal that took me up into the mystic night on this journey to my children.

I began daydreaming about Dmitri and what he might be going through. I imagined our possible pasts, and our possible futures. Letting my mind be free, I saw flashes of him in a string of various trailing identities, birthing and dying in the concept of linear time, like a thread of experiences that yielded similar but slightly changing scenarios, a warrior, a policeman . . . a spy. And I was another string of trailing identities that were similar, birthing and dying in linear time, a nun, a social worker, a therapist. The threads of Dmitri and I paralleled each other like the ribs in the tunnel of our Being.

My mind was so free that I couldn't tell what was real and what I might be making up. And then I thought about that. Perhaps we don't make things up. Perhaps we just tap into other realities. Can anything ever really be made up? Just how real are our imaginations? What is imagination?

And so, there on the airplane, I pulled out my Walkman and headphones from my bag, and played Anton Bruckner's *Symphony No.4*.

I went into meditation, clearing away thoughts of Dmitri, releasing my perceptions, and loosening my beliefs. And from this deep place, thoughts and ideas tumbled into my consciousness.

'Imagination is involved when projecting possible futures. We imagine what this or that might be like: *What would happen if I had a million dollars? What would happen if my mate left me? What will happen if I don't speak up and what might happen if I do?* All of these projections require imagination. Imagination is the ability to think outside the immediate box in which one lives.

'Imagination is involved in our creative pursuits: *We write a story, create a song, make a new recipe, conjure a fresh concept in the workplace, or find clever ways to parent our children.*

'Imagination is also involved with fantastical day dreaming: *I am a princess in a foreign land. I visit another planet and discover an alien culture. I am young again and romantically pursued by many. I can save the world!*

'Imagination is often shrouded in hope: *I hope I get the job.* And as we hope, we see ourselves in the work place. *I hope I find my soul mate.* And as we hope this, we see ourselves with the perfect mate. *I hope nothing bad happens to me today.* And as we hope this, we see ourselves having a perfect day.

'And when we close our eyes, the box we live in falls away, and we can dream of scenarios that in mundane reality might get us into trouble. *We beat up the boss. We have an affair. A monster gets us.* Or scenarios we wish would come true. *I dreamed I was in a beautiful exotic land. My dead child was alive again. I won the lottery. I was flying.*

'Sometimes we dream of other times and places: *I was a gladiator in ancient Rome and a lion killed me. I was a woman with sixteen children. I was the wife of an English sea captain.*

'Imagination helps us problem solve, form new ideas, rehash old ideas, embrace hope, play out our wishes in day dreams, and free us in our night dreams.

'In fact, the only time we do not use our imagination is when we initially receive information such as two plus two equals four, or we must stop at a red light. Or, when we are performing mundane tasks by rote such as brushing our teeth or doing fifty sit-ups.

'However, even the information received was first imagined, as in figuring out that two plus two equals four, or that stopping at a red light would help keep cars from crashing into each other. And mundane tasks, such as brushing our teeth or doing sit-ups, first were imagined as a method to keep our teeth from rotting, or exercising to stay fit.

'So, even the things that don't seem like imagination were actually born from imagination. Without imagination, there would be no scientific advancement, and nothing could ever improve. Without imagination, change is thwarted and life grows stagnant. So, in answer to what is imagination? It is the exploration of all that exists in the concept of time and space.

And then I was done thinking and ready for deeper insight. While the plane took me to Arizona and the music gave me its gift, I went to The Wall of Remembrance. My Fool appeared with bullhorns on His head and little white wings that seemed to sprout from the back of His violet sweatshirt. His white pants were now striped pink, purple, and blue. His orange socks that peeked through the cut toe opening in His jogging shoes were now red with a little white star on the tip of each toe.

I looked Him up and down, more than once, a bit tongue tied, and then I burst out laughing.

"Imagination," He said. "You forgot about humor. Humor is about looking at things from a comical angle."

I grinned. "Yes, that requires imagination."

He stroked a bullhorn, up and down. "The interesting thing is that while the dream was created outside time from one homogenized Creative Energy, imagination is what we do with the dream *inside* time."

I gasped with an epiphany. "Oh! So imagination is what we utilize while in the projection of Creative Energy, this projection that we call life. In this projection, we live the memories, already created, like living scenes from the great one dream, but the *way* we experience the scenes and the dream are born from imagination."

His wings fluttered. "Yes. Yes. Imagination is where we find free will. We can view life," rose-colored glasses appeared on His face, through the filter of ***beauty***. *All people are good. All stories end happy.*"

Then the rose-colored lenses turned gray, making His eyes look lifeless. "We can view life through the filter of **boredom**, blinded to beauty. *Life is monotonous. Life is stupid.*"

The lenses turned red, making His eyes look big and stressed. "We can view life through the filter of ANGER. *Everyone is mean. Life is bad. I hate the world.*"

I stepped back from Him, repelled by the look of anger. Then the lenses flashed from color to color to color. He said, "The choice of perception is endless. For as many shades of every color and every color combination there are, that is how many choices we have to imagine the world, like this, or like that . . . or like that, or this. These choices can remain the same for a lifetime, change periodically, or change moment to moment."

I felt glasses appear on my face, and through the lenses I saw a myriad of colors.

He said, "You are trying to view life through many perceptions in an effort to see everything from a more balanced point of view. Eventually, the colors will blend like a fiery opal where all can be seen simultaneously. This is called seeing life through the eyes of wisdom."

I said, "Well, right now, I see pink, then purple, then blue, then . . ."

"Try not to focus on one color at a time, but rather all colors at once. See through the whole lens."

"What if I removed the glasses?"

"Then you would remove your imagination. Imagination is what enables us to explore the wonderland of life on earth."

I recapped, "So, seeing life through no perception would take us out of the earth experience, but seeing life through all perceptions makes us wise?"

"Well, it can be enriching from time to time to view life from this perception or that. A scene viewed with anger can lead to an emotional explosion. It might mean that a passive person has found his power. Or that a hotheaded woman acts in a way that backfires on her, forcing a life change that will invite the next chapter in her story. She might even be forced to see life through a blue-colored perception and learn to calm down."

"Wow," I said, "imagination gives us a life."

"Yes," He affirmed, "yes. Without the changing colors of perception, all the color is gone, and there is but a sterile story with no impetus to live it."

"So, if I am wearing these multi-colored lenses, viewing life from multiple angles at once, what kind of life experience does that lend?"

"It lends a life experience void of moral judgment, brimming with loving acceptance, and a charge of wisdom from every life event."

I said, "It does change the flavor of life, like not tasting this spice, then that, but throwing them all in your mouth at once."

He said, "You might want to taste this spice and that, one at a time. Then again, there might be times when you don't want to taste the same thing over and over."

"Yes. I am tired of viewing things from this or that perception, bouncing around. I'd rather merge the perceptions and elevate my life experience. I think there is more to the spice of life than the spices commonly known."

"There is. And in the merging of perceptions, new perceptions are created. I m a g i n a t i o n."

Just as I felt I was beholding the wonders of imagination, My Fool and I seemed to turn into liquid color and we swirled together into a world of dripping shades and tones. We were like paints moving, mixing, into each other, away from each other, in circles, in squares, and in all kinds of lines and curves. We were on a canvas of air so expansive there was no end in sight. So even if colors blended in a way that seemed bogged down, there were other parts of blank canvas to drip upon.

On one level, colors mixed, or had a journey of their own in one solid shade. On another level, pictures formed, like houses, grass, mountains, a boy flying a kite, a girl throwing a doll at her baby sister, a couple getting married at the altar. But it wasn't the scenes themselves that were interesting, but rather *how* the people were *experiencing* the scenes: facial expressions, body language, and how settings affected mood.

Suddenly, I felt wings burst out of my back, and I was once removed from the canvas, flying over the great work of art in progress. I saw emotions as colors with tones dancing together, sometimes repelling, and sometimes mixing. I saw thoughts in the form of crazy boiling water birthing miniature bubbles that grew huge. Sometimes the bubbles blended with other bubbles, creating massive shapes that had varying energy currents. Sometimes the bubbles fizzed lightly or intensely. Physical energy in micro-particles permeated everything, creating small bursts and big explosions, amassing and disintegrating in multiple ways. I saw these micro-particles, thoughts and emotions actively moving over many kinds of lands: deserts, forests, cities, dream lands, fairylands, and future lands, and through many kinds of heads and hearts: flowers, fish, animals, people, incorporeal entities, and Beings.

Oh the majesty! Such freedom!

A mystical sigh sounded beside me as I flew over the infinite panorama. It was My Fool. And then we seemed stopped, though the panorama beneath us continued to move and change.

I looked to My Fool, His bullhorns gone, and wings too, but His eyes seemed like tunnels of stars that held the energy of inception, of birth, and creation. He whispered hauntingly, "This is the land of imagination. This is . . . earth."

And the way He said it was so beautiful, that even in my transcended spirit state, my cheeks welled with tearful joy.

My Fool said, "Open your hand."

And as I did, He placed a small blue and green earth in my palm. "This is the Gem of Imagination. Earth is imagination's playground. Beyond all tangible reality, there it is . . . waiting to be manifested into new and interesting things by earth's inhabitants."

Tears seeped from my eyes. And I was back on the plane, crying gently. My eyes opened as Bruckner's *Symphony No.4* ended. I was staring out into the dark night, high above the clouds, flying over the land below, on Christmas Eve, on the eve that always sent my imagination running wild.

I inhaled a sob that would have been too loud to expel on a plane full of people.

But the lady next to me heard, and she put her hand on my knee. "Are you all right?"

"Yes, yes," I said, "thank you." I had an urge to flow openly as usual and say, "Oh yes, I just had a beautiful experience in the land of imagination, and well, 'ain't life great!' "

Instead, I let the urge sink back into me that I might behold the gift I had received in revered silence. I resumed looking out the airplane window into the rich black air, but I did not see rich black air. I saw gremlins and ghosts, dragons and knights, and lords and ladies. I saw cherubic angels, and spirits that had left their bodies, and spirits moving into bodies to have an individual life. I saw births and deaths, celebrations and wars. I saw people laughing, crying, hating, and loving. I saw.

"I am that I am," I whispered to myself, "I *am*."

Behold it now. Your individuality. Your capacity to imagine, and your capacity to experience life as you yearn to experience it. Find a quiet place in nature or with music that moves you. Close your eyes and say, "I am." Feel it. As you move deeper inside yourself, say again and again, "I am. I am. I am." Soar into the inner world of you with reverence, with an open mind . . . and see . . . what . . . happens.

The Other Side of Life

"We die when we are born; we are born when we die."

GEM #11 TOTALITY

Seeing my children for Christmas took my mind off Dmitri, and lent passage for love's expression. Though grown, my children were ever flowers in my heart. I respected their individuality and their independence, but they were as much a part of me as my right and left arm.

Well regenerated by my human connection, I was back home on the computer recording my morning writing from what came to me in the night.

'Life rolls along, it seems, throwing punches and presenting prizes, often when we least expect it. A fire combusts in our backyard or a heart-warming package arrives at our doorstep. Our child dies in an accident or we are pregnant at long last. We are diagnosed with cancer or a loved one survives impossible circumstances.

'The seeming randomness of such events might be perceived as unfair or lucky. Or, the seeming deliberation of fate exacting these occurrences might be seen as punishment or reward. Or, the finality of such happenings might be interpreted as a forsaking of, or a miracle of—God.

'No matter which way the positive and negative events in our lives are viewed, we are often left with a sense that we are at life's mercy. Even if we do everything in our power to control our environment and the people around us, so that 'bad things' can't happen—the yard can still burst into flames, the child can still die, and we can still be diagnosed with cancer.

'This helpless feeling often generates anxiety and depression. It can fuel obsessive compulsions, neurosis, hysteria, paranoia, agoraphobia, and emotional paralysis. In an effort to quell the uneasiness, people often become excessive in their behavior and develop addictions to alcohol, cigarettes, drugs, gambling, television, virtual reality games, chronic exercise, or even work. They might become spend thrifts or misers, overeat or under eat. To guard vulnerability, people might chronically lie, cheat, brag, deny, complain, or blame.

'But what if our life events were not random or the result of punishment or reward, betrayal or miracle? What if there was rhyme and reason for every single event in our lives? The yard catching fire might be about instilling caution to avoid a future fire that would be far worse. Our child dying might be about a new adventure for her while gifting us with a needed set-up to fulfill *our* current life intent. A cancer diagnosis might be about triggering a sequence of events whereupon we must value ourselves enough to extract hidden inner strength, setting us on course to fulfill our life intent.

'And if we were able to step back and back and back from these challenging scenes, we would witness how *every* occurrence was relevant to the unfolding of our story.

'When I was going through my masters program, which was far from my house, I met a woman named Paulette, who asked if we could carpool. We became friends. In school, I was in love with a man, but I was too shy to let him know, even though he was flirting with me. Paulette was not shy, and knowing my feelings for the man, she steered us together. Once he knew I liked him, he admitted he was about to give up on me because he was under the impression I wasn't interested. We married. He was controlling. I fought being controlled. To fuel my self-esteem, I meditated daily and had life changing experiences that helped me strengthen my personal power. I became a social activist. I began writing books, which was not only therapeutic for me, but led me to become a professional writer. I divorced my husband, moved to my dream state, and currently live a life I enjoy deeply. My husband was the perfect choice for me because he facilitated my 'becoming.'

'So, Paulette saying, "Hey, do you want to carpool to school?" was a key event that unlocked a door that led me to my current life. Illustrating the synchronistic tributaries that sprung from this one act would fill a book, and illustrating the complete synchronicity in all my life events or anyone's, would fill volumes of books. But in short, the punches, (from stubbing our toes to losing a loved one), and the prizes, (from receiving a compliment to inheriting a windfall), are part of the grand design in our journey of self-discovery. Viewing life from this perspective can alleviate much stress and depression, and all the things that come with that.'

Upon completion of that last sentence, I felt like the wind had been knocked out of me. Breathing was hard. I had to lie down. Something was happening to me. My essence loosened from my body in a *very* strong form of astral projection.

As my body lay on my bed, my astral self journeyed over water. Moments later, I was in Russia, at night, in a dark alley. The street was wet from rain. Dmitri was standing in front of multiple garbage cans, clustered about a brick wall. His long hair lay over the front of his opened black trench coat. He was wearing a black dress shirt, black slacks, and boots.

He said, "Susan?"

"Dmitri?"

He didn't answer, but he was peering hard right at me.

"Dmitri?"

"I can see you faintly, Susan. You are almost transparent."

I moved up to him looking into his face. "Can you hear me?"

He didn't respond, but then he said, "I hear your voice in my head, but I don't know if you are talking to me or if I am imagining. Did you just ask if I could hear you?"

"Yes!" I cried.

"Did you just say, yes?"

"Yes!" I cried again.

He said with half a laugh, "Only you would come to me . . . at a time like this—in a form like this."

"My heart is with you," I said.

"I know," he said softly. "I have reclaimed my innocence. Can you feel it?"

"Yes, Dmitri, I can feel it." And I did. His eyes glowed with deep peace and sparkled with Creative Energy.

A sharp sound cracked behind me, and a small burning force shot through my astral body. Dmitri flew backwards, hitting garbage cans that fell over. He landed on his back, sprawled over downed cans. He had been shot!

I went to him and looked down. His eyes were open in a vacant stare, hair splayed over garbage. His open trench coat revealed a chest of blood. He was dead. It started raining—hard. I crouched over his body trying to kiss his cheeks and eyes, but I couldn't make contact. I started sobbing. The rain came down right through me, wetting his face.

I snapped back into my body at home on my bed. I was in a cold sweat, hands pressed over heart in physical pain. I could barely breathe. I thought, *What one identity in our Being feels, in some way, we all do.*

Dmitri was dead. Finishing his life story, he was moving on to the next adventure. I needed no proof. I knew what had happened and I needed to accept it.

I sank into a meditative state thinking about totality because it hurt less than focusing on separation.

My Fools calming words washed over me from wherever He was. "This day of days, after a night of nights, Dmitri's so-called life, as are all lives, and his so-called death, as are all deaths, integral to totality. Totality is the *complete* projection of Creative Energy configured. It is all that is. It is Creative Energy's masterpiece."

I nodded to myself, trying to reign in my woe.

My Fool said, "Totality has layers of countless vibrations, of all that can be imagined and even what cannot. In totality, science and its scores of theories are all correct. In totality, spirituality and its many faces are all correct. In totality, science and spirituality do not compete. Intellect, intuition, and imagination, do not compete. Every way of thinking is a thread in totality. Every level and kind of morality has a place in totality. Every thought, feeling, and action of any person, place, or thing, is precisely the way it is supposed to be."

I saw myself amongst countless winding tubes that emanated some sort of electromagnetic energy. It looked like infinite nerve bundles, or massive wiring.

My Fool said, "Pure Creative Energy is of a substance humans cannot fully understand or experience in projected realities, but the totality of these projected realities is a masterpiece to the square root of infinity."

Just as I was beginning to feel relief from the horror of the Dmitri incident, the pain returned. I felt the bed beneath me, and my white fluffy cat, Angel, curled up at my side, purring. My fist flew to my heart, cupped by my other palm. I pressed down trying to quell my sorrow.

All my life, on some level I used to cry out for my phantom warrior, at first to save me. I sought to merge with him and integrate warrior energy. In this effort, I mostly attracted physical warrior-type men who sought to control me. That was the old pattern.

But then I grew wise, and now the warrior that I, on some level, had called for was my diametric opposite, an identity in my Being who wanted to integrate heart as badly as I did the sword. He gave up his long cemented story in order to develop his heart, just as I had been giving up my long cemented story in order to wield the sword. He died to merge with heart that he may reunite with his compassionate self, and I lived to resurrect the sword that I might sing my foolish songs, instead of hiding from life. We had shifted our energy simultaneously.

And even though I knew Dmitri had simply shifted focus and had not 'ended,' a roaring grief overcame me. And even though I knew he'd completed his intent to reclaim his innocence from the grip of depravity, cruelty, and lack of conscience, I wanted him with me as I had known him, right now. Even though I liked being married to myself, I wished I was married to him. I felt like part of him was with me, but then again a part of him was very much—not.

I needed more help to deal with this event—much more. I grabbed my Walkman and headed outside to my hammock where Dmitri and I had once slept. With Walkman on my stomach turned off, I stared sadly at the daytime sky of endless blue. *Where are you Dmitri?*

A part of me wanted to chase after him on his time line, the way I had my mother and my cat, but no, I had to think polyphonically now. The small pictures of Dmitri's various existences were important, but the all-encompassing picture, I had to see it too.

I thought of the harsh profession Dmitri had experienced and all the harsh realities of everyone, everywhere, and of all the lovely realities too. Everyone's reality was pure and beautiful in meaning, even when in ugly situations.

Everyone's core is the same. Only on the surface do we appear different. It is as if on the surface we wear a mask of sorts, an image of who we think we are; but in the depth of ourselves—in the depth . . . we are all authentic and innocent. There in the depth, we reside in naked wonder of how we will experience the next adventure.

I closed my eyes, *Oh My Fool, I need more than your voice, or appearance. I need—more!* I put my headphones over my ears, and clicked on my Walkman. Gustav Mahler's fifth symphony played.

The first movement sounded horns blowing in such a way, as to blow the top off anything that was capped. And when I heard that, it was as if the cap of my composure blasted into the air, and my authentic self from deep inside, screamed, *I am! I am! I am!* Raw wounds from wherever and whenever were exposed, and I needed medicine to aid my badly grieving heart.

And during the second movement, I grieved. And when the third movement came, I felt cradled like a baby. My human self was raw without mask or cover-up, nakedly open and vulnerable to whatever 'is.' The nourishing tones seeped like water into the dehydrated places deep down inside me. I was receiving all the love I ever needed or wanted in the life of Susan.

My Fool's voice blended with the music. "Whatever you need, it can always be had here and now when you move into the moment. Following the version of Dmitri who moved on would not serve you, for you are not finished experiencing this version of Susan. Live *this* version great, Susan. Live it grand. Life is the same no matter which side of The Wall you are on."

I heard another voice, Dmitri's voice. "Trust me, it's true."

I opened my eyes, but I did not see my backyard or the sky above me. I was on the other side of The Wall in a more brilliant ethereal body than I'd ever consciously experienced. I was standing, facing My Fool who was smiling. Dmitri stood next to Him. And he was smiling too. He appeared as he was when we last parted, hair in a ponytail, light blue dress shirt, black slacks, and boots. The backdrop against Dmitri and My Fool was the diamond veil I had once fallen through to experience the lives of my trailing identities.

Dmitri was glowing. "I am free. I did it. If I had died before going through this transition, I would just continue it in another reality. But I did it. I found my heart."

My eyes were teary, torn between anguish and joy.

Dmitri reached out his ethereal hand, and stroked my cheek. "All is well Susan, all is well. If I have done this thing of heart, then it is true that you more tightly grip the sword, for we continue our adventures together, no matter what worlds we are in. Our Being is the same. Our mission is the same. The things we seek to experience compliment one another."

I nodded, anguish subsiding into joy. Then a form came up behind Dmitri. It was . . . me, Susan, in the black pants and midnight blue dress shirt I'd worn when we said goodbye at the airport. Had a version of me truly gone with him?

Staring at myself, as myself, rattled me to the core, as if shaking me awake, vibrantly awake even in this deepened state. It was as if I had opened my eyes to see the beauty in myself that I hadn't seen before—the beauty that was always there.

Dmitri turned toward that version of me, but said to this version of me, "See Susan, we are together. We are." And with one last affectionate gaze into my eyes, he, and the other version of me turned away and began walking hand in hand. Then, the other Susan looked over her shoulder—my shoulder and nodded with a knowing glint in her eye—my eye. I nodded back at me with that same knowing look. Me and myself acknowledged me and myself. And then me, the other me, and Dmitri walked through the Diamond Veil and disappeared.

My Fool said, "Ain't life great!"

I nodded, for it was. All the rumpled ridges of fear and grief within me, dissolved.

My Fool declared, "Move on Susan, move on. Fulfill your life intent, which is really just about moving into yourself, into the center of existence. The deeper you go into yourself, the deeper you are in Pure Creative Energy. So, you cannot lose by living your life. You cannot die, even when you feel that the living is done. So live your story, Susan. You have lingered now long enough in the shadows on the Other Side of Life. It is time for you to embrace your Focus Self in your Focus World, in your Focus Life, and matriculate your gathered experiences into your daily living." His eyes beamed profoundly. "Open your hand."

I opened my opened my hand, palm up.

He laid in it a miniature backdrop of the Universe.

He said, "This is the Gem of Totality. All the seeming separate parts are always connected. Everything connected is a projection of one homogenized Creative Energy. The journey into mundane reality requires a conscious leave from the other side of life, from all the realms that lurk on the boundary of the mundane world. It takes great bravery to die away from pure wisdom, and a sense of total connection. It is a most noble adventure to be seemingly cast adrift into what seems confusing and lonely. When we are born, we forget about the eleven gem odyssey of death which is really the life of life, pure beauty. What we call death is life, and what we call life is death."

He was right. In conscious life we were cut off from so much, for only in this manner could a great adventure be had. The mini Universe absorbed into my palm.

He said, "And now, I must, as you would term it, go. I will not be accessible in the manner you wish for some time, for your daily life awaits."

"Oh, don't go yet, not now. Teach me more!"

He said, "You are ever eager to see what is around the bend before you fully experience where you are. Digest these gained insights in your daily life and reap the rewards."

"But I want to know more."

"Beyond consciousness, you *already* know everything."

"But I don't want to lose you."

"You know, you cannot."

"Who are you, really? What are you? What haven't you told me? If am to end this chapter of my life, is it not time to unfold that mystery?"

"It is," He said hauntingly.

He began to whirl and grow and change into a kaleidoscope of panoramic scenes and people and creatures and particles—merging, separating, and swirling. The movement felt more and more like raw power merging into one solid, yet changing energy, so full of color that no color could be seen, and birthing unto itself a trillion times a second. Energy overlapped energy, rippling outward, while at the same time lapping inward upon itself. The energy mounted outward and inward, mounting, mounting. I began to lose my breath. "Who are you!" I shouted. "*What* are you!"

And a voice said, "I am beyond fiction. I am before stories begin. I am the seeds of all existence. I am energy. It is I. It is I. It is I. Don't you know who I am?"

Then the energy seemed to implode and explode simultaneously. And though I was in an ethereal form, I felt blown backwards into a tunnel where bands of brilliant light flashed so bright and fast, my eyes hurt. My hair blew straight in front of me, sheer force at my back. I was traveling backwards into time, toward a location, away from the experience of totality, while also moving deeper into the center of totality. Ever and always the counterbalance—ever and always.

Then I stopped moving. Everything was still, but I could feel massive energy all about me. Everything was dark, but I could see. Everything was silent, but I could hear. In my hand appeared a wand, dark, like anti-matter. Upon closer viewing, it was not a wand, but a sword—the sword of death from the other side of life. Embedded in the length of the blade were the gems My Fool had given me: transition, time travel, multiplicity, duality, the story, compression, fear, faith, dreaming, imagination, and totality.

And as in anytime I grip a sword, it becomes the most poignant moment of my existence. I folded into myself while moving outward. I felt the world's pain. I felt the world's beauty. Then I felt pain and beauty as one energy, total and perfect.

I was large and small, totality and the particle, everything and nothing, Pure Creative Energy and Susan. Would I be able to balance this expanded way of being with my everyday reality? Could I return to a singular existence where confusion lurks and death is feared, and still feel the infinity of this richer existence that I'd come to know? Yet, that was my destiny, was it not? I held the sword of all that generates everyday life, and My Fool bade me return. What was stopping me? I realized then that my hesitance was rooted in a fear, ironically, of Susan's physical death, yet to be.

It was then I noticed a dark wall of energy before me. It had been there, I just hadn't seen it. It was the wall of physical death, the wall that keeps the human self on one side, and mystery on the other. In staring upon this dark wall, I became aware of my secret fears in the life of Susan.

I hadn't thought I feared physical death, given I'd journeyed beyond it many times. But here it was before me, this wall of physical death. I was trapped in a paradox. I didn't want to go back to my body because I didn't wish to experience its eventual expiration, but if I didn't go back, it would expire anyway.

Then I realized that it wasn't physical death I feared, but leaving behind my *concept* of Susan's life. I feared letting go of who I thought I was in my everyday life. I feared uprooting myself from my familiar surroundings: my house, my computer, my cats, my bed.

To face this fear, I had a sense that I must walk through the wall of physical death and time travel into my future. If I could experience what lay ahead for me when I physically died, I could dispel this fear when I moved back into the physical reality of Susan.

With sword in hand, I rose before the shadowy wall of death. If My Fool and Dmitri could face it, why not I? What was this fear anyway, but fear of the unknown, fear of what I would become when I left Susan's life behind. I would meet it now. I would meet death—now. I would meet *my* death—now.

I released all I thought I was, and all I believed myself to be. I released my resistance to live a human life, as well as my resistance to release my human life. And with that mind state, I moved into the dark energy wall. I did not move through it, for it was more akin to a vast place. I was waist deep in a non-physical serene body of water. I was an energy form of sorts, a female with seeming boundaries, and yet I had no boundaries. I felt myself as a shadow, like a silhouette, like a nameless, faceless entity that was larger than I looked. I felt like my whole Being rather than one of its identities.

And though I seemed to be standing waist deep in this non-physical body of water with sword in hand, half immersed in the liquid energy, I wasn't actually standing on anything. It was as if there were no bottom, beginning, or end to this water.

My life as Susan, the mother and a writer, was left behind on the other side of the dark energy wall. I could see how Susan's writing was fueled by her fear of death as much as it was a passage to her life—to life.

Then there appeared before me all versions of Susan, *and* all the trailing identities I'd ever experienced, and all the counterpart identities in my Being. They had experienced the dregs of vicious hell and the heights of unimagined beauty. I swirled my free hand in front of my many identities, generating an energy that blended them all together, like gathering them up to bring them home from a story that had fully manifested.

Then they condensed into a point of light, a tiny star that I held in my hand. I released the star as one would a captured bird, and it went off into the night sky. The star was all the energy that my selves had generated by exploring an idea through living a great story with numerable sub-stories. I saw it then, that when a Being finishes a story, the energy born from living the story, becomes a star in the sky.

And it seemed then that all the stars in the sky were created from all of this living we have done. With each star, the Universe became more that it was. Our experiences made the Universe beautiful. The Universe was the reflection of Pure Creative Energy—coming to know itself.

I quite suddenly returned to conscious focus in the identity of Susan, staring at the blue, blue sky from my hammock. I sighed with a smile, replenished and sated with all I needed to feel *in The Zone*, once more.

I crawled out of my hammock with headphones on ears and Walkman on waist. Mahler's fifth symphony had ended.

I went to my bedroom, placed my Walkman and headphones on the bed stand, flopped on my bed, and stared up at my Wizard of Oz poster on the ceiling. I had been exploring the worlds beyond accepted reality. I'd had a great adventure. I would never forget it. I would never forget My Fool.

My Fool was beyond identity, even though I saw Him so. He was Pure Creative Energy, for I had softened my 'knowing' enough to have that experience. And it isn't that He wasn't My Fool, for what is not Creative Energy? What is not . . . of us?

I was learning to experience what was beyond imagination in earth worlds, and touch the dreaming outside time. And I was learning to behold the dreaming outside time, simultaneously with imagination inside time. I was living outside in, and inside out. I laughed a little. I kind of liked that.

I reached for the television remote, and clicked on the news.

A body was found . . . A bank was robbed . . . War rages in the country of . . . Expect rain showers . . . Concert playing at . . . Donated a million dollars to the poor.

I smiled. And that is life. Or one side of it anyway. My fluffy white cat, Angel crawled onto my stomach. I pet her. My fluffy black and white fur-masked cat, Baxter, came over and bit her rump, and she ran away. Baxter took her place. Did I mention I loved the black spot on his pink nose? Ah, life. *Finally,* I accept the way of it. I clicked my heels three times.

Welcome home, Susan. Welcome home.

And it is time for you to come home too, home to yourself, home inside yourself. Your story is all right. You are okay. All is well. A little step to one side or another, and it is right there, the okayness, the constant wellness of everything, in chaos and in harmony. It is right there in the periphery of your being. There is a reason we cry in the face of incredible beauty: pain and joy are one. Individuality and totality—are one. You and all whom you love and hate—are one. So, with that insight, live the mystery and have great adventures. In the words of My Fool, "Live with Gusto."

Ain't life great!

About the Author-Susan D. Kalior

Susan was born in Seattle, WA, raised in Phoenix, AZ, and currently resides in Oregon. In her first profession, she was a psychotherapist (individual, marriage, and family counseling) treating those suffering from depression, anxiety, post traumatic stress, substance abuse, sexual abuse, family violence, and severe mental illness. She employed therapies such as communication skill building, relaxation training, systematic desensitization, bioenergetics, and psychodrama.

She has, over the years, facilitated personal growth and transformation workshops that promote self-discovery and teach meditation. These workshops have aided in the psycho-spiritual healing of many.

She has lectured on sociological, psychological, and metaphysical topics, and been involved in various social activist pursuits.

Her education includes an M.A. in Ed. in Counseling/Human Relations and Behavior (NAU), a B.S. in Sociology (ASU), and ten months of psychological and metaphysical training in a Tibetan community.

Aside from facilitating workshops, Susan writes entertaining books steeped in psychology, sociology, and metaphysics in various generes: self discovery workbooks, visionary fiction, fantasy, dark fantasy, and fantasy romance. All her books are designed to enlighten and uplift the human spirit.

If you are interested in hiring Susan to do a group workshop, refer to www.bluewingworkshops.com for more information. She can be contacted at sdk@bluewingworkshops.com.

In her words: I love to meditate, play in nature, go outside the box, and read between the lines. I strive to see what is often missed, and to not miss what can't be seen. There is such a life out there, and in there—beyond all perception! So I close my eyes, feel my inner rhythm, and jump off the cliff of convention. And when I land, though I might be quaking in my boots, I gather my courage and go exploring.

Through travel, study, and work, I've gained a rich awareness of cultural differences among people and their psycho-social struggles. I have discovered that oppression often results from the unexamined adoption of outside perceptions. The healing always has been in the individual's stamina to expel outside perceptions of self and constructively exert one's unique core being into the world. I am driven to facilitate expanded awareness that people may separate who they are from who they are told to be. Embracing personal power by nourishing our *true* selves is the key to joyous living.

My motto is, *Trust your story. Live the Mystery.*

CPSIA information can be obtained at www.ICGtesting.com
Printed in the USA
LVOW11s1404170814

399532LV00001B/106/P